DAMI SALAKO

CHILDREN with GIFTS

Praise for Dami Salako

"Children with Gifts is a remarkable debut that will keep readers on edge until the final page—and long after. With cleverly interwoven character dynamics, jaw-dropping twists, and an exploration of trauma and its lasting impact, this is a story that must not be missed."

—Angela Montoya, award-winning and critically acclaimed author of *A Cruel Twist*

"Children with Gifts is fit for Regulars looking for familiar tropes in a deliciously deviant tale about found family, sacrifice, and the structures keeping all the power to themselves. A thrill ride from first page to last!"

—Amparo Ortiz, author of *Last Sunrise in Eterna*

"Children with Gifts is an electric debut that I couldn't put down! Salako weaves the multiple POVs together seamlessly and draws you in with intrigue from the get-go. She keeps the superhero genre feeling fresh, all while unfolding mysteries and masterfully tackling hard and real–life issues, For fans of Heroes, Push or X-Men, this one is for you!"

—Ria Parisi author of *Of Wolves and Stags*

CHILDREN WITH GIFTS

DAMI SALAKO

This is a collection of fictional works. Names, characters, places, and incidents are either a product of the author's imagination or are used fictitiously. Any resemblance to actual persons, living or dead, businesses, companies, events, or locales, is entirely coincidental.

Children with Gifts

Inked in Gray Press

InkedinGray.com

Copyright © 2025

All rights reserved.

ISBN Paperback: 9978-1-952969-45-4

ISBN Ebook: 978-1-952969-44-7

Cover Design by MILB Art

No part of this book may be used or reproduced in any manner whatsoever without written permission except for the use of brief quotations in a book review.

No part of this book may be used or reproduced in any manner for the purpose of training artificial intelligence technologies or systems. In accordance with Article 4(3) of the Digital Single Market Directive 2019/70, Inked in Gray Press expressively reserves this work from the text and data mining exception. in any form or used by, with, or fed into any electronic or mechanical systems, including information storage and AI, without written permission from the author

To the daydreamers who tend to live in their heads — don't forget to come out and tell us all about it.

Content Warning

This book includes content that may be upsetting to readers including suicidal ideation, mentions of completed suicide, symptoms of post-traumatic stress disorder, depression, anxiety, panic attacks, death, grief, violence, domestic abuse and manipulation, and references to incidents of sexual assault.

Part I: Me & the Devil

Ruth

The early morning air was crisp and taut, as if every molecule was held together by a tightrope. This was good; it kept Ruth awake. The air at dusk was always overwhelming and suffocating, so desperate to be needed and inhaled and felt. The early morning air hadn't yet been bastardized by the smog and smoke and filth of humanity. It was full of potential — before the inhabitants of the Earth woke up and discovered new, ingenious ways to ruin each other.

Ruth's mark was inside a black sedan that had seen much better days. The paint had chipped and faded, and the scratches had rusted over. Ruth left the overhanging shadows of the taller buildings and walked towards the rear door behind the driver's seat. Before she opened it, she took a moment to examine her reflection, readjusting a persistently disobedient loc. The rest of her dreads were bound together and formed a large bun at the top of her head.

The soft click of the car's lock beckoned her entry. Ruth

didn't bother opening the door, still adjusting her hair. Not until—

Oh my God, you absolute donut, your hair looks fine.

She grumbled under her breath. God, she hated him. *It.* That *thing* that walked beside her as she traveled the world, chattering incessantly. Her invisible companion that bothered her all day and every day for as long as she could remember, providing the endless commentary to the soundtrack of her life.

The vehicle reeked of molding sandwiches, take-out Chinese food, tacos, reefer, and cigarettes. Of sweat and salt and dirty laundry. And remnants of fear, pain and — indigestion? She sniffed again. That was new. She hadn't been able to smell indigestion before.

"Seriously?" the driver said, barely craning his neck to look at her. "You gotta fix your hair first?"

See? the Companion remarked, gesturing at the man. *He gets it.*

Ruth settled into the seat behind the driver. Despite the distinct smell of chemical cheese and flatulence, she inhaled deeply and folded her gloved hands in her lap. "I was told you have something for me, Mr. Barnes," she announced, ignoring the figure-less voice beside her. If her companion wanted attention, then it would have to find a way to be useful. Those were the rules.

The driver clearly wanted to say something. Ruth watched Mr. Barnes's mouth try to form the words. But the moment passed, and he turned back around and shuffled through a stack of papers in his lap.

"You shouldn't do that," Ruth said.

"Do what?" Mr. Barnes asked absentmindedly.

"Consider lying to me."

Mr. Barnes hesitated. This time, he put in that extra effort and hoisted himself up so he could turn and face her properly. He grinned, and for a moment Ruth's mind wandered. *Were those veneers?*

How on Earth can he afford veneers, the Companion wondered aloud. *They must pay really well. We should jump ship. We could be living in a high-rise. I could have my own room.*

Ruth allowed the thought to simmer. It had a good point. Mr. Barnes's current occupation clearly paid very well, didn't it?

Which meant he had an awful lot to lose in being here today.

"Why would I do that?" Mr. Barnes said, interrupting Ruth's internal dialogue. His grin broadened. "Lie to you?"

Lies, her companion groaned. It sang the words, as if practicing arpeggios. It had moved, too — now it sat in the passenger seat with its face just inches away from Mr. Barnes's temple, staring at Mr. Barnes as if he were something to eat. Its eyes shifted slowly, examining every open pore and every bead of sweat on Mr. Barnes's brow.

It always liked to play with its food.

He does that often, her companion said as it watched him carefully. *He's terrified but he lives terrified, doesn't he? Terrified of losing his job, of being sacked, or getting dropped in the Trinity River — or whatever's left of it this time of year. Terrified of being strung up by the people he hunts down. Lies and fear are his companion — like a wife or a seeing-eye dog.*

Ruth inhaled. She could smell it all over him now. The fear. Barnes's fear strengthened with each passing moment, until she couldn't even smell the dirty laundry or the marijuana. But there was something else; there always was. It was never *just* fear.

"I don't know why you would lie, you fumbling idiot," Ruth said. "I don't read minds. But I can read your emotions . . . I can *smell* them on you. You're scared. I'm a stranger who is threatening your livelihood and leaving you vulnerable to the whims of dozens of very rich and very important people. Your employers wouldn't hesitate to drop your carcass into an unmarked hole in the ground if it meant keeping their operation functional and lucrative. Important people are petty, presumptuous, and violent when cornered, Mr. Barnes. And that's what makes them so . . . well, so bloody terrifying doesn't it? But fear is boring."

Breathe. It was important she remembered to breathe. If she didn't, then she could miss new information. Emotions were whimsical and fleeting like that; it was imperative she keep up. The devil was in the details.

"Besides, we're not like that are we, Mr. Barnes?" Ruth uncrossed her legs and leaned forward, reaching for the side of his seat with the tips of her fingers. "We haven't the privilege to choose violence for no reason. We're more . . . purposeful in our chaos. For people like us, it isn't until hope is lost that we become utterly desperate. And for whatever reason Mr. Barnes, you are not yet desperate. And I find that insulting."

The Companion yawned. *Beautiful monologue, Sweetie. Now, breathe.*

She did. Then she waited for the air to change and her palette to adjust to something new.

And when it did, it was absolute heaven.

She closed her eyes, savoring it. The next time she opened her eyes, Mr. Barnes wasn't smiling. Instead, he had a gun pointed directly at her head.

There it was. Desperation. It smelled like chocolate chip cookies.

Ruth smiled. "Much better."

Her smile was tight and reserved but her companion's was broad, gleaming, and ravenous. It leaned back, propping its feet up on the dashboard and sitting back in the passenger seat. The Companion looked so out of place in that three-piece suit it insisted on wearing to every assignment.

"You're right," Mr. Barnes said between clenched teeth. "It would be very bad to put me in a desperate situation. Which is why you're going to tell me who hired you and where I can find them."

The Companion scoffed, leaning back slightly with its head in its propped-up hand.

Within a fraction of a second, Ruth had pounced behind him, her lips close enough to kiss his temple. She grabbed his gun with her right hand, her left holding a knife to his throat. With a sharp twist of her hand, she forced his palm up and dug the nail of her first finger between the tendons in his wrist. He dropped the gun, but she kept searching, her nail maneuvering slightly until — ah, yes. There it was. The median nerve.

With triumph, she drove her nail until she broke skin. Then further still.

Mr. Barnes screamed but she adjusted the knife in her left hand — a reminder that he could just as easily *stop* screaming as well.

"Mr. Barnes," she said clearly. "I really wouldn't."

"What the hell is your problem?!"

Oh, now look what you did, her companion said, examining its nails with a disgusted sneer on its face. *It's everywhere now. The fear. It's ruining everything. Get rid of it.*

The Companion was right, of course. That was the problem with physical pain. It was like dumping a jar of salt into a stew. "You're scared, Mr. Barnes. My coworker here is of the opinion that now you're a bit too far gone in the wrong direction."

Mr. Barnes blinked wildly. "Cowork — *what* — *what the hell are you talking about?*"

"I've been completely transparent since I first made

contact three weeks ago. I want to know the location of your arena's next posting."

Mr. Barnes was quiet. So, Ruth focused her attention on her index finger and dug a little deeper.

Mr. Barnes yowled. "Alright! It's at Saint's. It's at Saint's!"

Liar! The Companion said, looking bored.

Ruth released Mr. Barnes's wrist, but only to grab a fistful of his hair with her right hand and slam his head against the window. He didn't have time to scream before her knife was back at his throat and her other hand wrapped around his wrist at an almost impossible angle.

Almost.

Mr. Barnes stuttered, blinking wildly. She couldn't try that maneuver again: another hit to the head and he'd simply be unconscious. But now, he was dazed and confused. His emotions dulled, the tastes and smells less potent than they were moments ago. He was getting tired.

"I want to know the location of your arena's next posting," she repeated.

"I told you," he gasped. "It's at S—"

She yanked her grip downwards, breaking his wrist.

Mr. Barnes howled and this time, Ruth allowed it. When his breath returned and his pupils widened, she asked her question again, her tone just as even and soothing as it had been the first time. "Mr. Barnes. I want to know the location of your arena's next posting." She allowed her blade to dig into his skin, a tiny bit deeper. "Please."

He changed his answer. "It's *here*," he said through clenched teeth "It's . . . here, downtown. Below Old Red. They use the tunnel systems."

Her companion sat up, opening its eyes dramatically as if waking up from a nap. *Yay*, it sang, its voice pathetically flat. *Can we go now?*

"When?" Ruth asked.

Mr. Barnes was silent.

Ruth rolled her eyes and released her tight grip around his wrist. Her fingers found the letter opener tucked between her locs. She slipped it out of the knot, allowing her locs to tumble around her face.

Then she stabbed him in the upper thigh.

He let out another pointless scream. After a beat, she asked again, "When?"

"This Saturday," he said. "They transfer the kids in the middle of the night usually; I don't know what time—"

The scent in the air changed, and Ruth's nose curled in disgust. People always had so many *feelings* — fear, sadness, anger, worry. It was impossible to find the dominant emotion in these situations, especially when pain was involved. So she waited as the poor excuse of a man cycled through them. His pain blended with putrid hatred and noxious fear until all of it disappeared, drowning in the sea of—

Despair.

He was telling the truth. Because now he knew he was a dead man.

Ruth cleared her throat. "Thank you for your time."

She released him, leaving the letter opener jutting out of his thigh. "I would suggest you leave that in until the ambulance arrives," she told him as she opened the car door, sure to confiscate Mr. Barnes's firearm on her way out.

Have a good day at work! the Companion said as it waved goodbye to the weeping man. Ruth slammed the door before the man had the opportunity to hurl a flurry of expletives.

It didn't take long before she heard the car door swing open behind her. She rolled her eyes and changed course, ducking behind a parked truck in an alley. Barnes wouldn't make it very far, not with a broken wrist and an injured leg. But nevertheless, it would be wise to become scarce.

That was unnecessary. The Companion's voice was low and moody. Despite its cane, it matched Ruth's gait perfectly.

Ruth rolled her eyes. "Not everything I do has to be necessary."

Perhaps not, but I'm pretty sure you're supposed to be efficient.

"So, I'm not allowed to have a bit of fun?"

Have you considered taking up roller-blading?

"Would you be able to keep up?"

Twat.

Ruth's lips curled into a smirk as she yanked at the tips of her gloves. She shoved the pair deep inside her coat pockets before pulling off her coat. She turned the sleeves inside out before donning it again over her shoulders.

It was nearly five in the morning, and she was bordering the edge of downtown near the farmer's market. The air had started to change here — no longer crisp and fresh, but polluted with the hot breath of retailers hoisting crates of fresh fruits and boxes of artisanal bread, craft beers, honey, and waxes.

Your protege seems a bit miffed, her companion announced.

Ruth paused, now sensing Vashti's presence.

I saw her first, didn't I?

She briefly considered sticking out her foot and tripping the Companion, but she knew it was no use. That *never* worked.

You're getting sloppy, it teased. Its footsteps stopped, its presence was replaced by another: a softer, younger voice, lacking in the Companion's commanding timber.

"That was reckless," Vashti scolded.

"*That* wasn't your business," Ruth said back. She shoved her hands deep into her now deep green coat pockets and fished out a pair of round glasses. "Mr. Barnes will be fine as long as he remembers to call for an ambulance."

Vashti's brows furrowed. She was a good half a foot shorter than Ruth but was able to match Ruth's pace step for step. The two of them weaved between different vendors, crates, and boxes creating a winding obstacle course. "What if he goes back to them? Tells them what happened?"

"And says what, precisely? That he sabotaged a multi-million dollar operation? That would make him a dead man."

Vashti ignored the excuse. She jumped over a crate of cheese and plucked a wheel of brie from the open container. Before the vendor noticed, Ruth's shoulder collided against his. She quickly apologized for her clumsiness then slipped a ten dollar bill into his coat pocket. By the time Ruth was shoulder to shoulder with Vashti again, her protege had already fully unwrapped her wheel of cheese.

Ruth glared at her. "Thanks for that."

Vashti narrowed her eyes. Ruth expected to smell pride, perhaps some unwarranted confidence at her petty thievery. But instead, Vashti only stank of anger.

Ruth had learned long ago, from the moment she came into her Gift, that everyone was angry. People trudged through life, accumulating anger like waste in a growing landfill. It seeped from their bones and lifted off their skin like beads of sweat at the end of a long day. Anger was everywhere — which made it useless.

"You should have killed him." Vashti said flatly.

Oh.

That wasn't *just* anger — that was disappointment. Vashti wasn't upset because Ruth had gone *too* far . . . she was disappointed that she didn't finish what she started.

"Is that what you would have done?" Ruth asked.

"Kill an arena handler? You shouldn't have to ask."

Ruth sighed and decided to move on. Given Vashti's history with the arenas, her response was no surprise. "And what about you?" Ruth asked. "I believe you had your own assignment."

Vashti huffed but pulled out a folded slip of paper from her inner breast pocket. "Hardly an assignment."

As if on cue, a heavy weight fell on both Ruth and Vashti's shoulders. A blonde woman slipped between the two of them, grinning as the rays of the early dawn caught the mischievous glint in her eyes. "Yes, well Vashti's mark didn't really need much persuasion, did he?" she said.

"Nina, you broke his hand," Vashti said.

"He's lucky I didn't break his di—"

"What happened?" Ruth interrupted, snatching the slip of paper from Vashti's fingers. She opened it and perused the laundry list of names scribbled on it.

Nina sighed and rolled her eyes. Nina was, to put it plainly, gorgeous in every sense of the word. Blonde hair framed an angular face, harsh jawline, and a pair of sharp cheekbones while her blue eyes assumed curiosity and something akin to friendliness. But it was her charm that made her perfectly ideal for reconnaissance and infiltration. She was intelligent, personable, and had once managed to get a room full of national diplomats to drunkenly sing Katy Perry's *"I Kissed a Girl"* at a private dinner (that she had also happened to crash). She'd left with a full belly, many new, and *very* useful, friends, and the names of six sitting presidents and chancellors' current mistresses. All in all, it had been a very successful assignment.

Everyone loved her, and Ruth was hopelessly and entirely jealous of this effortless skill. Ruth could sense emotions. She could taste fear and hear paranoia and feel someone else's envy on her own skin. If it was a very good day, she could even influence those emotions to her liking. And yet Ruth couldn't land a second date. Although, admittedly, the Companion's nonstop distractions didn't help with that, either.

And the worst part of it all? Getting people to like her wasn't even Nina's Gift.

She just happened to be good at it.

"What happened, Nina?" Ruth repeated, perusing the list of names.

Nina scowled, blue eyes dark and furious. "He wanted to go back to *his place*."

Ah.

Ruth shifted her attention back to Vashti. "And you just *let* her break his hands?"

"Right, because stopping Nina from doing anything is within my repertoire. Why are you even upset? All Nina did was break his hands. *You* killed your guy. Well, *half*-killed him anyway."

Nina gasped and covered her mouth with her hand in faux surprise. "Did you really? Temper, temper."

"He's going to die anyway," Ruth grumbled.

"Dying to the elements is cheating," Vashti said.

Ruth led them towards one of the many breakfast caravans along the street. Ruth had hoped they could debrief back at her apartment, but Vashti had been stealing quick glances at the food trucks for the last several minutes and Nina kept trying — and failing — to swipe what was left of Vashti's cheese.

They ate biscuits, egg sandwiches, and muffins on the side of the road just off the edge of the curb. Despite their varied spread, Nina begged Vashti for a bite of whatever she happened to be eating. With a muttered curse and a grunt, Vashti would begrudgingly allow it.

"What about you?" Nina asked, pointing at Vashti with

half a sausage. "Didn't *you* have a job to do or did you just watch me maim belligerent idiots?"

Vashti couldn't be goaded into an argument, not when she had a jelly donut in one hand and a sausage kolache in the other. "There are twenty-three Gifted in Arena Rho," she said. "The club owner is some balding nobody called Russell. Well, he's not a nobody. Apparently, he's Christian Loubiton's cousin or something."

Ruth nearly choked. "Wait—"

Vashti nodded. "Wild, isn't it? Anyway, Russell's just the arena's benefactor. He handles the money. But day to day management is handled by Brandon Wayne." She licked stray jelly off her finger. "*He's* actually a nobody as far as I could tell, but his resume is impressive. He's managed multiple arenas over the last decade. And his records are clean — just one arrest for a possession charge four years ago. But that was dropped, obviously. Nina, can I have the rest of your donut?"

She looked at Nina, who was holding the last jelly donut between her fingers. Nina handed it to her with a slight shrug. "How did you find all that out?"

Vashti hummed, pleased with herself — but only because the donut was now in her possession. "I stole his phone and wallet while Nina broke his hands—"

Nina growled, narrowing her eyes. "*Hand*. I only broke one of them."

"He's staying at a hotel close by. So I used his keycard to check into his hotel. Found his ID — the *real* one and a second phone in a lockbox. I saw him unlock his other phone a few times before he started chatting up Nina. And like a moron, he uses the *same* password for both phones. Brandon Wayne — real name, Irving Weiss, may run a few arenas, but his security sucks."

Vashti finished the donut with another two bites. Nina

supplied her with another donut. "He gets paid every two weeks by Lincoln & Co."

"Lincoln & Co?" Ruth frowned. "What is that?"

Vashti's answer came with a full mouth. "Absolutely nothing. But on paper, a fashion company based in Los Angeles. And Russell is a majority shareholder."

Nina looked surprised. "They really have their little piggy fingers in everything fun, don't they?"

"I'm guessing that's the information Min cares about?" Vashti asked.

"Surprisingly, no," Nina said, leaning back on the curb. "But we do enjoy incidental findings. The job's unchanged: the extraction in a few days."

"At Old Red," Ruth supplied. "Somewhere underground."

Vashti beamed. "Oh, that's exciting! I've never been to Old Red."

"This is an extraction, not a field trip," Ruth said. Then to Nina. "So? Who are we picking up?"

Nina pulled a folded photograph from her back pocket and handed it to Ruth.

It was a photograph of a teenager — maybe seventeen or eighteen years old, with dark brown hair and loose disheveled curls framing a long face. It looked like a picture from a driver's license.

"And . . . who exactly is this?" Vashti asked.

Anthony

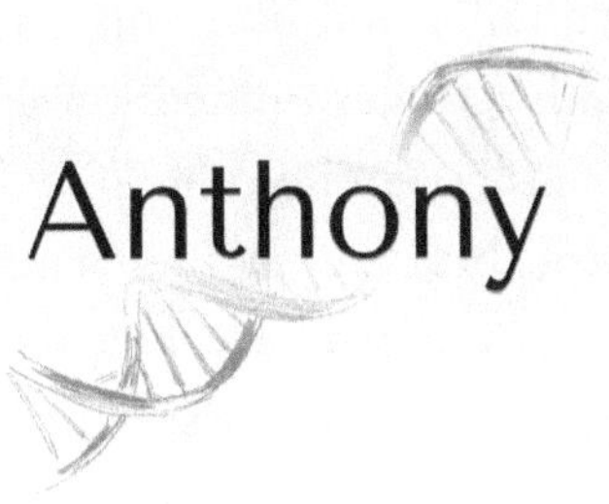

Anthony stood at the sink and allowed the faucet to run, even though he knew the drain was clogged and it wouldn't take long for it to overflow. His hands gripped either side of the metal until his knuckles turned white and his nails scraped the rust around the bowl's edges.

Just breathe.

He inhaled slowly, like he'd been practicing, hearing the whistle of the stale air as it moved into his nose and filled his lungs. He held it there, allowing the air to work its magic where it belonged, before exhaling again—

Too fast.

He gasped and coughed, his right-side aching and throbbing.

Idiot, Anthony thought to himself, clutching his side. His rib didn't feel broken — and he knew exactly what that felt like: the throbbing misery that accompanied stretching, bending, breathing, sitting, and standing. There was no relieving a fresh or healing rib fracture other than bedrest and *really* good pain meds.

Anthony stood taller and lifted up his shirt, holding it in place with his teeth as he examined his skin under the single dim, flickering incandescent light hanging from the ceiling. An angry red and purple bruise the size of a grapefruit marked the right side of his abdomen like a botched tattoo. Maybe he could ask Eric for some pain meds before he went up for his round of fights.

A loud bang on the door yanked Anthony out of his own head. He released his shirt from between his teeth and turned off the faucet — the water was getting dangerously close to the top anyway — and opened the door.

Speak of the devil.

Eric raised an eyebrow. Two years ago, Anthony might have wet himself just at the sight of him. But now he knew that even though the man was over six feet tall and nearly two hundred and fifty pounds of pure muscle, he was all show: an over-glorified bouncer. He could take anyone out, if necessary, but preferred to spend his free time treating his fighters to burgers and milkshakes after fight night.

"What's up, Eric?" Anthony hopped up and down on the balls of his feet in a desperate attempt to release the adrenaline coursing through every blood vessel in his body.

"You know the rules, man. No locked doors on fight night."

"It's the bathroom."

"And you know the rules."

Anthony rubbed the back of his neck. Yeah, he knew the rules — and that rule had only been put into place after Asha, a new "recruit" had been found swinging silently from the light fixture, just minutes before his fight. He had used his shoelaces.

Now nobody was allowed any sort of privacy.

Eric paused, his blue eyes soft, yet piercing. "You doing ok, Anthony? You almost got taken out yesterday."

Anthony grinned. "Almost," he quipped.

Eric reached over and ruffled Anthony's hair — an infantilizing reminder that Anthony would need to put his hair up later that evening.

"You're fighting Wyatt tonight," Eric said.

Anthony faltered. "I know."

"He can't hold back tonight."

"I—"

Oh.

Oh.

Anthony stilled. His restless feet now felt like lead. "Yeah, sure thing. You got it, Chief," he said, but his voice fell flat, like a deflated balloon.

Eric's mouth opened slightly, but he swallowed the words that nearly tumbled out of his lips. Instead, he gave him a curt nod before retreating into the main hallway, leaving the bathroom door open on his way out.

As soon as Eric was out of sight, Anthony twisted the faucet until lukewarm water spilled into the bowl. He gripped the edge of the sink and focused on his reflection in the mirror.

He was still sporting the black eye he'd earned about a week ago. The bruise had faded and changed over the course of the week. Once a deep and angry purplish blue, it was now a yellowish sickly green. But his brown hair distracted from the ugliness that had taken over the right half of his face. Thick and disheveled curls tangled into one another. It was longer than it had ever been in his life, brushing past his shoulders.

He hated it.

Anthony pulled a hairband from his wrist and tied his hair up into a messy knot at the back of his head behind his ears.

Another knock on the bathroom door.

"Not necessary," Anthony said with a harsh tongue and biting bitterness. "Seeing as the door is already open."

"Sorry."

Anthony stiffened, his anger immediately quelled by the meekness in the girl's voice. She'd only been here for a few weeks, but she'd already grown accustomed to the tension that filled the arena on fight night.

Anthony swallowed. "Sorry . . . wait, what are you doing here?"

Sarah shrugged, holding her left shoulder with her right arm. "The water's running."

"Yeah, I—" Anthony stuttered. The water in the sink was just millimeters away from the bowl's edge. Before he could turn the faucet, the handles straightened and stiffened back to its locked position. The drip stopped and the water in the sink went still.

He glanced at the young girl. "Thanks."

Sarah shrugged. She twisted her lip to the side, quietly deliberating her next words.

"What?" Anthony pressed, the annoyance and hatred in his voice replaced by something gentler, but still firm. The girl wasn't going to survive here if anyone treated her like a child. Unfortunate, really, since that's what she was. She had to be the youngest "recruit" he'd ever seen.

"You're fighting Wyatt tonight."

Anthony scowled and tried not to roll his eyes. He could handle Wyatt. Why was everyone making a big deal out of nothing? "Yeah, I know."

"What happens if he loses?"

His chest tightened. "He . . . can't," he admitted. Then he left the bathroom to find Eric.

To a Gifted, recruitment to the arenas was a worst-case scenario, and its traders and handlers were the boogeymen — villains of stories older Gifted told their misbehaving younger siblings to convince them to stay in line. As if the systemic oppression of an entire subspecies of human wasn't enough. Don't run off, don't start a fuss, don't get into arguments with the other kids in school even if they started it. *The handlers will come for you. They'll take you away and you'll never see your family again.* When Anthony was six, his older sister threatened to 'call the handlers' on him for eating the last bag of salt and vinegar chips.

Deviants eventually grew out of the old wives' tale, realizing there were more real and imminent dangers just around the corner: like prison and labor camps where Gifted were allowed the opportunity to pay off their debts. But every so often a sibling, a nephew, a *child* — but somehow, always someone Gifted — would disappear. Their families would raise hell in the streets and occupy police stations, telling different versions of the same story.

We saw it happen! We were there when they took my brother.

They broke in and they just took my niece!

We came home and my sister wasn't there! We haven't seen her in three days.

They wouldn't just run away . . .

The stories were all written off one way or another: The abductee had been affiliated with a gang activity. She'd been present at an illegal gathering after curfew. He was in debt and owed several loan sharks. He may have been assigned to one of the state labor camps. Crime ran rampant in the Sectors, anyway.

Sometimes, Anthony wondered what excuses the police had made for his own disappearance two years ago.

He's a teenager. Teenagers run away.

Eric was waiting for him in the infirmary: a dark, sullen room with no windows and three rows of rickety, wooden benches where Gifted sat and waited for Holly to take care of their injuries. Holly's back was to the door, her thick red curls shielding her current patient from his view. But her shirt clung to her back and her upper arms glistened with sweat. Fight nights were too much for just one person. Couldn't they find another healer to help?

Almost immediately, guilt clawed at the back of his throat. Was *that* what he truly hoped? That the handlers would kidnap some other teenager and force them to heal their own fighters?

Eric cleared his throat. "Ready, Sampson?"

Anthony ground his molars together and yanked the hairband out of his hair. It snagged on a few loose curls and his scalp stung as strands were pulled free from the follicle. He didn't care. He could pretend that's why his cheeks flushed and the back of his eyes stung.

Anthony followed Eric through the meandering halls of the dilapidated warehouse. Fights usually took place in locations like this: abandoned schools and warehouses deep in an industrial part of town, where late night construction could mask the cheers of contestants, buyers, sellers, and gamblers alike. Today, the fighting ring was sequestered in the middle of a wide-open space about half the size of a basketball court. The surrounding area was filled with hundreds of people. But perhaps the most impressive feature of the arena was the plexiglass dome that encapsulated the central fighting space, separating contestants from spectators.

The noise was deafening.

Anthony had no idea how many arenas existed. Traders and what the other fighters jokingly called "upper management" kept that information to themselves. But over the course of the last two years, he learned that each arena had, at most, twenty-five fighters. Some arenas were stationary, like the ones in Boston and Baltimore: The "Ivies." But most arenas were mobile like theirs: an entire group of fighters, traders, and security relocating from one venue to the next to fight with other arenas who were doing the same thing.

Nearly every shape, size, and creed of person was represented. There were middle-aged men who had stopped by on their way home from work. He spotted a group of college students, likely some millionaire's kid and his friends judging from the Greek letters on their sweatshirts and the Rolex on their wrists. Anthony even recognized some of the faces: the frequent flyers. Businessmen and businesswomen in perfectly tailored suits. Diplomats, rappers . . . one time, Anthony had spotted the current vice president (and a *ton* of security) hidden among the crowd.

Brokers and middle-men organized bets along the east wall of the arena, exchanging earnings for ticket stubs and convincing other betters to put just a *little* bit more on the line. The yells and demands of the egregiously wealthy filled the space until there was little room for thinking, breathing, or morals. Entrance fees to the arenas were not cheap, and patrons often put hundreds of thousands on the line to bet on their favorite local or visiting deviant.

Usually, the fights were between two different arenas: massive weekend long tournaments that brought fans from all over the country.

But matches *between* fighters from the same arena were exceptionally rare. Like tonight's fight between Wyatt and Anthony.

"AND JOINING NUMBER ELEVEN IN TONIGHT'S FINAL FIGHT," Ender's fourteen-year-old voice boomed throughout the arena, courtesy of his Gift. "A FACTION FAVORITE, *SAMPSON*, NUMBER FORTY-NINE, RANKED AMONG THE TOP TEN FIGHTERS IN HIS REGION!"

The room shook as the guests roared in excitement.

Anthony kept his head down, his black hoodie pulled up

over his head. Eric pushed through the crowd ahead of him while two other handlers flanked either side of him. All Anthony had to do was follow Eric, step by step.

But he could *feel* them. The heat of the crowd, choking his airway as people pushed and shoved so they could get a better look at one of their favorite fighters. The occasional grasp and groping as fans screamed his number, or worse, that stupid nickname: *Sampson.*

He'd heard that some of patrons followed their favorite arenas across the country, like dedicated football fans who hoped this was the year their team would make it to the Superbowl. *Arena groupies* the handlers called them. Rowdy and insatiable animals with voracious appetites for blood and violence.

Out in the real world, before he'd been taken, Anthony lived in an assigned Sector with the rest of his family. He couldn't be outside his home after ten o'clock at night. Because of his status as Gifted, he was branded a "possible threat to national security" and therefore, was not allowed to leave the state unless he completed a very tedious application and waited six months for a response that was probably going to be a "no." He couldn't go to college unless he managed to get into one of the six universities in America that accepted Gifted (but no more than ten Gifted students each academic year for safety reasons). There were jobs and fields of work he had no chance of entering. An entire world he'd never get to see.

But in the arena, Anthony was an icon. A legend.

A celebrity.

"LIKE I SAID," Ender continued, bellowing. "THIS IS THE FINAL FIGHT OF THE EVENING AND ALL BETS ARE COMING TO A CLOSE WITHIN THE NEXT SIXTY SECONDS! PLACE YOUR BETS, LEAVE YOUR KID'S COLLEGE FUND TO CHANCE AND LET'S HAVE A GOOD TIME!"

The crowd ate it up without pause, cheering with abandon.

Ender's voice dropped in pitch, and the crowd quickly hushed to hear it. "My fellow Americans, I have one more question for you . . ."

Anthony raised an eyebrow as the room buzzed.

"ARE YOU READY TO *RUMBBBBLEEE*!"

Anthony couldn't help but smirk as the crowd, quite literally, went wild. He approached the uneven steps that led up to the square-shaped ring.

"Knock 'em out, kid." Eric said from the foot of the stairs.

Anthony glanced over his shoulder. "You got it."

"You wearing the shoes?"

"Of course."

Eric's shoulders fell slightly, and he nodded.

"Don't worry, I won't die." *Probably*, he added beneath his breath.

The fighting ring was bright, almost glowing with light from the floodlights fixed onto the ceiling and walls of the plexiglass. Wyatt's back was towards him as he faced the crowd on the other side of the arena. His lucky Pink Floyd shirt was ripped at the back, as if it had been slashed with a knife. His khaki cargo pants were muddy and crusted at the bottom and caked with blood at the heels.

Wyatt finally turned around, his white hair flat against his forehead and around the edges of his face. His nose was bleeding, his left eye was swollen, and there was a fresh cut along his right cheek from his earlobe down to his upper lip.

Anthony's heart dropped. What in the fresh hell? Had he been fighting *all night*?

"Wyatt . . ." he started, but Anthony noticed Wyatt's right hand was already moving. Painful exhaustion pulled him side to side, swaying him like a gentle breeze. He had two tightly fitted metal cuffs around both arms, just above his wrists:

suppressors. Wyatt didn't have access to the full strength of his Gift.

Which was good, because Wyatt's Gift beat just about everything else on the planet, every single time.

Wyatt's body came alight as he reached for his Gift. The white glow traversed his skin forming an intricate pattern of intersecting and parallel lines along both of his arms.

Oh, so they were doing this. *Right now.*

"You're right," Anthony muttered to himself. "Fight now, talk later."

Anthony felt the chill take over as the familiar pattern of light and ice spread across his skin, from his chest up to his neck and finally to the left side of his face. He was used to it now; the fluorescent white glow and the broad strokes of light that meandered over his skin like an ancient rune. His own unique pattern, every time he reached for his Gift. He'd rarely seen it before the arenas. As soon as their Gift manifested, the first thing all Gifted learned was to *never* use it. But after he was taken and his monitoring chip was removed, his own pattern had become novel, a part of him he finally had a chance to understand. But two years had changed his perspective. Now, when he experienced the familiar chill and saw the light appear from just beneath his skin, he remembered that he wasn't just fighting for the entertainment of the barbaric gawkers.

He was fighting for his life.

Wyatt snarled as if he already had a dead animal between his teeth. A white-hot light danced across his fingers, and with a savage yell, bursts of lightning surrounded him, zig-zagging, raging and wild.

Anthony swallowed. *That* was with the suppressors? Were they even on?

Anthony dug his heels into the sand. He had known what

he was up against long before he stepped foot in the arena. So he had come prepared.

Ice and lightning? According to high school science, not the best combination. General recommendation: avoid if possible. But since water and ice were his only form of offense, he tried to be more intentional with his defense. The shoes that Eric had fetched for him were made of rubber soles. He wasn't wearing a single piece of metal on his body; he'd even removed zippers and buttons. He'd rubbed oil all over his torso, which he was a *little* nervous about. Oil was a good electrical insulator, but also highly flammable. Anthony figured his Gift could take care of that, though. The entire arena floor was covered in sand, and the dome surrounding them not only protected the crowd and their well-lined pockets, but it also protected Anthony. No metal or electrical conductors in the dome meant less chance of death by electrocution.

The handlers didn't want him to die in the arena either. A dead deviant was a lost investment. Training a new one was a tremendous loss of money, time, and resources. Besides, Anthony was one of their best. *"Ranked Top 10 Fighters in the Region."* Anthony knew it. His handlers knew it. Every handler south of the Bible Belt knew it. And everyone in Arena Rho knew it.

Wyatt threw the first blow, sending a bright shard of white-hot electricity directly at him. Anthony retaliated quickly: the air around him condensed, forming a well-defined giant shard of ice that traveled towards Wyatt at lightning speed. The wall of ice intercepted Wyatt's light, shattering just meters in front of Wyatt, which was precisely where the ice needed to stay. He could not have the ice melt anywhere near him if he had any intention of walking out of here.

He heard a desperate yell from Wyatt followed by a hot streak of lightning that rushed towards him like a missile.

Anthony defended, directing his Gift towards it, but he was milliseconds too slow. Wyatt's surge of energy met the ground just meters in front of him and the blast threw Anthony a dozen meters back like a rag doll. He landed on his back. The world spun.

Anthony rolled onto his side and tried to catch his breath. His head was throbbing and the bright lights weren't doing him any favors. With a grunt, he shifted onto all fours before pulling his right leg in front of him, foot planted firmly on the ground. Anthony nearly collapsed again as a sharp pain tore through him from the small of his back up towards his chest in an arc. He looked down and saw it — a huge gash along his right side.

He gritted his teeth and before he could change his mind, he grabbed his side and let the cold take over, numbing the area. The pain was hot and sharp at first, but within moments, it became a blunted and dulled ache. The surrounding skin was so cold he couldn't feel anything at all. He rose to his feet, heaving through clenched teeth, his hands and arm now streaked red with his own blood.

Wyatt's eyes were whiter than pearls as he balanced sparks of lightning in each of his hands. Wyatt was already prepared for a takedown: to end it all now, quickly.

He can't hold back tonight. You know this.

Anthony *knew* Wyatt needed this win. Eric had already warned him. But now, Anthony was bleeding and the room was spinning. So he didn't care.

Besides, he needed this win, too.

Anthony feigned another collapse, knowing Wyatt wouldn't go for an offensive strike if his opponent couldn't stand and take it — customary arena fighting etiquette. They weren't savages. But, as soon as Anthony was steady on his feet, he dashed towards Wyatt. Frost and ice churned from every crevice of the arena. Every molecule of water his surroundings had to spare bonded together forming an angry swirling mass of tiny crystals. They chased after Wyatt like a rabid dog with a scent.

Anthony's hands glowed as his pattern burned brighter. His jaw locked as he focused. Ice, snow and hail: every form of condensed vapor moved as he instructed.

Faster. He created a whirlwind of ice and chaos. All anyone could see were the cracks of lightning and bright flashes trapped within Anthony's storm.

Faster.

There was nothing except ice and chaos. Destruction and anger. He noticed the frequency of Wyatt's attacks decrease and the intensity of the electricity dulled, like a receding storm. Was he giving up? Growing weary? Biding his time?

It didn't matter.

FASTER.

Anthony screamed, commanding and pushing his power even harder as his side ached and blood spilled onto the ground. The edges of his vision blackened but Anthony wasn't paying attention to anything outside of the scene playing out in front of him.

Then . . . the floor *moved.*

The ground beneath his feet wavered and trembled like a violent earthquake, sending Anthony to his knees. His concentration on his Gift lapsed. The flurries of ice disappeared and the swirling mass of water splashed to the floor. He tried to stand, but the ground still trembled and he could barely make it back to his feet. Dazed and confused, he looked past Wyatt and into the crowd.

It was pandemonium.

People screamed and ran in every possible direction, colliding with each other, pushing, shoving, and falling to their feet as the ground shuddered beneath them. In the distance, near the arena entrance, a fire had broken out.

Eric appeared at the foot of the arena steps, frantic and chest heaving. "Come on!"

Anthony spun around and hobbled towards Wyatt. "Fights off! We gotta go!"

Wide-eyed, Wyatt grabbed his arm and followed him out of the dome and into the fray.

Ruth

Ruth had picked up this shift for the same reason she picked up every weekend shift: guilt. As if two overnights and a few Saturdays at the hospital could redeem the murders from earlier that week.

As soon as Ruth badged onto the unit, she instantly regretted the decision to come in with every fiber of her being.

"Good morning, Doc," One of the techs greeted as he wheeled his WOW — workstation on wheels — down the hall.

She forced a tight smile. "Morning, Wes. Have a good weekend?"

"Nope. You?"

Just a murder. But he was a bad guy, the Companion recommended, trailing after her. Its cane hit the ground with a soft *thunk* with every step.

"Uneventful," Ruth answered as she walked towards the physicians' workstation.

She could *feel* everyone.

Half a dozen patients were wandering the hall aimlessly. Some were talking to themselves. A dozen other patients were still in their rooms. Four were sleeping — she could tell because everything went quiet when she walked past their rooms. But the other eight were wide awake, their minds busy and active, their emotions ranging from labile to blunted to flat.

It felt different from walking into a busy mall or even a chaotic festival. In public open spaces, people's emotions were constant, but smothered. Like a pot left on simmer. People's minds were too occupied with remembering if they had eggs at home and if they had sent that one email last week. At more excitable venues like concerts, emotions were unified in unyielding glee and euphoria. Loud, but not necessarily distracting.

But every time she walked through the double doors of the Dallas County Psychiatric Hospital, her mind endured nothing short of an emotional assault.

Ruth adjusted to the onslaught of stimuli, though. She always did; usually by the time she made it to the workstation behind the glass doors. It was still uncomfortable, and she had to focus *very intently* to think. But eventually she adjusted.

But today, routine was not on her side.

Just before she turned the corner, she heard a loud crash and a surprised yell.

Ruth sighed, but maintained her current gait and stride as she walked towards the sounds of chaos. One of the patients — not hers — was yelling and a swarm of technicians and nurses were handling it like a well-oiled machine. Some nurses carefully and quietly redirected curious patients back to their rooms while the techs focused their attention on the cause of the commotion.

The man who had disturbed the tenuous peace was nearly six feet tall, hair tangled and a dark, chestnut complexion that compounded any and every reason to take less . . . conservative safety measures. The floor technicians were standing closest to the patient and they nearly matched him in height.

"No!" the man yelled again. His feet shuffled as if trying to back further away. But he had backed himself into a wall and had very limited options. "I don't want that. I don't want another shot!"

"Mr. Harrison, you can take a pill or a shot," the tech explained, for the third or fourth time judging by his tone. "You can choose which one you'd prefer."

"I don't want none of that shit!"

"Well, you have to choose one. You're walking around, hearing things and yelling at people and getting aggressive . . ."

Mr. Harrison's eyes widened at that and his brows furrowed. *Uh oh,* Ruth thought. "He started it!" Mr. Harrison accused taking multiple steps forwards towards the tech. "He's telling people I'm in here! And . . . and . . . and he stole my stuff!"

"Hey, wait, wait," Ruth interjected. "What's going on, Mr. Harrison?" She lifted her usually deep and monotone voice half an octave.

His words weren't terribly important. He claimed he couldn't find one of the forms that was in his room earlier, and he swore up and down that he hadn't touched them. So, *obviously,* someone had stolen it from his bedroom. No, he didn't lose it — yes, he was *completely* sure. It had to be the people who were always following him. They were definitely in his room stealing his things.

Ruth didn't believe any of it. Mr. Harrison was one of the few patients on the unit without a roommate because he refused to shower (six days and counting), convinced there were nanobots in the water that would give him leprosy. And his room was an absolute disaster: food everywhere, copies of court mandated forms wet because they've spent some time in the sink, dirty sheets on the ground that he wouldn't allow *anyone* to touch. The other day she caught him stuffing muffin wrappers into his pillow. Whatever form Mr. Harrison thought he was looking for, nobody would be able to find it, even if it *was* somewhere in his room. For all they knew, Mr. Harrison may have already flushed the damn thing down the toilet.

And to top it all off, now he was angry.

Fortunately for Ruth, she had a *slight* advantage.

Mr. Harrison gave off a stench that tasted like six . . . oh, today would make it seven-day old body odor, sweat, dried blueberry muffins . . . and jealousy.

"Why did they take your stuff?" Ruth asked.

Mr. Harrison hesitated, startled that his monologue — external and likely internal — had been interrupted. But after a beat he continued, "They're taking my stuff! They're gonna keep me. You're gonna lock me up!"

Nice try, the Companion said, leaning against the wall next to Mr. Harrison, arms folded across his chest. *Would you like to reason with him next?*

Ruth felt something stir, sensing something else in Mr. Harrison.

". . . and I won't get to go home! Everyone else gets to go home," Mr. Harrison said. Ruth reached again, desperately grasping for whatever that *thing* was, buried so deep below Mr. Harrison's rage and paranoia. "I won't get to go home! I want to go home!"

He was crying.

I want to go home.

Ruth froze. She remembered wanting that too.

That had been a long time ago. Years and years ago when there was only terror and constant fear. When people in lab coats and large eyeglasses, wearing purple latex gloves scanned her entire body, took vial after vial of her blood, told her to hold her knees to her chest so they could put a needle into her spine and test that, too. They shaved her head so the EEG stickers wouldn't keep slipping. All because of her dangerous, impossible Gift. She had tried to explain that she couldn't read minds, that feelings weren't the same. But they didn't care. So she stopped saying it.

She had wanted to go home *so badly*. She didn't even know where home was, hardly understood the concept after spending over a decade in a facility with scientists as rotating surrogate fathers and schoolteachers who taught her math in the morning and how to control her Gift in the evening.

For science, they said. It's because you're special. You're going to change the world. This is very important, do you understand, Ruth?

I want to go home! When can I go? Stop it! That hurts. You're hurting me.

You're hurting me!

"I want to go home . . ."

Mr. Harrison was crying.

Ruth blinked.

"Well, of course, you'll get to go home," she said quickly, forcing herself back in the present. Ruth was safe. She was home. "We'll find what got lost and get you home. We don't want you to stay here forever. How about you come with me and tell me what's gone missing?"

Mr. Harrison continued to mutter to himself. Ruth doubted he heard half of what she had said, but something about *how* she had said it was convincing enough. She took a step back and held out her hand towards a conference room. "Let's find your stuff. I'll talk to your team, too, yeah?"

She would be working an extra half an hour later than usual because of this little detour. But at least she wouldn't have to write a personal hold note and go through the emergent medication paperwork.

Right. That's why you do it, the Companion said, rolling its eyes. *Out of the goodness of your murderous heart.*

Ruth opened the door to the conference room and Mr. Harrison grumbled but walked in, eyes a bit drier. "When can I go home?"

I want to go home. You're hurting me! Ruth remembered. *When can I leave? Can I go home now?*

Can I go home now?

Can I go home now?

Ruth bit her tongue and held in a pathetic whimper. *No, no . . . not now.*

Ruth was *there* again. She was a name and a number, enduring never-ending days of tests, puzzles, games and experiments. But she was still *here*, with Mr. Harrison. And it was suddenly impossible for her to distinguish between her own fear and Mr. Harrison's. Ruth was trapped somewhere in space and time and memory while occupying this body and holding a very heavy door that led to a quiet conference room.

It only took a moment and Ruth was nothing more than an empty container for someone else to fill. A pure vessel. The perfect empath.

Mr. Harrison walked past her, barely grazing her arm. And as he did, he stood up a little straighter, his eyes brightened as his mind was cleared of the worst of his acute anxieties, fears, paranoia, and panic. It wouldn't last, but the day would be a little easier for him.

He turned around and looked at Ruth. His brows furrowed. "Are you alright, Doc? You seem . . . a bit nervous."

Ruth smiled, her vision swirling as different thoughts that didn't belong to her slipped in and out of her own mind like powder through a sieve. Her emotions were a kaleidoscope of colors and vignettes, none of which she could name or recognize as hers or as anyone else's. But she smiled anyway, somehow remembering that as long as she smiled, these feelings of fear, paranoia, and loss and the vestiges of memories she didn't recognize would pass.

It had to pass.

"Doc?"

Perhaps it would be different this time. Maybe this would never end and she'd be trapped in feelings and emotions that didn't belong to her and stuck in memories of loneliness and isolation.

What if her coworkers knew her secret? That she was not just Gifted, but an empath, capable of altering minds?

They'd find her, lock her up again. She'd never leave.

They'd come and get her.

I have to leave. I need to leave.

They'd get her. Take her stuff.

I want to go home.

"Doc, when can I go home?"

Ruth opened her eyes. "Sorry, about that. Got a bit lost." She closed the door and motioned towards one of the chairs in the conference room. "Let's figure out how we can help you out, today."

Vashti

The rest of the week had been largely uneventful. And Vashti hated that.

She didn't do well in times of quiet and stillness. She preferred it when the surrounding air breathed and swelled, when the leaves rustled and the world moved in its predictably chaotic fashion. But in periods of peace, every vagrant sound was amplified and every wayward movement destabilizing.

Like the air conditioner, for example. It groaned more frequently. Ruth didn't know and nobody else could tell. But Vashti could hear it wheeze every seventeen seconds, as if on its own internal clock. There was a mouse stuck in the crawl-space between their apartment and the neighbor's. It was dying. Over the last three days its scurries had become less frantic as it starved. But there was nothing Vashti could do about it, other than bear witness to its demise and mark its time of death.

Vashti sighed and sat back on the couch, springs and questionable lumps shifting underneath her weight. The couch had more in common with a sack of lumpy potatoes than living room furniture, but Ruth refused to invest in a new one. She generally refused to invest in anything new, unless it was a new set of IDs and documentation.

She shouldn't complain. Min had hired Vashti two years ago and Ruth had immediately taken her under her wing. They worked together well and their Gifts complemented each other perfectly. Vashti saw subtle movements, felt the air move and heard footsteps from half a football field away — her sensory perception always tuned up to one hundred percent. Ruth could sense a person's emotions swarm and settle into what would eventually become a motivation. Vashti saw change happen in real time while Ruth sensed the changing tides before the crash of the waves.

But, for the first six months, the two kept their proverbial cards held desperately close to their chest and their emotions tucked away under layers of mistrust and suspicion. Eventually, Ruth found out Vashti had been spending those months crashing at shelters or squatting. And Ruth had decided that was entirely unacceptable. Ruth took her in, introduced her to the old man who owned the only donut shop that mattered, and told her to sleep on her lumpy, potato sack couch. A few days later, Ruth had purchased a bed and they'd put it together in the spare room.

And the most surprising part? Ruth and Vashti happened to *like* each other. The two of them hated virtually everyone else in the world. Well, except for Nina to an extent. And the old man who owned the donut shop across the street. He could do no wrong.

Everyone else could burn in hell.

Vashti learned that Ruth did her own hair, everything from box braids, crochet braids, plaits and wig installations. But even though Ruth groaned and moaned the entire morning of her wash day, she nearly glowed with a sun-hot anticipation when she was almost done six hours later. And her hair was truly transformative. Box braids seemed to clip her already very short fuse further, as if her patience was tied right into the knots on her head. She was also more likely to wear heels. She smiled more when in plaits, but it didn't necessarily mean she was happier. She seemed to be the most comfortable in faux locs. Sometimes she even laughed. *In public*. The scandal.

She also learned that if Ruth didn't remember to take her meloxicam before work, her left knee would ache by the time she got home. Which meant that by the time Ruth was in the hallway of their shared apartment after a full day at the hospital, her gait was slightly uneven and she was desperate for the comfort of a chair.

That was the uneven gait Vashti could hear approaching the front door right now. Which meant two things:

First, Ruth was now about three steps away from the front door. And second, she was in pain. And *that* meant when Ruth found out Vashti hadn't folded up her share of the laundry and let the dishes pile up in the sink, she would be more annoyed than usual.

Ruth opened the door.

Ugh, Vashti groaned. Box braids. Wonderful.

Ruth shut the door with her foot and kicked her heels off into the corner before reaching for her knee and massaging the joint absentmindedly. Her eyes scanned the apartment. It was a mess. A total disaster. Vashti shrank, wishing she could become one of the lumps on the couch. "Sorry," she mumbled.

Ruth's eyes narrowed.

"How was work?" Vashti tried.

Ruth limped past her, muttering to herself, articles of clothing trailing behind her. She jumped out of her pants, threw her blazer onto the couch and lifted her blouse up over her head before crossing the threshold into her bedroom.

Vashti peered around the corner. "Ruth?"

Ruth was back at the door, glaring at her. Then she glanced at the front door. "Did you lock it?"

Vashti blinked. "Um. No. You're the one who came in."

"Lock the door."

What the hell? Vashti wasn't in any position to argue given the state of this place, so she did as asked, adding an eye-roll for emphasis.

"How was work?" Vashti repeated.

Ruth half-stumbled out of the bedroom in an oversized Rolling Stones t-shirt. "None of your business. Why are you asking?" Then she jumped over the console table, nearly toppling the thing over in a hasty attempt to get to the window and close the blinds.

"Ruth, wha—"

Oh. *Oh, no . . .*

Vashti inhaled — *hold, release . . . hold, exhale* — just like Ruth had taught her.

"Hey, Ruth," Vashti said a few moments later. Her voice was soft and smooth like churned butter. Sensitivity had never been Vashti's strong suit. Hopefully she could fake it well enough.

Ruth ignored her. She closed the remaining blinds and ensured all the windows were locked for good measure.

Vashti glanced at the clock. It was nearly eight in the evening. Usually the paranoia lasted a few hours, a fraction of the time Ruth had spent on the unit, absorbing the emotions of everyone around her as if by osmosis. It wasn't like this every day, though. Most of the time, Ruth came back from work her usual irate and indignant self. But on bad days — and Vashti had no idea what *made* it a bad day — Ruth came back home a little . . . different.

Vashti *knew* this job had been a bad idea. But Ruth had been so determined to "help people." Seriously, an inpatient psychiatric unit? For a Gifted empath?

"Ruth?" Vashti whined again.

Ruth didn't even acknowledge her. Instead, she held up one of Vashti's daggers — where the hell had she found that thing? — and stabbed repeatedly into their lumpy couch.

"Hey!" Vashti yelped. She tried to grab the knife from Ruth but she had the wherewithal to dodge Vashti's wayward hands as she dug a crater into the settee. She pulled out lumpy, old, white and yellow stuffing as if it were wrapping paper on Christmas Day.

She glared at Vashti. "Stop being an idiot. She's being an idiot," Ruth muttered.

Oh, great. *He* was there, too. It. Whatever Ruth called it . . . her conscience? The devil on her shoulder? Her "companion."

"Ok, my bad," Vashti said quickly. "Can I — just, can I have my knife—"

Ruth twirled the dagger in her hand and held it by the blade, hilt facing its rightful owner.

Vashti carefully accepted. "Uh. Thanks."

Ruth stuck her left arm into the couch until she found what she was looking for: a small, metal black box.

Vashti's eyes widened.

It certainly wasn't where Vashti had expected Ruth to store her Box with a capital B. Vashti kept hers under the floorboards, hidden beneath a rug in the dining area. But there it was: Ruth's various identifications and aliases, likely dozens that Vashti had never even had the pleasure of meeting yet, as well as a couple thousand dollars in cash. And yen. And pounds. And euros.

Ruth looked at Vashti, terror and mania masking the quiet fortitude Vashti was so used to seeing.

"Yeah, it's still there, Ruth," Vashti said. It was a feeble attempt to sound reassuring. Vashti felt like a helpless child tugging at a mother's arm, desperately trying to wake her up from a deep sleep.

Ruth's upper lip twitched and she whimpered, shaking her head. "No, we — look, trust me, right? Yeah? No, shut up, just *listen!*" Ruth's right hand gripped Vashti's shoulder. "It's always — *shut UP!* — it's always you and me, right?"

"Yeah," Vashti's throat itched and her throat tightened. "For sure, Ruth. It's you and me."

"So, we need to go." Ruth stood up, pulling at Vashti's arm until they were both on their feet. Ruth held her box close to her chest. "We have to go right now, we—"

The phone rang. Vashti's cell phone, for once in its miserable existence, was not silent. Instead, it blared Queen's *Bohemian Rhapsody* with reckless abandon.

Vashti reached for it but before she could even fully turn, there was a knife at her throat. *Vashti's* knife. Somehow, at the height of her transient psychosis, Ruth had managed to get the drop on *her*, the Gifted with enhanced sensory perception.

"Don't answer that," Ruth warned.

Vashti considered going for the knife in Ruth's hand. She could take it before Ruth realized Vashti had even moved. But that would scare Ruth, and she couldn't afford to have Ruth suspicious of her. Not *now*.

"Yeah, no problem," Vashti said, reaching for her phone in her back pocket. Slowly. She let it ring all the way through until Freddie bellowed *Mama...ooooh,* and the phone finally went silent. Vashti turned the damn thing off, holding it up so Ruth could see what she'd done, then tossed it on the floor beside them. "See? We're good. Always you and me, yeah?"

Ruth's eyes were wide and unblinking. And even though it freaked Vashti out, she didn't move.

Finally, Ruth lowered the knife.

"Look. My phone's off, see? Yours . . . is probably off already," Vashti guessed.

"I tossed it."

Goddamn it. They'd deal with that tomorrow. "Great," Vashti said between clenched teeth. "The doors are locked. Our stuff is here, you're holding your Box. We're safe. What if we camp out here, take it easy. Wait it out," she suggested. "I'll stay up and take first watch. Make sure we're safe."

Ruth nodded slightly, but her eyes were unfocused. It didn't seem like she'd heard most of what she'd said.

"So we can stay here?" Vashti tried.

Ruth looked at her this time. "What?" Then, to nobody, to *somebody*, she muttered, *"No, we can't."*

"Can we stay here, Ruth?" Vashti asked again. She knew she sounded desperate. But she was so tired. She just wanted to sleep. She wanted Ruth to tell her she should have done the dishes. Then Vashti would do them, whining the whole time, while Ruth made them dinner. They'd watch reruns until they dozed off on the couch.

But instead, Vashti asked, as if Ruth truly had any say in the matter at all, "Can we stay, Ruth? Please?"

Maybe Ruth trusted her. Or maybe she just sensed the pathetic begging of a tired and hungry teenager. Regardless, Ruth nodded. Then she stood up, and slowly shuffled back into the bedroom before crawling under the sheets, leaving Vashti alone in the living room with a knife and the broken remains of a lumpy potato couch.

Vashti

The Dallas Pedestrian Network spanned nearly forty blocks downtown and connected buildings, garages, and parks through sky bridges and undercover tunnels. It housed its own collection of high fashion designer stores, shops, eateries, and boutiques. It was an excellent way to navigate the city without having to deal with the bludgeoning Dallas heat or the suspiciously fresh scent of urine that wafted through the air on the street's surface.

Unfortunately, most Dallas citizens didn't even know the network existed.

In an effort to encourage pedestrians to use the underground system, and therefore encourage more ground level activity for the street shops, the network had expanded further and further, throughout all of downtown and towards Dealey Plaza and the Old Red History Museum. Since upstanding citizens weren't using the tunnel system, it was readily available for virtually any other activity: drug deals, gang fights, temporary shelter for the unhoused . . .

And the occasional arena tournament.

Vashti and Ruth sat with their legs dangling over an overhanging balcony that overlooked an empty cavernous space below ground. There, they waited for a boy with curly brown hair.

They'd been waiting for nearly an hour. The entire time, Ruth had been stretching her empathic tendrils into Vashti's mind. Vashti wondered if other people noticed Ruth digging around in their mind trying to figure out what they were feeling.

Probably not. People were generally painfully unobservant.

She had half a mind to grab that letter opener right out of Ruth's hair and bring it towards the woman's throat. Rummaging through her mind like that was rude, as if Ruth's own mind hadn't been a disheveled mess only yesterday when she showed up after work, threatening her, tearing apart their couch, trying to convince her to run away from mysterious problems that didn't exist while muttering paranoid nonsense.

The *audacity*.

Vashti rubbed her eyes. "Just *ask*, Ruth."

Initially she didn't, and Vashti could still feel Ruth clawing in her head. Finally, Ruth announced, "You're angry."

"That's not a question."

Another pregnant pause. Ruth was always so stingy with her own thoughts. Meanwhile she found no issue violating everyone's sanity with a fine-toothed comb.

"And?" Vashti pressed, growing impatient.

"There's nothing else. You're angry. With me."

"Everybody is angry." Vashti said. "As you've said. Ad nauseam."

"So you don't deny it?"

"Deny what?"

"That you're angry with me."

Vashti clenched her teeth and focused on the opposing

tunnel wall. Someone had graffitied an offensive word on the other side with great artistic flourish, as if to complement the slow, rising arch of the wall.

"Vashti," Ruth started. "I—"

Ruth had only moved to readjust her position, bringing her left knee up so it wasn't dangling over the banister ledge. But before Ruth could complete the movement, Vashti raised up her arm, knife in hand, and held it against Ruth's throat.

"You're wrong. I'm not angry," Vashti spat, remaining perfectly still otherwise. "I'm livid."

Vashti felt the woman's pulse halt for a full second before galloping wildly. Ruth's empathic Gift retreated from Vashti's mind.

"You need to get your shit together, Ruth. You can't keep coming home looking like you're a supporting cast member of *One Flew Over the Cuckoo's Nest*."

Ruth hesitated but Vashti's hand remained still and poised in its position. And when Vashti finally looked at her, her eyes burned. "You can't *work* like this . . ." Vashti's voice wavered and cracked and she hated herself for it, that she'd somehow become so hopelessly attached to another person in just a few short years. "What if Nina sees? Or Min finds out?"

"I have it under control."

"No, you *don't*. It's been getting worse for months!"

"Stop yelling."

"There's no one here!"

Ruth closed her eyes. "Vashti, my Gift has . . . side effects. Min needs me for my Gift. I have it under control."

"It's *not* your Gift that's the problem. You've had your Gift for your entire life. You started working at that . . . *place* last year." Vashti shook, her fury and rage washing over her in waves. Why was she so stubborn? "It's those people you work with, it makes it worse! They—"

Vashti stopped as an odd awareness flooded her senses. Ruth's muscles tightened. Then she reached for Vashti's outstretched arm. Vashti pulled her hand back, tucking her hand — and the knife — out of reach and tumbled backwards, landing on the ground.

Ruth swung her legs over the ledge of the balcony and rose to her feet. She offered Vashti her outstretched hand.

Vashti reached up and accepted it. But instead of hoisting herself up, Vashti grit her teeth and violently yanked Ruth's arm. With a surprised yelp, the older woman fell forwards. Vashti grabbed Ruth by the collar of her shirt and smashed her head directly between Ruth's eyes.

Ruth rolled onto her back, dragging Vashti with her. It was just a distraction. Ruth was going for the throwing knife strapped to Vashti's leg, and she was counting on the roll to disorient Vashti to not notice.

Idiot. Of course she noticed. She—

Cool metal pressed against the hollow of Vashti's neck. Vashti seethed, perfectly still, while Ruth pressed the barrel of a pistol against Vashti's jugular.

Blood dripped from Ruth's nose like the waters of a macabre stream. "I *told* you. It's under control. As for *you* . . ."

Ruth shoved Vashti off to the side, coughing as the wind rushed out of her lungs.

"Your anger makes you careless and overconfident," Ruth berated. She wiped her nose with the back of her hand and spit out a chunk of bloody sputum to the ground. "Even with your Gift. If one of us should be practicing control, it's you."

Vashti's jaw clenched and her fingers twitched, itching to grab her knife and prove Ruth otherwise.

Which, Vashti realized with frustration, would likely prove Ruth's point.

Ruth held out her hand but Vashti smacked it away before

trudging towards the ledge. She leaned over the banister, admiring the graffiti-art on the other side of the cavern.

Behind her, Ruth sighed. "Quit pouting."

Vashti glowered at her. "You just held a gun to my face."

"Yes, and you *disfigured* mine," Ruth countered. She hoisted herself up onto the ledge beside Vashti, her legs swinging over the ledge.

"I can't believe you got the drop on me," Vashti muttered. She kicked at a rock jutting out of the cement, firmly embedded in the ground.

"It's because—"

"Yeah, I heard you the first time. Because I'm angry and unlike you, apparently, I'm shit at controlling my emotions."

Ruth sighed. "Vashti, I . . . apologize if I scared you yesterday."

Vashti's eyes stung. Adrenaline from the fight blended with the concern and trepidation that had been simmering beneath her skin. She would *not* let Ruth see her cry. It was one thing for Ruth to snatch the feelings right out of her skull, but she wouldn't allow her the privilege of seeing them blatantly on her face in real time.

Still, Vashti couldn't suppress the wavering in her voice when she finally admitted, "I *need* you."

"No," Ruth vehemently denied. "You don't."

"I *do*. I can't do this . . . any of this." Vashti swallowed. "Min is a psychopath. I can't handle her—"

Ruth jumped to her feet and grabbed Vashti's face, forcing her gaze. "No. *No*, you *can* do this. Alone. You don't need me. Do you understand?"

Vashti's throat tightened. She pushed against Ruth's chest. "I get it," she spat angrily before resting her head on the balcony banister. She *did* understand, but that didn't mean she had to like it. Anything could happen in their line of work. And

Ruth had a *lot* of time left on her contract. She was much more likely to see the inside of a body bag before she saw her final paycheck.

And for the millionth time, Vashti wondered what fresh hell Ruth had left to agree to a thirty year contract with Min Liu in the first place.

"Nina said their last arena fight was cut short," Vashti said, eager to change the subject.

"Since when do you and Nina talk?" Ruth asked.

"Every Thursday is girls' night. We do our nails and catch up at brunch with bottomless mimosas."

"Vashti."

"She called. While you were *working*," Vashti answered honestly. "There was some sort of explosion. No casualties. It ended their tournament early. Maybe a bomb?"

Ruth shook her head, sighing. "Unlikely. The arenas are careful with weaponry." She looked pointedly at Vashti. "You should know."

Vashti stiffened. "We aren't exactly made privy to the security detail protocols. For obvious reasons."

"Fair," Ruth answered as she rubbed her eyes lazily. "Most arenas usually have a Gifted who is able to detect metals and alloys specifically for this purpose. Besides, why risk bringing in a weapon when you have so many walking weapons of mass destruction to choose from?"

"You think maybe it was a Gifted? Like a fighter for the arena? That one of them . . . just had enough and blew the place up?"

"Did they?" Ruth asked. "Blow the place up?"

Vashti shook her head. "No, it was contained. Like I said, no casualties. That's why they expedited their relocation to Dallas."

Ruth hummed. "Stay alert, then. People do desperate

things when cornered. Or . . ." She tilted her head, a new idea digging its heels in the crevices of Ruth's mind. "Maybe we have some competition."

"Seriously?" Vashti scoffed. "Who else would want this kid?"

"Just a thought. Like I said, stay alert and stay sharp." She looked down at Vashti. "Do you understand?"

Vashti noticed the air shift, as if someone had opened a window and let in a draft. She stood up tall, lifting herself away from the banister and ledge. Someone else had just entered these tunnels.

They were coming.

Vashti brought her hood up over her head and lifted her black neck scarf until it was just above her nose. Then she stood on the balcony's banister.

"I understand perfectly," Vashti said before she stepped off the ledge.

Anthony

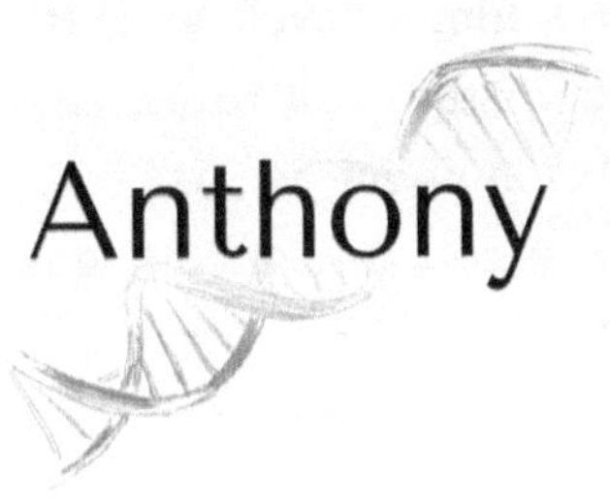

Anthony woke up to someone lightly jostling his shoulder, but the best he could do in response was groan, cry (only a little), and mumble something about feeling like he had to throw up as he rolled onto his side like a bowling pin.

Then, true to his word, he proceeded to projectile vomit over the side of the bed.

"*Dude!*"

Anthony blinked, willing the colors in front of him to form a cohesive image as his head bobbed and the world spun in circles. His eyes wandered up until he caught Neal's disapproving scowl. Anthony blinked twice. Surely Neal didn't have *two* pairs of eyes, right?

"What?" Anthony said. But the sound that actually came out of his mouth was, "Wh-aurgh-*GER*?"

"We're hauling ass, man!" Neal yelled. "And you puked all over my sneakers!"

Anthony rolled his eyes and moaned before collapsing back onto the mattress and staring up at the ceiling. The light fixture above him swayed as arena fighters ran from one room or hole-in-the-wall to another in a mad dash to find all their belongings or, as was usually the case, commandeer a few new ones from unsuspecting and still sleeping peers. Kids and teens screamed and shrieked at one another as the handlers did their best to rally the group. Eric's loud and booming voice echoed through the halls, the only discernible one among the general chatter and noise, "FIFTEEN MINUTES, PEOPLE! LET'S GO, LET'S GO, LET'S GO!"

"Holly already checked you out," Neal told him just before throwing a half-empty duffel on top of Anthony.

Anthony groaned. "What the hell, man!" he spat between clenched teeth.

"Stop whining. It's just a concussion."

"What happened?" Anthony grunted. He shoved the duffel off his lap.

"I just told you. You got a concussion. Something fell on your head and you passed out."

Anthony racked his muddled mind, trying to remember what had happened last night. But navigating his thoughts felt a bit like trying to read a map with the lights dimmed to low. He couldn't remember anything hitting his head at all. He'd been fighting Wyatt, and then the fight had been cut short.

"Now gimme your shoes," Neal demanded. "Mine are gross now."

Anthony waved him off as he sat up. The nausea returned, but this time, he was able to force the rising bile back into his esophagus. Neal, however, saw this as an opportunity to relieve Anthony of his shoes and scurry out the door.

Just like that, Arena Rho's time in Chicago was over. Most residencies lasted at least a week, but they'd only spent three days in Chicago. And yet, it wasn't even their briefest visit: a few months ago, they'd spent a grand total of thirty-four hours in Las Vegas.

Hosting arena fights in Vegas was an astronomical risk. The FBI's Gifted Services Division, primarily involved in trafficking cases, spent a lot of their time in Vegas to ensure those working in the clubs and casinos weren't being exploited. Which was preposterous. Gifted who were employed at any legal establishment in Vegas were one of the lucky ones. Nine times out of ten, they had a good gig, an air-tight legal contract, and the opportunity to show off their talents on a stage. Some Gifted saw them as sell-outs, obsequious grovelers who belittled and debased themselves and their powers for inconsequential things like a stable salary and basic human rights.

Despite the FBI's presence in Vegas, arenas risked the visit because there was good money to be made. Earlier that year, Arenas Rho and Epsilon had hosted a very exclusive, $2 million minimum buy-in round of fights.

It had been the most stressful thirty-four hours of Anthony's life, especially since he was the night's headliner. Right before his fight, he'd pissed himself in the hallway. Eric had helped him clean up as he stood there, feeling dumb and absolutely petrified that the arena would be found out by the authorities, that he'd be taken out of the arena, only to be dumped at the nearest labor camp instead.

Anthony had won both of his fights that night.

He sighed, shoving the memories into the back of his skull. He swung his legs over the side of the bed, and his feet landed directly in a puddle of his own sick.

ANTHONY and six other Gifted were huddled in one of the warehouse rooms no larger than a bedroom in Queens. Casey, a sixteen-year-old new recruit, had her head buried between her knees as she hugged her legs to her chest. Sarah, the eleven-year-old telekinetic sat next to her, drawing small circles on her back. Anthony sat in the opposite corner, his back against the wall and his right leg stretched out in front of him. His right hand was deep in his pocket, playing with a small ball he'd lifted from another recruit a few months after joining Arena Rho.

"You're staring," a familiar voice whispered in his ear. Anthony didn't so much as blink as Wyatt sat down beside him, groaning like a fifty-year-old man before he finally settled on the hard ground. Wyatt had a jagged cut across his cheek and stitches along his hairline.

Anthony gestured at his hairline. "Paolo?" he guessed. If Holly had healed him, there wouldn't be so much as a scar remaining. Paolo, however, wasn't Gifted, and relied on old fashioned methods to patch up the fighters: like stitches and ice packs.

"Paolo always takes care of me," he said with a grin. Then he then stuck his tongue out, just for a second, showing off the small pink pill.

Anthony wanted to strangle him. "How many of those did he give you?"

Wyatt clicked his tongue. "This is the last one."

"Those will mess you up."

"He doesn't give me enough to get messed up," Wyatt argued, rolling his eyes. "Chill, *Mom*."

"Where was Holly?"

He shook his head. "By the time I needed her, she was tapped out. I heard they're looking for another healer."

"*Hey*," one of the handlers bellowed before kicking Antho-ny's propped up leg from under him. Anthony lurched forward but caught himself with an outstretched arm. He looked up and glared at Clay, his least favorite handler.

"Both of you! Quiet!" Clay warned again as he shuffled to the other side of the room. Anthony imagined all the different ways he could freeze him to death.

"You guys still aren't friends, yet?" Wyatt joked with a snort. Suddenly his face fell, and his cheeks turned bright beet red. "Wait, sorry, I forgot . . . he was the one who recruited — I mean, picked you up, wasn't he? Shit, sorry. Clay's just . . ."

Anthony pulled his foot back up again and rested his free hand on his knee.

"The worst?" Anthony finished for Wyatt. "I don't know, man. They all seem a bit . . . on edge today."

"Oh, you didn't hear? A bomb went off yesterday."

Memories of last night flooded his mind with such profound intensity he nearly lost his breath. The fire, the shuddering ground beneath them — *that's* what ended their fight last night.

"Ok, well nobody actually knows what happened," Wyatt amended. "But there was some sort of explosion in one of the tunnel systems last night. So they shut down the fights early . . ." Wyatt trailed off as the elephant in the room made itself known and comfortable.

Anthony nodded to himself, squeezing the ball in his pocket. He might as well get this over with. "I'm . . . sorry about last night."

"You *knew* I needed to win that fight," Wyatt said.

"I — You . . . *I thought you were gonna kill me!*"

"I wouldn't and you know that."

"Well, it's hard to remember that when your best friend is throwing lightning at your face."

"I had my suppressor on!"

"It didn't look like it was up very high!"

"They were going to trade me."

The confession shriveled Anthony's tongue. It was extremely uncommon to trade Gifted between arenas. Arena managers were always skeptical when a trade was suggested. The only reason to trade a Gifted was to get rid of the weakest link. Even so, a bad fighter could still prove useful in the arena: cleaning, cooking, even spying on other fighters. But Wyatt wasn't some washed up fighter. He was one of their best. Which meant . . .

"How much?" Anthony asked. Not trade. *Sell.*

Wyatt picked at his cuticles, brows furrowed. "I don't know exactly. Eric said it was a *lot* . . . like Ivy arena a lot. And I sure as hell am not going to get transferred to an Ivy. So, I volunteered for the marathon. I figured if I could prove I was worth more than what they were offering, maybe they wouldn't do it. I won all of them, man. And then they stuck your *popsicle* ass in there."

Anthony flinched.

"Eric said he *told you* I had to win."

"No one said anything about being *traded*."

"What other reason is there? I had something to prove last night. But you couldn't just throw *one* match. You — you're . . ." Wyatt looked like he was about to break into tears. "You're supposed to have my back."

"I needed the win, too," Anthony admitted.

Wyatt scoffed. "Why?"

"Because we're going to Dallas next."

Wyatt's jaw dropped. "How the hell do you know where we're going?"

"I have my ways," Anthony said. His ways included giving up all of his extra blankets, his only pillow, and his favorite pair of socks to Bryce so he would spy on Mitchell and Clay and figure out when the arena would touch base in Dallas. Anthony had slept uncomfortably for four months but the boy had pulled through. Granted, the boy's gift was light refraction — invisibility, in other words. So, it wasn't a particularly dangerous or difficult favor for him. Regardless, his services came at a premium.

Wyatt shook his head. *"Don't."*

"I have to try."

"You smooth-brained idiot," he whispered. "You think you're the only one to try and run home when we land in someone's hometown? It doesn't matter that you're at the top. Clay and company will cut off your legs if they even suspect you plan on running."

Before he could argue, the ceiling above them shivered and shook. Loose gravel fell to the floor. Anthony and the others looked up expectantly as the low rumble evolved, growing in volume and timber until the tell-tale signs of Holly's portal came into view: a soft blue circle and a shimmering image of what was to come.

Holly herself ducked her head from the space above the ceiling. She grinned like a Cheshire cat and her red thick curls stretched towards the floor. Holly jumped, or rather, fell through the holes she had created. Just before she landed on her feet, the portal above her snapped shut, collapsing into itself like a black hole.

The wall behind Anthony softened, as if he was leaning against a massive stick of butter until it disappeared completely. He yelped as he almost fell into the new portal Holly had just created.

Holly winked at him, her blue eyes electric and as bright as her the pattern that glowed along her arms. "Who's ready for Dallas? Welcome home for the next couple of days. Or maybe we'll be there for a few weeks this time, they don't exactly give me a schedule around here."

Nobody else seemed bothered by the lack of itinerary as they jumped through the portal, eager to move on to their next stop. A new location usually meant a break, even if it was only for a few days while security surveyed the location to make sure it was truly secure.

And most importantly, one Gifted fighter would have the opportunity to head into town. They called it an "excursion," usually rewarded for ranking as the arena's top fighter at the most recent round of fights. Usually, the fighter returned with an impressive haul for the rest of the group, like an assortment of food from local drive-thrus and bags of sour candy. The Gifted teen wouldn't be traveling alone. They'd be with three other handlers to ensure they didn't make a run for it.

Since Anthony was currently ranked the arena's number one fighter, he would be the lucky Gifted selected for today's excursion. He'd made rank and gone on excursions before but today's ranking was important. *Finally,* after two years, they were back in Dallas. This was his chance. He just needed to give the handlers the slip.

He could go home and find his family.

He could go *home.*

Anthony waited for everyone else to go through Holly's portal. Once they were the only ones left, Holly snapped it shut, then faced Anthony.

Anthony dug his fingernails into his palm. "*Well?*"

He knew exactly what she was going to say before she said it, could see the truth in her slumped shoulders and eyes that refused to look into his.

"I'm sorry," Holly said. "I . . . don't think they're there."

Anthony swallowed the lump in his throat. "Sure. Yeah, no worries."

"But I didn't get a chance to look very hard," she added.

"You know they keep me on a tight leash. I only get a few hours when I scout ahead, and I'm with a handler most of the time."

Anthony clenched his fists. "You don't have to—"

"But I visited the address you gave me. I only had a few minutes to portal in. Sector 16 B, right off of eighth street, right? But no one's leased the place in—"

"It's *fine!*" Anthony yelled. His Gift lashed out, pulled violently by his anger. The temperature in the room plummeted.

Anthony kept his gaze down, shoving his hands into his pockets. "Sorry. It's fine. Let's just go . . ."

Holly held out her hand. Anthony hesitated but Holly held her hand up a bit higher. Eventually, he took it and stood at Holly's side, facing the concrete wall.

"Are you still going to do it?" Holly whispered.

Anthony sighed. "I have to *try.*"

Holly inhaled sharply. "Anthony—"

"Wouldn't *you*?" he pushed, squeezing her hand.

"Do you seriously think you're the first person to try?" she spat, her eyes wet and glassy. "What do you think they'll do to you? And if you get caught, I'd be in trouble too, you know."

Anthony tilted his head to the side, doubt finally settling behind his sternum. "Holly . . . what aren't you telling me?"

She shook her head. "Nothing! I'm just saying . . ."

Anthony squeezed her hand and Holly gasped, wincing. Her knees buckled. The air around them turned cold and thin. "Holly," Anthony warned.

She whimpered, her bottom lip trembling. "You're hurting me."

"Then what is it?" he asked again. He released her hand only to grab her by the wrist.

"They're letting you *go* on the excursion, aren't they?"

Holly screamed, clawing at her wrist. "You think they'd let you walk around your own hometown if there was anyone left?"

Anthony's heart stopped. What was she saying? He *had* to go home. Why did she think . . .

"It was Eric's idea," she said finally. "You'd been feeling down. Like *really* down. He was just worried. And after Asha . . . he thought maybe this would help. The fight with Wyatt didn't matter, Eric was always going to get you an excursion day here in Dallas. But the only reason he was even okay with it was because he double-checked ahead of time. Your family isn't in Dallas. There's no one *there*."

What did she mean? That there was no one at home?

He *needed* to go home. He'd made plans. He was going to go home and see his family. His sister would be there. He'd thought it all through, imagined it every night for five hundred and eighty-nine days. His sister would still be there. She'd be making dinner just like she had the night they took him. He had to get home first — just in time for dinner. Before Clay showed up and the door exploded and everything was just so *loud*.

His sister screaming.

His father, Logan, *begging*.

Gunshots.

It was so *loud*.

"Anthony, stop!"

He whirled around at the sound of his sister's voice. They couldn't take her — had to stop them. Vanessa wouldn't survive here. She was too good, too . . . *fucking* optimistic. She belonged in university, eating tacos at midnight and discovering something important but confusing in a lab somewhere. Vanessa had never even been in detention, let alone a fight. He couldn't let them take her. He had to—

"Anthony, *stop*, please!"

He groaned and fell to his knees. Why was everything still so *loud*? He looked up. Vanessa's hair was different. What was she doing here? And why—

His sister's face disappeared. It was Holly. And her face was wet with tears. She was on her knees, desperately trying to pry Anthony's fingers away from her wrist.

Anthony let go, eyes wide with terror.

"Holly, I-I'm sorry. I'm so sorry." There were large, tender blisters on her wrists. They were already changing color, now bright red and angry. He reached towards her but at the last second, pulled back. He couldn't touch her. He'd probably just hurt her again.

Holly cradled her wrist to her chest. "I-I'm sorry I lied. When they told you that you could go on an excursion . . . I already knew it didn't matter." She stood up and Anthony followed suit on unsteady legs. She was already starting to heal her own blisters, the angry boils receding back into blemish-free skin. "They don't let you go on an excursion if you have family living in the area. They double-check, follow up on records . . . that's why they trust us to go on them. Trust *us* to go."

And then, one more time, she held out her hand.

Anthony stared at her uninjured, completely healed hand. He took it carefully, but he had a hard time feeling her skin underneath his or the clothes on his back.

Holly's portal opened up. "I'm really sorry."

He nodded, dazed. Numb. Exhausted.

God, he was *so* exhausted.

The two of them walked through the portal. And on the other side, they were met with absolute chaos.

Vashti

This was supposed to be a simple extraction.

The Arena Rho fighters poured into the tunnel in groups, seemingly out of thin air. They were all coming from one direction. That suggested a portal system rather than travel via teleportation. Most of the Gifted here were barely teenagers, and they whooped and hollered like kids arriving at summer camp, backpacks and sleeping bags in tow. One fighter had already dropped his bags and was crawling along the walls of the tunnels. Vashti would have to keep an eye on him.

In total, nineteen Gifted flooded into the warehouse. But then, after a few minutes, they stopped appearing.

"He isn't here," Ruth said from behind her.

"I'm not blind," Vashti said, but her attention was else-where. She noticed something shift in the air. But she wasn't sure what it meant. She hated when that happened. "Wait."

Ruth did wait — for three seconds. "We need to move. The east side is a dead end and they're coming from the west. And

I'm not sure if you noticed Spider-Man over there crawling all over the walls. He's going to make us."

"Of course I noticed."

"We're in a room with nineteen Gifted and we have no idea what their Gifts are."

There it was again, that shift in the air, a ripple coming from the ceiling. Gravel floated through the air like miniature fireflies.

Vashti sprinted towards Ruth, knocking both of them to the ground just as the roof of the tunnel collapsed. Pieces of rock, cement, and century old piping landed in the same spot Ruth had occupied just moments ago.

Vashti stared at Ruth, wide-eyed. "Meet you at the rendezvous?"

"*Ye-ah!*" Ruth moaned, rolling onto her side.

Vashti jumped to her feet and ran into the fray. Massive cracks in the ceiling lengthened as rubble crumbled to the ground in heaps. No one seemed to notice her presence among the chaos. The other kids were screaming, trying to find cover. A few people were unconscious on the floor, including a young child — judging by his size — who had his leg pinned underneath fallen debris.

"Hey!"

Vashti stood, reaching for her knives as she rushed past terrified teens and dodged flying pieces of debris, shoving aside any person who happened to be in her way.

"*Hey!*"

A low voice, deep and masculine. It was either a handler or a trader. Either way, she didn't care. She threw her knife to her right as she leaped over the rubble. The knife found its home in the man's throat.

Two other arena handlers ran towards her next, coughing

into their arms. Vashti grabbed another pair of knives and threw them both in a single synchronized motion, one in each hand. Each of them found their home in the men's eyes. They crumpled to the ground and Vashti yanked her weapons from their eye sockets on her way past them.

Where the *hell* was that—

The boy she was looking for stood in the middle of the cavern. Somehow, he looked even more lost and confused than everyone else. His dark brown eyes darted around the room, struggling to make sense of the surrounding pandemonium.

Understandable, Vashti thought to herself. There was a lot going on. She broke into a sprint, jumping over a body as she made her way towards him.

Unfortunately, that body was not unconscious.

The handler grabbed her boot. Vashti stumbled, landing on her chest. She twisted onto her back with a curse and kicked the handler in his forehead until he let go. Then she leaped up, and without hesitation, dragged her knife over the handler's throat. She didn't wait to see his blood spill onto the broken ground. Before he was even dead, Vashti had closed the distance between her and her target, barreling into him just before another rockslide could crush him.

"Pay attention!" she yelled.

He looked around. "What is — Who—"

"I'll explain later but we have to get out of here *now*," Vashti yelled, yanking him by his wrist. He stumbled forward like a drunk. Impatience bubbled beneath Vashti's skin, so she grabbed him by the hand and ran.

"Hey, who are you—"

Vashti reached for her knife again and spun around, her arm already above her head, hand and knife by her ear, poised and ready to throw. But she wavered when she saw who it was:

a boy with stark white hair. His hands were alight with crackling electricity that danced erratically at his fingertips. Vashti threw her knife at him. He dodged easily but the distraction served its purpose. When the white-haired teenager looked up again, Vashti stood behind her mark, her knife to his throat.

"Wyatt, it's fine," the boy said, holding his hand out, his voice surprisingly steady. "Don't do anything stupid."

The white-haired boy, Wyatt, glared at Vashti, teeth clenched, eyes wide and wild. But his hands remained at his side as electricity surged and pulsed at his fingertips.

Then his head jerked to the side and his eyes rolled back. Ruth stood behind him, a lead pipe in her hand, as he collapsed.

"Let's go," Ruth said, dropping the pipe and nodding towards their new escape route: a precariously balanced collection of rocks, concrete slab, and rubble.

Vashti yanked the boy by the collar of his shirt but his eyes were focused on the unconscious deviant. "No!"

Another loud explosion shook the ground. Vashti ducked, shoving the boy's head lower as she surveyed their rapidly disintegrating surroundings. The next time Vashti tried to pull him towards their exit, the boy nearly tripped over his own feet. His eyes glazed over, horrified as he noticed something directly behind Vashti. Vashti turned, knife at the ready, but the person that had captivated the boy's attention was already dead — killed by Vashti's hand only moments ago.

"*Eric?*" Anthony mumbled.

Ruth was beside them in an instant. She grabbed the boy's shoulder, forcing him to look at her. "Come with us *now*. Or I will knock you out and take you anyway. And I'll have my friend here to kill every single one of your friends here. Do you understand?"

The boy's breath caught in his throat but he nodded.

"Okay," he muttered over the sounds of screams and collapsing debris. "Okay, okay . . ."

This time, when Ruth ran, the boy followed. Initially, they'd planned to escape through a restricted access elevator shaft, but that tunnel had collapsed in the first explosion. It wouldn't be long until the police arrived. They needed to get out. *Now.*

The three of them traversed through the debris, hoisting themselves over rubble, broken bricks, and jagged pipes of steel. The boy followed suit silently, but Vashti could sense his racing heart and haggard breath.

Ruth led them toward an intact door with the words RESTRICTED ACCESS painted in red. The three of them burst through the doors and Ruth grabbed hold of the ladder on the other side.

"Move it," Vashti said, shoving their latest recruit up. He followed Ruth blindly and Vashti trailed him a few rungs below. The light from the fluorescent street lamps nearly blinded the three of them as they climbed out the hatch and into an open, empty parking lot.

Nina was waiting for them, her backside resting against the car door of a ghost-white Bentley, arms folded over her chest. She wore a black, perfectly tailored suit. Her hair was up in a tight bun without a singular strand of hair displaced. She looked like she'd just come from a business meeting.

"You guys look like shit," she said. She opened the door and climbed into the driver's seat.

Ruth scowled and pulled the boy towards the vehicle. She whispered something in his ear, and he stiffened, then nodded before climbing into the backseat.

Vashti sat beside him and pointed at the hole in the ground they'd just climbed out of. "Was this you?" she asked Nina.

Nina shook her head. "Absolutely not. I thought it was you."

Ruth scoffed and buckled her seat belt. "Please. We'd never be so messy."

Nina

All three of them — Ruth, Vashti and the boy — smelled of charcoal, sweat, and singed hair, but Nina couldn't risk winding down the windows and an archaic traffic camera snapping a photo of them looking like burnt toast just minutes after an explosion that rocked most of Dealey Plaza. She was positive Min could make it go away if it came to that, but it would be a waste of time and resources. And Min *hated* wasting both of those things.

Nina glanced at the rear-view mirror and took in the boy sitting in the back seat. The photograph they had of him was from a two-year-old driver's license. The softness in his cheeks had fallen victim to the years and his hair now fell past his shoulders in a mop of disheveled curls. Years of fighting in the arenas had earned him a smattering of scars along his cheeks and arms and strengthened his muscles. Nina had done a little extra digging and learned he was one of the arena's most impressive fighters. Powerful. Resilient.

In other words, Min's favorite type of gun-for-hire.

And yet, that wasn't why Min wanted him. Min had

recruited Vashti because her Gift perfectly complemented Ruth's. And she'd chosen Ruth because her Gift was like no other.

Now, Min wanted *this* boy. But only because he was a means to an end.

The kid sat on the far-right side of the vehicle, taking up the least amount of space possible as he crushed himself against the window. He kept his hands wedged tightly between his thighs and his eyes closed.

His eyes shot open, staring straight at the rear-view mirror, somehow sensing Nina's eyes on him.

Nina offered a tight smile. "What's your name?" she asked. She knew it, but she figured a formal introduction would be a good place to start.

"What's yours?" he asked instead.

"Nina," she answered. "I've been told to take you somewhere safe."

"You could have let *us* know that," Vashti said.

"*I* knew that," Ruth said without opening her eyes. Her elbow rested against the passenger window as she held her head in her hand.

"But I *didn't*," Vashti mumbled. "It would have been nice to know there was a Plan B regarding extraction."

Nina scoffed. "I'm sorry, what?"

Vashti didn't take the hint. She rarely ever did. "I don't like being kept in the dark," she said, clearly enunciating every syllable.

"You *could* just say thank you," Nina suggested.

Vashti grumbled beneath her breath.

Goddamn teenagers.

"Today it was my job, not yours, to have Plan B. Besides . . ." Nina's voice turned sweet and viscous, like cough syrup. "When have I ever let you down?"

"Bosnia, D.C., Waco—"

Nina's smile fell. "Well, that's not fair."

"Girls, settle down," Ruth whispered.

"You're just jealous you weren't invited to mimosas," Nina countered.

Ruth frowned. "I thought that was a joke."

"It *was*," Vashti argued hesitantly. "Mostly. Happy hour is on Saturdays, not Thursdays."

"Are you kidding me? What the hell do you even get at happy hour anyway, V? You're not twenty-one."

Vashti canted her head to the side, lips pursed, as if she couldn't believe Ruth's questions. "Mozzarella sticks. *Obviously*."

"You can never make it anyway, Ruth," Nina argued. "You're working all the time. *Every* weekend. Guess when brunch is. *Weekends*." Nina paused, then added, "And sometimes Thursdays."

There was a hardness in Ruth's eyes, but she leaned back in her chair and said nothing as Nina pulled up to their destination: The LIUYEN Building, the tallest building in Dallas. It had adopted many names — and nicknames — over the last several decades. For years it had been informally called "The Pickle Building" due to the green argon lights that outlined the entire skyscraper at nighttime.

Min and Nina liked to call it "home."

Nina's window slid open, and she handed her building ID to the security guard at the tenant entrance. The gate to the parking garage glitched for a fraction of a second before stuttering open. This late at night, the building was almost completely empty, except for its residential tenants. Nina descended down until they were eight floors beneath the surface and not a single vehicle was in sight. She parked, and all four doors unlocked and opened.

Ruth was immediately at the boy's side. She shouldn't have bothered. Anthony was as lost as a goldfish in a fishbowl, and he soaked everything in with hungry, disbelieving eyes. Pity pierced her familiar shroud of uncaring detachment. This was likely the boy's first time outside since he joined the arena, at least without a handler on his heels. She'd seen this wild-eyed and desperate expression before in dozens of others Gifted they'd found.

In Vashti, two years ago.

Speak of the devil, Nina thought as Vashti walked past her towards the elevator.

Before Vashti could cross her, Nina grabbed the girl's ear between her thumb and third finger.

Vashti squealed, knees buckling. "When you next open your mouth, you will speak to me clearly," Nina whispered into her ear. "I do not like to repeat myself, and neither does your boss."

"*Nina,*" Ruth warned.

Nina pinched harder, cartilage bending between her fingertips. "*Do you understand?*"

Vashti nodded. Then, realizing her mistake, she hurriedly added, "*Yes!*"

Nina released her and Vashti nearly tumbled to the floor. Her palm cupped her ear but she composed herself and hurried towards the elevator with her head down. Anthony's eyes met Nina's, but instead of seeing remnants of the annoyance and hatred he'd been wearing so effortlessly moments ago, he seemed . . . calm.

He followed Vashti towards the elevators.

Ruth sighed beside her. "I already warned her today. About her . . ." Ruth hesitated. "Attitude problem."

Nina sniffed. "She's petulant."

"She's a child."

"She's eighteen and she works for Min. Being a child will kill her," Nina said with finality as the two of them approached the elevator. "She doesn't have the luxury of being a child or teenager. She should know better. Min doesn't have that sort of patience."

"I know."

"It's our job to protect her."

"I *know*," Ruth said in a hushed tone before the two of them joined Vashti and Anthony in Nina's private elevator.

The last leg of their trip was bathed in silence. Nina kept her eyes focused on the space between the sliding elevator doors, watching as the light from each floor peeked through as they climbed higher and higher until they reached their floor. *Her* floor.

Home.

Nina kicked off her heels by the entrance and her toes melted into the cool marble beneath her feet. Ribbons of silver light poured into the room through the open curtains, illuminating the foyer of the penthouse.

"Vashti, show Anthony where he'll be staying tonight," Nina said motioning towards the hallway on her left. "Call Max. He'll bring up dinner. You remember how to call for Max?"

"I'll take care of it."

Nina tousled her blonde hair and headed towards the bedroom she shared with Min. Muttering and grunting to herself, she reached for the clasp at the back of her blouse and pulled down the zipper. "Come on," she said to Ruth. "Get me out of this stupid thing."

Nina and Ruth had known each other for the better part of the decade, but Nina had the advantage of meeting Ruth at her most desperate — back when Ruth was still a teenager and barely had a handle on her Gift. Back when she was just a terrified girl who had been trapped in a box with curious scientists that lacked any semblance of a moral compass. For years Ruth suffered in the name of science and the pursuit of knowledge.

Nobody would ever be able to prove it, though. Those secrets remained buried with the dead.

But in the many years following, Ruth had matured into a woman who wielded her Gift with prowess and precision. Her fear had long been replaced with anger and disdain.

And, apparently, impatience.

"What are we doing here?" Ruth asked as she collapsed onto the deep marigold chaise couch at the end of the bed. Nina suspected she'd chosen that delicate settee on purpose: Ruth was covered in soot and grime and hadn't bothered to even remove her boots. And yet there she sat on a fifty thousand dollar chaise lounge with her feet up, one arm propped up against the back of the couch.

Nina leaned against the vanity and set down the glass of wine she had poured for herself. "You've stayed at our place before. My wife and I are hospitable people."

"Are you joking?"

Nina snorted. "Fine . . . *I* am hospitable."

"Your *wife*," — Ruth spat, irritated — "isn't even here."

"Why are you always so angry?"

Ruth stood up and approached Nina in just a few strides. She stopped when she was a mere handful of inches from her face, breathing the same air. "You've seen me angry," Ruth reminded her. "Do not make me angry."

Nina knew what she was doing — searching, tasting, sensing — whatever the hell it was that gave Ruth a perpetual advantage. Anxiety and dread flooded through Nina. She tried to suppress it, but of course Ruth could sense even that.

After a moment, Ruth took a half-step back. But not before reaching for Nina's glass of wine and bringing it up to her own lips.

Nina exhaled. "That's mine."

"Piss off," Ruth said before taking a sip of wine. "Whenever you bring me here, it's always bad news. Or another suicide mission."

Nina rolled her eyes. "It's not a very good suicide mission if you keep coming back." It was supposed to be a joke. But Ruth's eyebrows only furrowed.

Nina sighed as she wandered towards her wife's side of the bed. Min was many things: vicious, wicked, driven. But she also had an impossible and insatiable sweet tooth. Nina grabbed a cookie for herself, then snatched her glass of wine out of Ruth's hand.

"Min . . . lost something. She wants us to find it," Nina explained.

Easy enough. Ruth got up and claimed a cookie for herself. "What is it?"

"Information."

"Who does she want on the job?"

"*All* of us, actually. You, me, Vashti . . . and the boy as well."

Ruth coughed, nearly choking on her biscuit. "Who the hell is this kid?"

"You know, I thought the same thing when I picked *your* ungrateful ass up from that basement ten years ago."

It was the wrong thing to say.

Ruth's eyes darkened and she clicked her tongue. "What *I* do," Ruth said between bites, "is so novel that dozens of institutions and twice as many labs still study it under the chapter of their textbook labeled, 'theoretical.'" She pointed at the door, a half-eaten biscuit in her hand. "*That* child makes ice cubes."

"Min wants him on the roster."

Ruth scoffed, rolling her eyes. "Of course she does."

"And what's that supposed to mean?"

"That's why I'm here, isn't it? Min wants me to convince the boy to sign away another decade or two of his life to work for her. Doesn't she have enough guns for hire?"

"No, she isn't planning on—"

"I agreed to pick him up," Ruth said, her voice tight and strained. Her eyes glazed over, unfocused and distant and her chest heaved with every harrowed breath. "I'm not — I swear to *God*, Nina, I'm not doing the sales pitch again. Vashti was the last one, I warned you. I warned *both* of you that I wouldn't be your wife's telemarketer for—"

"What the hell sort of hypocrisy is this?" Nina spat. "If the boy works for Min, he'd be fully employed *with* a stipend. Yesterday, he was just another missing teenager. You like to paint Min and I as the villain but a few days ago you killed a mark because he smelled like suspicion and tasted like corn chips."

Ruth stiffened. "That's different."

"Of *course it is*," Nina said with a roll of her eyes.

The two of them fell silent. Nina cursed under her breath. This wasn't going the way it was supposed to go. "Look. Min isn't in the market for a new hire so relax. Min has *good* news, for once. That's why she wants all of you here."

Ruth rubbed her eyes and sighed. "Fine. What does she want?"

"She wants to write off the rest of your contract. And Vashti's. And she's *not* looking to make a new one with the boy."

Ruth's right eye twitched and she shook her head slightly. "That's not funny, Nina."

"I'm dead serious. No more extractions or sale pitches. No

more *favors*. The extortions, the bribery, the . . . occasional assassination—"

Ruth canted her head. "*Occasional?*"

Nina waved a noncommittal hand. "It's all done. She wants to completely terminate all of your contracts. You and Vashti can leave and do . . . whatever the hell you want to do. No strings attached."

"Nina . . . what did you do?"

Nina huffed before raising her glass to her lips, finishing the last vestiges of her wine. "I didn't *do* anything."

"Your wife is not altruistic. What's the catch?"

Nina sighed, massaging her temples. "The company is planning on making a major announcement in a few months. It's a huge, long-term project that's finally ready for release."

"Incredible," Ruth said without even the faintest hint of interest.

"It is," Nina said, blatantly ignoring her tone as she poured herself another glass of wine. "But now everything is on hold. Our hands are tied."

Ruth connected the dots immediately. "Min's being blackmailed."

Nina nodded.

"What do they have on her?"

There was a long pause as Ruth waited for her answer. Then, a realization dawned on her.

"Oh my God," Ruth gasped. "You don't know what it is."

Nina's silence was deafening — and she knew it. Ruth's laughter felt like a slap across her face.

"She won't tell me," Nina groused, and she hated how timid she sounded. So uncertain and desperate.

"She needs to tell *someone*. Nina, come on you know this. Blackmail is . . . tricky. We need to know the stakes so we can establish our necessary losses."

Nina rolled her head back, staring up at the ceiling for a moment. Mostly, it was to avoid looking at Ruth. "You really think I didn't tell her this? That she doesn't know this? All I know is that if this . . . secret gets out then she and the company are ruined. And the company is all that matters right now. The information that was stolen needs to be contained by any and all means necessary. You're asking about necessary losses? *Everything else* is considered a necessary loss. Nothing is worth more than this."

Nina could see the thoughts swirl behind Ruth's eyes, folding and marinating as she thought things through.

"This better have been a damn good affair," Ruth muttered.

Nina scoffed. "She would have just told me if it was an affair."

"I know."

Nina knew Ruth could sense her rising shame, but also her anger. Min had revealed all of this to Nina only three days ago and since then, Nina had spent every waking moment trying to imagine what on Earth her wife could have possibly done that she couldn't tell her. They were all supposed to be a team. Her personal team of dirty secret keepers. They'd handled mysterious disappearances, briberies, corporate espionage, assassination, theft and — just an hour ago — a kidnapping. What was left? What could be worse?

Nina raised her glass to her lips and engulfed the remaining contents into her mouth. "I'm going to tell you something, Ruth. And it's very important that you tell *no one* else."

Ruth leaned forward.

"LIUYEN's Genetically Gifted Division has fully mapped DVNT-29, the gifted gene. And we've identified all of its associated proteins."

Ruth frowned. "That's not—"

"Five years ago."

She shook her head. "No, that's impossible. Half of the labs around the world are still working on it. It's supposed to be . . . the next frontier of genetic medicine or something."

"Yes, on the same level as the isolation of stem cells," Nina confirmed. "We already did it. And three years ago, our genetics department successfully mutated a rat."

Ruth balked. "Nina . . . entire countries are pouring billions of dollars into their research into this. You expect me to believe LIUYEN did it five years ago?"

"First of all, I don't expect. I *know* you believe me. You know what Min's capable of achieving with enough resources and money to throw at a problem. But if you're interested in the details . . . we've been operating on faulty assumptions. Everyone assumed the genetic code was in the nucleic DNA. And they're not wrong. There are dozens of genes associated with deviancy all wound up in there. But the important genes — the productive ones that we can link to *specific* Gifts — those are in the mitochondria."

Ruth scoffed. "Surely a lab *somewhere* would have figured that out."

"I can take you down to R&D right now if you want to see it yourself," Nina said with a smirk. Hard sciences were never her area of interest, but over the last several years she'd managed to pick up the basics. "I'm not a scientist but I'd be lying if I said it wasn't interesting. Gifted and Regulars have the same number of mitochondrial genes. *But* one of those genes has a very small mutation. And because of that mutation . . . Gifted produce an additional twenty-nine proteins that are required for deviancy expression."

"Alright. . . so why are you telling me this?"

"Because in six months Min will host a symposium in Silicon Valley. She's going to announce that LIUYEN has successfully mapped DVNT-29 and report our preliminary findings regarding the successful mutation of *several* animal species.”

Nina slowly sucked in a large, exhausted breath. “*But* if this . . . secret of hers gets out to the public first? Min tells me that the company won’t make it to the next quarter, let alone another six months. Our reputation will be marred and the company will go bankrupt in a blaze of glory that rivals the demise of Enron.”

“Impressive.”

Nina glowered at her.

“What about . . . getting rid of the gene?” Ruth asked carefully, as if her words were tip-toeing between broken shards of glass. “You said LIUYEN’s figured out how to mutate the gene and cause deviancy in normal people. What about gene suppression?”

“You mean . . . curing deviancy?”

“Isn’t that what everyone’s wanted anyway?”

Nina played with the stem of her empty wine glass, rolling the thin glass between her fingers. “Don’t be naive, Ruth. The general public doesn’t have a problem with Gifted. They have a problem with lacking Gifts of their own. People *want* to be us. They just don’t want . . . well, *us*.”

“I’m being naive?” Ruth spat. “You can induce deviancy but the company’s put no money into suppressing it. You can’t give the world a bomb without creating the kill switch!”

“Yes, well . . . the bomb is worth a lot less money if it has a kill switch, isn’t it?” Nina answered. “Come now, Ruth. It’s just good business. And we haven’t induced the mutation in humans, yet. We’re at least a decade and a half from that.”

“Are you listening to yourself?” Ruth had a wild look in her eyes. “She’s *selling* our genetic codes for a payday. Nina, we can’t even fucking vote. We’re second-class citizens but from your wife's perspective, the reason we can't walk across state lines freely is your wife's next payday? And who do you think this will benefit? It will be people like Min, who lie to their wives and blackmail the competition and sell people's genetic code — *that's* who you want with powers like ours?"

"You're being outrageous and unfair—"

"I am not being outrageous. This is . . . it's—"

"How the world ends?" Nina suggested.

"Well, I'd hate to be dramatic."

Nina set her empty glass of wine on the bedside table and folded her legs beneath her on the bed. "Do you really think that *this* is the beginning of the apocalypse? Every scientific advancement in history has been met with gloom and doom and cries that it would bring about the end of humanity. The Regulars kill each other in *droves*, Ruth. They already hold all the power in this world. And yet, here we are. There's enough money in this world to feed everyone a dozen times over and yet they allow entire countries to starve. They blow each other up and kill thousands before lunch without raising a finger. We have rockets that have taken men to the moon, and yet people are killed for believing in the wrong God or because they live on the wrong side of the made up line drawn in the sand that separates one country from the next. Don't give us too much credit, Ruth. Access to deviancy won't end this world. Sure, they'll invent new ways to kill each other, but the Regulars are cockroaches. They'll live. And since they don't give a damn about the planet they live on, why the hell should we?"

Nina leaned back until her head hit the pillow, sighing as the down feathers hugged her neck and upper back. "I'm married to one of the richest women in the world, Ruth. And I can't travel to another country without paperwork that states that she's responsible for any damages or perceived threats caused by my Gift. Like I'm some sort of dog on a leash. This world isn't ours. We lost it when our genes lost the plot, about thirty trillion cells ago. What makes you think I care about protecting it?"

At first, Ruth was silent. After a few tense moments, Nina wondered if she'd quietly left in the middle of her tirade. But then the bedsheets shifted and Ruth sighed as she settled onto the bed next to Nina, occupying Min's side.

Nina cleared her throat. "In a year, governments and nations will argue and bicker and probably kill each other to get their hands on a dose of the deviant gene. But today, Min is hiring you to bury a secret. And if we can do it, then you and Vashti will get to do something no other Gifted can do. *Leave.* Your chips are already out. She'll get you both new identifications. You can live as Regulars — completely free. You won't ever hear from us again. Now, look at me. And tell me if I'm lying to you."

Ruth turned her head, but Nina kept her gaze focused on the ceiling. Nina could feel Ruth's Gift rummage through her, peering into every crevice and leaving no stray thought untouched.

Ruth would sense *so* much. And Nina could only hope the woman would never mention it again.

Love.

Disgust.

Guilt.

Desire. That pathetic desperate yearning that consumed Nina from the moment she had understood what it meant to have family. Her own parents had fed that desire with painstaking care until it had firmly taken root in her soul and invaded every thought and decision Nina could ever remember making. She had loved her family with everything in her being. Even after her family had changed their mind about love and left her behind.

Nina needed love. She needed to be loved. To be desired. To be needed in any capacity.

But now she had Min, and her craving had evolved into a destructive ravenous hunger. Nina dedicated her life to fulfilling every nefarious whim of the only woman who mattered. But despite the thorns of disappointment and the jagged edges of jadedness, Nina hoped that maybe, just *maybe*, if she was able to do *this one last thing* . . . Min would finally see her.

Ruth didn't flinch. She just looked at her for what seemed to be an eternity, until the invasive claws in Nina's mind retreated.

"I believe you," Ruth said simply.

Nina nodded and sat up, eyes burning.

"You deserve better," Ruth added.

"*Don't.*"

"*We* deserve better," Ruth insisted, unable to mask her frustration. "Your sociopathic wife is going to single-handedly destroy the planet."

"Possibly."

"*Probably.* And you don't even care."

"I don't." There was no point in pretending. She didn't care about this world or its future. Of petty things like politics and the preservation of humanity. What had the world ever done for her? All she had, all she'd *ever* had, was Min. So she would do whatever Min wanted.

And Min wanted to take over the world. So why not let her have a go at it?

"Do *you* care?" Nina asked. "About . . . the preservation of humanity, or whatever?"

Ruth laughed. "Sometimes. When I go to the hospital and go to work like a normal person. It's . . . easier to believe in those things when I'm with one person. But out here doing *this* work?" Ruth shook her head. "Morals and values are meant to guide people who lack the resources to behave otherwise. If Min hadn't made the discovery first, someone else would have. I'm lucky it was your wife. It's the reason I'm being given the opportunity to leave. Working with Min has afforded me many privileges, I won't pretend I don't know and appreciate that. But . . . I'd like to try my hand at making my own rules for a while. At least while the world still spins. Could be fun." After a beat, she sat up, massaging the back of her neck. "The information Min wants us to retrieve, where do we find it?"

"The information is secure for now. It's in a biologically encrypted hard drive. One of those newer models from Bio-Sec. The drive was stolen but without Min's fingerprints and a sample of her blood, it's impossible to share, open, or even copy the contents."

"So the information is contained."

"Correct."

Ruth sighed. "Great. All we have to do now is find the moron who had the audacity to steal it in the first place."

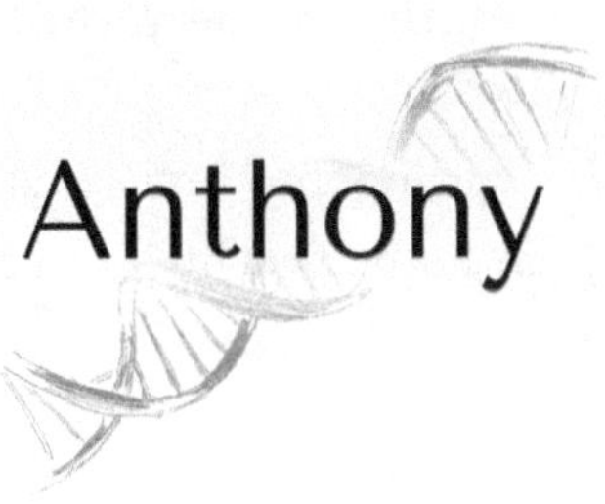

Anthony

The girl, Vashti, had largely ignored Anthony ever since their escape. And for that, he was grateful. She had shown him to his room, explained that the door was locked from the outside, and reminded him that they were on the seventy-fourth floor and the windows didn't even open so he shouldn't try anything clever. There was a change of clothes in the closet. Something in there should fit. Feel free to use the shower. There would be breakfast in the kitchen at seven tomorrow morning.

"Min will want to talk to you then," she said. As if that explained anything at all.

Then she left.

The bedroom was attached to his own full bathroom — shower, toilet, a bidet and a set of clean towels.

The first thing he did was check the doors and windows anyway, just in case. When he confirmed that Vashti wasn't a liar, he took a shower, then changed into a clean pair of pajamas.

He climbed into bed and sank into the sheets, the memory

foam beneath him shifting as he turned onto his side and reached for his pillow.

He sank further, curling into himself and covered his head with the duvet. Then he buried his head into the pillow and screamed.

Anthony

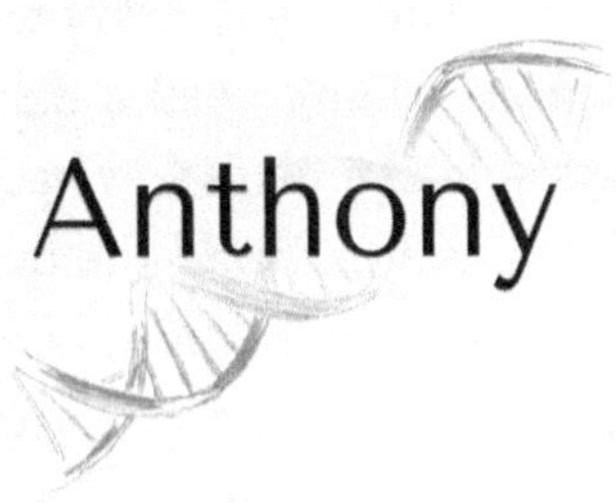

The evening air draped over Anthony and buried him like a heavy, oversized blanket: thick and smothering and in need of a very good power wash. It reminded him of the very heavy blanket he and his sister, Vanessa, used to share when they were children. Logan, their adopted father, would bury the two of them in the heavy sheets while they scrambled inside their cocoon of imagined danger, squealing in their attempt to escape the Jabberwocky or whichever mystical animal Logan had borrowed for the evening. And between the tightly woven layers of fabric was the light from their bedroom, and beyond that still, Logan: the only family they'd ever known.

But there was no light in this sector after hours. Once dusk had surrendered to night, the street lights dimmed and the neighborhood drowned in darkness. Blinds closed and every home, apartment, and corner shop in the sector was immediately inaccessible to visitors. But Anthony had lived in this sector his entire life. He didn't need a light to illuminate his path, he was always able to find his way back home.

The wind howled and he heard the quiet crunch of dead leaves and shifting shrubbery. Anthony whirled around, holding his breath. His eyes had long adjusted to the dark so he watched closely, waiting for any sort of movement. A few moments passed, then seconds.

Anthony scowled but turned back around, this time hurrying his pace. The last thing Anthony needed this evening was to run into a patrol officer who needed to get his numbers up for the month.

He couldn't see the names of the streets or make out most of the towering buildings that comprised Sector 16B, but he had no issue navigating through the broken chain-link fences and potholes between him and the southeast entrance of his apartment building. There was an ID scanner at the entrance, just below the intercom system. A small, metal box no larger than a pack of cigarettes. He held up his arm, wrist facing the scanner and within a moment, the door unlocked and Anthony was home.

The building had once been a luxurious high-rise. But twenty-five years ago, when the Gifted had first appeared, state officials chose which cities and neighborhoods the Gifted could legally occupy. In Texas, three small cities were chosen. And one of them was a small, quickly growing suburb in north Texas called Las Colinas. In a matter of weeks, the state of Texas had renamed Las Colinas "Designated Gifted Sector 16B."

Apparently, prior to what the Gifted un-affectionately called "The Reconstruction," Las Colinas had been an inviting, growing city that attracted successful businessmen, growing families, and some of the best restaurants in the Dallas area. Seemingly overnight, apartments that had once boasted of six-month long waitlists were vacant and begging for tenants. Theaters, cinemas, and convention centers went empty and unoccupied for months. Restaurants went out of business. It seemed that as Gifted gained entry into the city, Regulars picked up their bags and fled.

Anthony held his breath and bounded up the steps in the stairwell two at a time. At the landing at the second floor, he turned quickly, holding onto the banister to propel himself forwards. Mid-turn, he ran headfirst into a group of irritable tenants.

"Hey!" one of them yelled before making a half-assed attempt to shove him aside.

Anthony ducked and bounded up anyway. *Dick*, Anthony thought.

It wasn't until he had made it up to the third floor that he realized he hadn't heard the stairwell door slam shut. Curiosity sufficiently piqued, Anthony stopped and peered over the stair ledge.

There were three men at the landing. He didn't recognize them. He knew all three hundred and forty-one residents of Sector sixteen, as well as the fifty-four who resided in Building B. Well, fifty-five, after the Pattersons had their baby last week.

One of the men, the balding one, met his eyes. "The hell are you looking at?" he spat. His two companions looked up as well, snarling. Between all three of them they had approximately seven and a half teeth.

Nope, Anthony had never seen these men in his life. But since he had no intention of formally introducing himself, he continued his ascent up the next several flights of stairs until he reached the sixth floor.

"WHERE THE HELL have you been, Popsicle?"

Anthony kicked shut the door to their unit with the side of his foot. His older sister stared at him from the kitchen island and Anthony could have sworn her black eyes glowed red for a fraction of a moment. She held a wooden spoon in her right hand, the bowl of the spoon close to her lips. Her thick brown hair was tied loosely at the top of her head while a few rogue strands hugged her face, kept in place by the steam escaping the pot of food in front of her.

"Smells good," Anthony said, ignoring her question. "Careful, it's hot."

Vanessa's lip twitched. "Shut up."

"Careful, V, you're gonna burn it," Anthony smiled a little too broadly as he approached her.

"Anthony, I swear to God—"

"Let me help."

"No, st—*Logan!*"

Anthony leaned over and blew a small puff of air directly onto the spoon. Nebulous condensed vapor escaped his lips, churning and dancing as it engulfed the contents of Vanessa's spoon. In less than a second, Vanessa's wooden spoon was completely frozen and small, tack-sized icicles settled on her lips.

She yelped, rubbing at her face, her cheeks beet red. Anthony grinned and shoved his hands into his pockets, but paused when he entered the dining room. His sister had gone all out this evening: spaghetti with meatballs, chicken piccata and garlic bread. "Shit, V, are we feeding the whole—"

Anthony heard the profound *CRACK*! before he felt it, and for a split second he thought something had fallen from a ledge or a shelf.

Then came the rush of pain.

"OW!" Anthony yelped as he grabbed the top of his head. His sister, a foot shorter than him, stood behind him holding a broken, frozen wooden spoon. Her thick eyebrows furrowed and she lifted the spoon again, gearing up for a second bludgeoning.

Anthony ducked. "What the fu—"

"Is that Anthony?" Logan's deep baritone voice was coming from upstairs. Each step creaked as he half-jogged down the stairs. "Vanessa, is that your brother?"

"She hit me!" Anthony yelled, cradling the back of his head.

Vanessa scowled and this time, he *definitely* saw flashes of red in her eyes, like the glowing embers of fireworks. "You better . . ." she muttered threateningly, pointing the broken spoon at his face.

Logan let out a long, exhausted breath. "Anthony, what did you do?"

Anthony's jaw dropped. "Are you serious?"

Vanessa grinned, showing off her crooked teeth. "Don't mind him, Logan. Anyway, I think everything's ready. I had a feeling the two of you have been eating fish sticks and Anthony's famous pre-cooked grilled cheese or whatever. So, I figured I'd treat you guys." She bowed dramatically, then motioned towards the table. "You're welcome. Now sit down."

Logan's nose wrinkled. "That's hardly true. We also eat rice and beans."

Anthony sputtered. Unbelievable. "She broke a *spoon* on my head."

Logan helped himself to some bread. "Which spoon? Not the one with the red handle, right? That was my grandmother's."

Vanessa snorted. "Stop whining. I made dinner. Say 'thank you.'"

"Thank you," Anthony seethed. "I think you should still apologize for assaulting me."

Vanessa pointed her fork at him. "I don't think it counts if it's your brother."

"Uh, I'm pretty sure that's not—"

Vanessa held her hand up, silencing him. She cleared her throat. "Anthony, I'm sorry."

"Thank you."

"Sorry that you're being a little bi—"

Logan spoke before Anthony could interject. "Anthony, get some ice for your head."

"Yeah, Anthony," Vanessa teased. She looked up at her brother with sad eyes and a pout, a pitiful imitation of remorse. "Would you like me to get you some ice?"

Anthony rolled his eyes. "So how's life out in the real world?" he asked, eager to change the subject.

Vanessa's eyes widened and glowed with excitement. For a moment, Anthony almost forgot she had just made a possibly lethal attempt on his occipital lobe.

Almost.

Then came the familiar onslaught of one of the most aggressive bouts of verbal vomiting Anthony had ever witnessed:

"It's been *amazing*. I mean, it's a smaller college and super liberal obviously, so I know it's not like, you know, the real world. For example, ok, so get this: Gifted get extended curfew hours if they're college students. Even on the weekends. I didn't know so many taco joints stayed open after midnight but they somehow taste even better at one o'clock in the morning—"

Logan quirked a brow. "And why would you be up and about at one o'clock in the morning, V?"

Vanessa blatantly ignored his question. "And everyone

there is really nice. All the students *and* the professors. No one cares if you're Gifted. Well, for the most part. And I *killed* all my classes this semester and now one of my professors wants to let me work in their lab. She's a geneticist. And I got a job! Well, the genetics lab job is just an internship, but also like a *real* job that pays money. There's this tattoo parlor a couple minutes from campus and I think I can do both. The job and the internship, I mean. Plus, my manager says I'm really good. The manager at the tattoo shop — she says I'm one of their best artists and people *actually* request me now. So one of my clients bought one of my custom designs for a sleeve and I'm gone until January for the break, right? And I told him that Katie could work on it while I was gone if he didn't want to wait but he was like, *nope*, I'll wait until you're back."

Vanessa stopped to take a bite of spaghetti. Anthony wondered if she should have used that pause to do something more useful — like breathing.

"That's great, V," Logan said with a broad smile.

Anthony reached for Logan's glass of wine but before Anthony could lay a finger on it, Logan picked up the glass and moved it out of his reach. Anthony scowled in response and reached for a glass of water instead.

"What type of tattoo artist doesn't have a single tattoo?" Anthony asked Vanessa, feeling petty as he drank his water.

"I just don't know what I want yet."

"Or you're a chicken," Anthony said plainly.

"What about the research," Logan interrupted. "What does your professor do?"

Vanessa stabbed at a meatball. "She studies the Gifted gene. Looking mostly at epigenetic factors."

Anthony frowned. "Wait, isn't that . . . like trying to get rid of Gifted people?"

"Eugenics is a different word, Popsicle," Vanessa said with

a sigh and roll of her eyes. Anthony looked down at his plate, an uncomfortable heat rising up towards his cheeks. He hated when she did that. It made him feel dumb. Which, unfortunately, was often and not particularly difficult to do when she was off studying epigenetics/eugenics or whatever in college and he had to retake geometry over the winter break.

Vanessa, completely unaware of Anthony's shifting mood, continued. "She's trying to understand how the Gifted gene works. The gene doesn't kick in until puberty so something is suppressing it prior to that, right? And there's a big range in strength between people. One person with telekinesis may be a lot stronger than someone else. Which means maybe something genetic is enhancing the gene. It's a huge project and tons of labs are studying it all around the world."

Anthony frowned. Suppressing the gene? Enhancing it? "Wouldn't people just use that research to control Gifted even more?"

"Shouldn't we be trying to understand ourselves?"

"If people *actually* wanted to understand us, they wouldn't have dumped us in this building."

"Anthony . . ." Logan warned, but he wasn't looking at either of them. His eyes wandered towards the door and his brows stitched together in confusion as he slowly rose to his feet.

"The scientific community *should* be studying this stuff, Anthony," Vanessa said. "And at least this lab is willing to employ Gifted. The military funds their own research. Do you want *them* to figure it all out first? We should be trying to learn more about ourselves before someone else takes advantage of that information first."

"Quiet, both of you," Logan hissed.

Vanessa looked as if she was ready to turn the dinner table into cinders and ash. "You're an idiot."

"Your lab is literally studying how to *suppress* the Gifted gene. How am I the idiot? *You're* the idiot."

Vanessa's hands started to glow, red, hot, and fiery as her pattern traversed the length of her arm. "*I'm* the idiot? You were today years old when you found epigenetics and eugenics are two different things!"

"Quiet!" Logan yelled. The glasses on the table shuddered. Vanessa and Anthony glared at each other, their indignation teetering on the edge of outright rage.

Vanessa tried to speak first, lips parting slightly.

The front door exploded with a loud bang as pieces of the wooden frame splintered off and clattered to the floor like rain. Logan rushed towards the crash, Anthony on his heels.

"Hey!" Logan yelled. "What are you—"

The culpable party stepped through the demolished doorway. As soon as Anthony laid eyes on them, his stomach hit the floor. It was *them,* the three men and seven teeth from the stairwell.

The balding one appeared to be their leader. He walked a few paces ahead of his companions with a firearm in his right hand, pointed directly at Logan. But he grinned when he laid eyes on Anthony, showing off a handful of teeth, each of which were just a little too white.

"There's not much here," Logan said steadily. "There's cash upstairs . . ."

The balding one ignored Logan, his eyes fixed on Anthony. He looked him up and down, as if inspecting a new appliance for his home kitchen. Without a word, he pulled up the sleeves of his jacket. The sleeves bunched at the elbow, revealing a tattoo on his forearm: an image of thick barbed wire that formed a near-complete circle, with fraying ends that never touched. It was an old tattoo, faded. But every Gifted knew exactly what it meant.

The arenas. The boogeyman had arrived. And he had come to collect.

Anthony's knees went weak.

"Don't worry, kid," he said. The man's gaze shifted, and his eyes settled on something — *someone* — behind Anthony. "We're not after you."

Anthony glanced over his shoulder, and just out of the corner of his eye. His sister stood at the dinner table, her hands gripped the edges so tightly her knuckles turned white.

Anthony saw red.

All rational thought fled his mind as he shoved Logan aside and ran — literally head first — into Balding's center of gravity. With a cry that found its home in desperation, Anthony's entire body grew cold and heavy, as if he had taken a dive into the ocean in the dead of the winter. He collided into Balding's abdomen and sent them both flying to the floor. The gun that was once in the man's hand now lay on the ground. Anthony felt a wave of heat behind him and an enraged howl as his sister reached for her own Gift of fire and flame.

After a moment of shock and disbelief, Balding looked up at Anthony with a renewed fury. Before Balding could attempt to jostle out from under him — or, judging from the look in his eyes, just kill him — Anthony grabbed the side of his head and shoved it into the ground, so the left side of Balding's face kissed the carpet.

Fear roared through Anthony like a tempest. It molted into an untamed and unbridled fury that bubbled and boiled over until it became a physical force of its own, filling his mind and his entire being. His body grew heavier, cooler, his arms translucent like glaciers and equally immovable. Even as Balding screamed, Anthony continued to push into Balding's blistering face. He grabbed Anthony's arm in a desperate attempt to sever the source of his pain.

This was a mistake.

Anthony didn't think it was possible, but Balding's screaming intensified the moment he touched Anthony's frozen and impossibly cold arm.

It was the gunshot that shattered Anthony's concentration.

"THAT'S ENOUGH!" another voice bellowed.

Anthony looked up. Worry smothered his anger until it was forced to retreat into the tips of his fingers. Balding trembled and shook like a leaf. Anthony felt something warm and wet on his knees and he looked down. The man had pissed himself.

The third intruder held Vanessa's arm behind her and had her shoved and pressed up against the wall, a gun flush against her temple. Logan had his hand out, quietly pleading with the man holding Vanessa.

The tips of her fingers twitched, growing warmer and hotter despite her attempt to hold back her Gift.

"Okay!" Anthony said as he rolled off Balding and onto his knees. He kept his hands up above his head. The chill in his fingers retreated. "Okay, just stop. See, we're good? I'm good."

Balding took advantage of the moment. He grabbed Anthony's collar, dragging himself up from the floor before delivering a swift punch to the side of Anthony's head.

Anthony stumbled and his vision spun. He would have keeled over completely were it not for Balding, who had a tight grip on the collar of his shirt.

Balding punched him again. Anthony saw stars.

"STOP!"

"Anthony!"

"Come on, Clay," the man holding onto Vanessa warned. He yanked at Vanessa's arm, pushing her towards the demolished front door. "We got what we came here for. Let's go."

No, no, no. They couldn't take her. Not her. *Not Vanessa.*

Not his sister.

Clay apparently agreed. "Forget her," he said. Clay brought Anthony to his feet, until his face was mere centimeters from Anthony's unfocused eyes. The right side of Clay's face, the side Anthony had mercilessly frozen for the better part of fifteen seconds, was blistering, red, and inflamed. Larger vesicles near his brow leaked blood and colorless fluid and his right eyebrow was nonexistent.

"Change of plans," Clay said with finality. "We're taking this one."

Vanessa's eyes widened. *"NO!"*

Clay ignored her. "And as for you . . . if you even *think* about turning those little fists of yours into ice cubes again, I'll slit your throat and take your sister instead. Understand?"

Anthony blinked. At least, he thought he blinked. It was getting harder and harder to follow the conversation. His vision darkened, edges blurring, color bleeding into nothingness. His stomach twisted in knots, and he wanted to throw up.

"Please." That was Logan's voice. "We won't say anything, we won't tell anyone just—"

"You know that's not how this works," Clay said.

The man holding Vanessa shrugged. He shoved her aside, then aimed his gun at Logan.

"Can't have you two following," he said, before firing at Logan's abdomen.

"Logan!" Vanessa screamed, rushing towards him.

"Call 911. Get him to a hospital, he'll be fine," Clay said. He held on tightly to Anthony's collar, half-dragging him out into the hallway like a stubborn dog on a leash. Anthony tried to turn, tried to say something, tried to do *anything*, but he couldn't move. He could barely keep his eyes open. The last thing he saw before the group turned the corner out the apartment door was his sister, her hands and arms stained in Logan's blood.

"Welcome to the arena, you little shit," Clay muttered before Anthony finally lost consciousness.

Part II: I Think, Therefore I Am

Interlude I: Raahi

Raahi harbored immense pride in his ability to change.

Yesterday for example, he was a good son: reliable, ensuring his sister had eaten dinner and had her bedtime story read to her (the same one again about the princess and that goddamn cricket). She was fast asleep long before their father came home from an unexpectedly long day at work at the Immigration and Census Office.

The day before that, Raahi had been a good student, earning top marks on his placement exams. The exams were the first step of a long, winding journey that could lead to a top position at the ICO where he could finally be The Boss.

Today though, Raahi Varo had every intention of becoming a dragon.

"But you got to play the dragon last time!" Raahi huffed and whined in a high-pitched voice that nearly rivaled his sister's. And to make matters worse, Ruth was four years younger than him. It was *embarrassing*.

Whenever Raahi found himself lost in an emotion, especially an uncomfortable one, like anger or sadness, his chest tightened, and his vocal cords followed suit. Raahi's eyes burned and he furiously rubbed at the wetness on his cheek before his sister noticed. If she knew he was crying, she'd probably get nervous and let him be the dragon anyway. And that was *much* worse. He was eight years old, for crying out loud.

Fortunately, Ruth didn't notice. Instead, she lifted both of her arms above her head and bared all her tiny, crooked teeth in the most vicious growl she could muster. "*Rawwwrr! I'm gonna eated all your children!*"

Raahi blinked, for a moment forgetting why he was so upset in the first place. Maybe he shouldn't have read that Princess and the Cricket story to her again last night. Other children her age were terrified of the Queen in the story: hoarder of children that she'd bake into pies and serve to her favorite woodland creature, the Cricket. But his sister, for whatever reason, seemed to identify more with the Queen. Raahi wasn't precisely sure of the origin of his sister — or children for that matter. But surely it wasn't too late to return her back to . . . well wherever it was she came from. He and his father could exchange her for something less . . . odd? Preferably a boy, like Raahi. Or a parakeet. And they could play Dragons instead.

Ah, right, of course. *That's* why he was so upset. She was hijacking his game! *Again.*

"No!" Raahi said loudly, in a scary deep voice. The one Dad used when Raahi tried to eat another sweet before bedtime. "No, *I'm* the blue dragon and I *don't* eat any children."

Ruth was unimpressed. She stomped closer to him, lifting her arms up a bit higher and standing on her toes. "I eated ALL the children! I eat *you!*"

Her eyes widened, as if she had just realized the magnitude of her own imaginary power. Then she growled again, just to drive the point home.

Raahi panicked. His sister's growl grew louder, the sound resonating from her chest and dropping half an octave as she started to chase him around their father's workroom. Raahi screeched as he and Ruth ran laps around the workbench. On his fourth go-around, he reached up, hoping to grab something from the table that could serve as a weapon. His arms repeatedly found nothing as his sister stomped and roared and giggled. Eventually, Raahi found himself smiling too.

After seven laps around the workbench, Raahi grabbed hold of something hard, cold . . . and very heavy. He stumbled, ill-prepared for the weight and his sister ran directly into him with the grace of a newborn giraffe. She fell and Raahi took a step back holding out the . . . wrench? His father tried to teach him all the names, but he kept mixing them up. But instead of standing up and continuing their game, his sister looked up at him, surprised that she'd taken a tumble. For a tense moment, all seemed well.

Then his sister's lips trembled and she closed her eyes and opened her mouth.

Uh oh.

"No, no, no!" he tried to warn desperately, flailing his arms in front of her. But he was too late.

Ruth sobbed? Wailed? Screamed? All of the above. Raahi dropped the wrench. "No, it's okay!" he said, walking towards her to give her a patronizing hug. "Stop that. Dragons don't cry, remember? RAWR!"

His sister only sobbed louder. "I'm . . . the . . . *QUEEN!*" she hiccuped between deafening sobs.

A loud, booming voice broke through. A deeper, very grown-up voice. "What's going on down there?"

Great.

The steps to the basement creaked and groaned as their father forged down the stairs that led to the basement. "What are you two doing down here? I told you not to play in the shop!"

This time, Raahi forgot to wipe away the stray tears that escaped his eyelids. Now he was *really* going to get it. Playing downstairs *and* his sister was crying. And he was the only suspect at the scene.

His dad's cheeks were as red as ripe tomatoes and when he looked down and saw the wrench on the floor, his eyes widened.

Then his dad looked at his sister.

"What happened?" he rushed towards her, then lifted her up in one fell swoop before maneuvering her about as if she was one of her own dolls. He removed his glasses from his balding head and placed them on the bridge of his nose. "Alright, Princess, let's see."

"It wasn't me!" Raahi said, crying freely now. His nose was running, and he wiped the snot away with the back of his hand. "She was the dragon!" he tried to explain.

"I'M THE QUEEN!" Ruth yelled.

Their father ignored both of their weeping, inspecting his sister's finger, toes, and exposed kneecaps — both of which were scraped and bleeding.

"It's alright, you're just fine," he repeated as he hushed her gently over and over until she finally stopped crying.

Then she looked at Raahi, eyes wide as a realization dawned on her. Her eyebrows furrowed like dancing caterpillars.

Ruth pointed at him. "He pushed me!"

Raahi was going to kill her one day. If they couldn't find the proof of purchase and exchange her for something more appealing, he'd just take matters into his own hands and dispose of her himself. "I did not!" he yelled, stomping his foot. Then he started crying again. "She ran into me!"

Ruth narrowed her eyes at him. She looked like she was ready to let it rain baby tears once more, but with feeling. But Dad just lifted her further away from his shoulders so he could look at her face. His sister abruptly closed her mouth again.

"Was it an accident?" Dad asked slowly, looking at her above his eyeglasses.

Raahi sniffed and nodded. After a careful moment of deliberation, his sister nodded too.

Dad sighed. "I told you not to play here," he repeated.

Raahi bit his lip in thought. They had been told this many times in the past. He couldn't remember why they didn't listen this time. When he looked up again, he saw that Dad was looking right at him. His stomach felt funny. Like when he had to go to the bathroom or drank sour milk.

"Raahi—"

"I know I'm s'pose to look after her but . . . but . . . she started it! She's . . . *infuriating*."

"That's a very big word."

"Thank you," Raahi sniffed with a slight nod. Then he continued, "We were supposed to play Dragons upstairs and if I was the Dragon we would have been upstairs but she wanted to be the Dragon and she came down here because Dragons live in the dungeon and—"

Raahi was up in the air. His sister was squealing and their dad was holding them in each of his big arms, initiating their solemn retreat from the Dragon's lair and back to the real world.

"You're going to have to outsmart your sister one day, you know," his father said. He didn't seem very upset, though. In fact, he was smiling. But Raahi didn't know what there was to be so happy about. His dad whispered to him, so his sister couldn't hear. "You're older, yes? And smart, using big words like *infuriating*."

Raahi rolled his eyes but nodded.

Dad laughed, a low chuckle that started in his belly. It made Raahi's leg tickle as the sound vibrated between the three of them. Raahi giggled.

Something behind them also thought it was all very funny and started laughing too. But it was a different sound — a low buzzing like a swarm of bees. His dad turned around slowly. In the corner of the room, behind a draped curtain, something was *humming*. Raahi, tilted his head in thought and started biting his fingernail. Maybe it was a robot. Varas had told him about those . . . people that weren't real people but looked like people and tried to take over the universe. He doubted Varas, his friend at school, had ever seen a robot in real life, though. Varas liked to make things up. A *lot*.

Wouldn't that be something, though? If Raahi got to see a real robot? Varas would be so jealous.

"Maybe it's a robot," he finally said aloud.

Dad ignored him. He set both Raahi and Ruth and shoved them towards the stairs. "Raahi, take your sister upstairs, alright?"

"Is it a robot?"

"*Raahi*," he warned. The deep, grown-up voice was back.

Raahi shuddered but followed his dad's instruction . . . kind of. Once at the top of the landing, he looked at his sister. "Go upstairs to your room. I'm gonna spy."

"But Dad said—"

"Dad said to take you upstairs. So beat it."

Raahi doubted that if he got caught his father would agree with his interpretation of these instructions. But nevertheless, his sister scowled at him and retreated. Once Ruth was out of sight, he tiptoed back down the stairs avoiding the side of the stairs that creaked. Slowly, carefully, he squatted and peaked just behind the banister.

Raahi's face fell when he caught a glimpse of what was causing the mysterious sound.

It wasn't a robot. It was just a mirror. He huffed, annoyed.

His dad spun around.

Oops.

"Raahi!" Dad scolded.

And then the impossible happened.

Someone stepped *out* of the mirror.

Raahi rushed up the stairs and slammed the door to the basement behind him. Ruth, just as disobedient as he, was waiting for him.

"What was it?" Ruth asked as she bit her nails

He grinned, his body itching with excitement. "A robot."

Min Liu

"Ms. Liu, CNN wants a statement regarding the recent layoffs in the R&D department." Min's assistant, Sarah Lennox, held the elevator door open with the toe of her stiletto shoe, blatantly ignoring the elevator's infuriating whine in protest. "One of the scientists is threatening to talk. Barry something."

Min hid her left hand behind her back and pressed her fingernails into the palm of her hand, focusing on the uncomfortable prick to keep from screaming as her frustration pounded against the walls of her skull. "Didn't he sign an NDA?"

"Obviously."

"So he's testing us," Min said.

"Deflect or defame?"

Deflect the claims the scientist — Barry something — was making and ignore them, or defame his character. The former sent a message: that his claims were unfounded and that they didn't warrant the company's attention. The latter could backfire if the defamation wasn't substantial enough to make Barry stand down.

"Dig first. See what you find, then talk to PR."

Sarah nodded and stepped away from the elevators. By the time the doors finally closed, Sarah had already lifted her phone to her ear, prepared to carry out Min's instruction with faithful precision.

Min released a drawn out sigh, rubbing the side of her face. She was exhausted. Ever since she'd learned of the private information that had been stolen from her, she'd hardly slept. She could barely eat and her thoughts were always occupied, creating the most elaborate of worst-case scenarios. Concealer and eye-shadow covered up most of the evidence from her sleepless nights and constant worry. No one at work suspected that she was barely paying attention in meetings and conversations. Besides, she'd long learned how to fake intrigue for hours at a time.

But Min's next meeting was with her wife, and even though she hid the details of her most loathsome secrets from her, Nina could always plainly see the cost of those secrets etched into Nina's frown lines.

I should tell her, Min considered for the third time in as many hours. *This* was why she couldn't sleep. She wanted to tell Nina the truth, but if she did, then uglier, fouler secrets from Min's past would also see the light of day.

And she wasn't ready for that.

Min's office was on the fifty-third floor of the seventy-story building. The general aesthetic of the building was minimalist and simple: neutral tones, blacks, whites, and grays. Min, on the other hand, hadn't cared to match the building's color scheme.

Her office was eclectic and vibrant, furnished with a

vintage oak desk, a long white couch, and an antique Persian rug threaded with shades of mahogany and gold accents.

She found Nina waiting for her in front of the art gallery, carefully inspecting one of the paintings: a watercolor of a boat, careening in the midst of a brutal storm with its sails swaying wildly to the side and the men on the boat holding onto the mast and each other. Some of the boat's inhabitants were mid-fall, rapidly approaching the raging sea below.

"You seem worried," Nina said. Min hadn't even looked at her.

"I'm fine."

Nina sighed and took Min's hand in hers, tracing her palm with her thumb until she found four sharp divots, painful grooves where Min's fingernails had repeatedly found purchase.

"See?" Nina said. "*You are* worried."

Min inhaled sharply but didn't retract her hand. "Of course I'm worried. The most valuable asset I've ever owned is missing—"

"Blackmail isn't exactly an asset," Nina corrected.

"Well, yes, some of the information on that drive *could* be used as blackmail," Min huffed. "But there was also . . . delicate information. I don't want it falling into the wrong hands. Or any hands. Not yet."

"Your *delicate* information will be fine," Nina said. She turned and looked at Min with blue eyes as turbulent as a storm.

"And who the hell was that last night?" Min continued, her mind racing. "The explosion at the arena?"

"It wasn't us."

"Obviously."

"I'm sure we'll find out sooner or later, though."

Min groaned. "None of this would even matter if that drive

wasn't stolen. I thought that was the whole point of that stupid bio-security company."

Nina squeezed her wife's hand. "Your data, even if missing, is still perfectly safe. No one can open it."

She knew Nina was right. Biological encryption had only recently gained traction among the pretentious and wealthy. Within six months of it hitting the international markets, every tech mogul, big shot executive, and CEO that had the expendable income was completely outfitted with bio-encryption technology. To open biologically encrypted data, the person needed the right passcode, the entire DNA sequence and the unique proteins specific to the owner of that data. And since each person was biologically unique, it was very difficult for any human or program to decrypt the data.

All of Min's little secrets were safe. Nobody except for Min could open the drive.

In theory.

Nina released her hand and Min closed her hands to form a loose fist. The four sharp divots that Min's fingernails had created over the last several hours had disappeared. Her skin was now fully healed and blemish free.

"Try and keep it that way this time, yes?" Nina said before leaning towards her, capturing Min's lips in hers. Finally, for the first time in hours, Min's mind emptied. There was only this, Nina's assurance, her presence. Her loyalty. Her undying trust.

Nina didn't deserve this.

You should tell her.

All too soon, Nina slowly pulled back. Min sighed, already mourning the loss of her touch, and she rested her forehead against Nina's and closed her eyes. "I . . . I'm sorry," she whispered.

"I know."

You should tell her.

"You don't have to tell me."

Min's eyes flew open. Had she said that out loud?

Nina chuckled and lifted Min's chin with her index finger. Even though Min wore her tallest stiletto heels, Nina was still several inches taller than her. "You'll tell me when you're ready," Nina said. "I'll still be here. Besides, you know what we do is dangerous. Perhaps . . . it's a good thing I don't know. I can't divulge any secrets unknowingly."

"That's not my concern," Min said, eyes hardening. "That's *never* my concern. I trust you implicitly."

Min wanted to take back the words as soon as she said them. Of course she trusted her wife. *Completely and totally.* But if that were true, then she would have told Nina the truth about what was *on* that damn hard drive. Min could declare her love and trust as much as she wanted, but her actions today — *right now* — suggested otherwise.

And yet, Nina trusted her anyway.

"You'll tell me when you're ready," Nina repeated. "In the meantime, your team and newest recruit are ready to meet you. They're at home. Max is taking good care of them. Which you would have known if you had come home last night."

Min glared at her, but the words stung, nevertheless. "I know," she said softly. "I know. I'm sorry I was—"

"Working," Nina finished. "I know, it's alright. But *fixing,*" she held Min's hand, the one she had just healed. "That's my job. And we will fix this hard drive problem, too. The others are at home whenever you're ready. And Ruth is on board."

"Is she?" Min raised an eyebrow. "I expected at least some defiance."

"She needed some convincing," Nina admitted. "I told you, fixing is my job."

Min hummed as she shuffled through her desk drawers. To

an outsider, she seemed composed. But Min felt like her entire body was vibrating with anxiety. And she was certain Nina could see her other hand already balled into a tight fist again.

"What do you need me to do?" Nina asked.

Bless this woman.

"The attack at the arena this morning. I want to know more about it."

Nina nodded, standing up a bit straighter. Like a switch, Min was no longer exchanging concerns and anxieties with her wife. She was engaging with a business partner, delegating an assignment.

"I'll have a report for you in twenty-four hours," Nina promised.

"When you have it, show it to me first."

"You don't want Ruth to know?"

"I want to see it first. I have a suspicion I want to confirm. And if I'm right, I want to get ahead of it."

Nina nodded. "Consider it done." Before she could take a step towards the door, Min had slipped her hand in Nina's and tugged. Nina pivoted back until she was facing Min who then took her face in her hands, carefully, as if holding glass.

"Thank you," Min said. Her exhale became Nina's inhale and the space between them closed completely.

Ruth

Ruth was surprised to see Anthony the next morning, eating breakfast and *smiling*.

Max had truly outdone himself that morning in curating the expansive breakfast presented at the table for all of them: pancakes, fruits, sausages, eggs, and biscuits to start. Never one to skip a sampling of his own creation, Max had opted to take a seat beside Anthony and the two of them were muttering to each other in hushed, whispered tones. Every now and then, Anthony's tight smile would broaden and the skin around his eyes would crinkle while Max's hearty laugh echoed through the dining area.

"Morning."

Ruth nearly jumped out of her skin as Vashti walked into the dining room from behind her. Unlike Ruth and Anthony who were in nightgowns and robes, Vashti was already dressed in her signature color: black. Her hair was in a singular long braid that trailed down to the small of her back. She took a seat next to Max.

"Oh, Vashti. Good, you're awake!" Max exclaimed in his

welcoming mid-western accent, clapping his hands together like a showman. "I have something for you."

Vashti raised an eyebrow and reached for a strawberry. "Really?" she said flatly, but a knowing smile betrayed her.

Max held up one finger before slipping into the kitchen. Anthony leaned back in his chair to get a better view of where Max was going. When Max returned, he held up a plate of small, perfectly round bite-sized fruit tarts.

Her eyes widened and her grin grew as she snatched a tart. She shoved the whole thing in her mouth. "*God* I missed these."

Max winked and set the tarts on the table.

"Now, I do take requests," Max said to Anthony, reclaiming his seat. "So let me know what you're craving for next time, alright?"

"Why would there be next time?" Anthony said flatly.

Max frowned, hesitating but Ruth rescued him from further explanation. "Max, could you give us a minute. And thanks again for breakfast. It looks and smells excellent — as usual."

Max nodded, starting his retreat. "Sure thing."

Ruth sat down between Vashti and Anthony, taking Max's place. Vashti sat almost perfectly still, her hands tightly gripping the spoon in her hand. Anthony's hands were balled into even tighter fists with his wrists resting on the edge of the table. The muscles in his arms tightened rhythmically as his hands squeezed, then relaxed. Malice and anger practically evaporated off Anthony's skin.

To Ruth, it tasted like pickles.

Ruth reached for her coffee cup. "How did you sleep last night, Anthony?"

"Eat shit."

Excellent start, the Companion said in between bites. It

crunched loudly on a pear, a fruit that wasn't even present at the table, and had settled on the couch in the living room behind the breakfast nook.

Ruth ignored it. "I'm sorry that your retrieval was so traumatic," she said. "We generally err on the side of covert."

Vashti scoffed before stuffing a piece of toast into her mouth.

Ruth ignored her outburst. "Vashti, Nina, and I were hired to rescue you."

Anthony's eyes narrowed. "It didn't feel like a rescue."

"Yes, well—"

"Everything *exploded*."

"That wasn't us," Vashti said quickly, mouth half-full. "I don't disagree, your extraction felt a bit more like an . . . oh, I don't know . . . an absolute shit show?" Vashti looked at Ruth and blinked expectantly.

Yeah, what was that about, anyway? the Companion asked, now at the table, peering over the breakfast spread. It picked at a grape and threw it up in the air before catching it in its mouth.

Ruth closed her eyes and massaged her temples. "We suspect the person who attacked your arena yesterday was also behind the bombing of your prior location . . . in Chicago? There was another incident there before you arrived here, yes?"

Anthony's eyes darted between the two of them. "How did you know about Chicago?"

"Because it's our job to know these things."

Anthony's hands relaxed. "Who hired you?"

Bright one, isn't he? the Companion snatched an apple from the table. Nobody noticed. *Finally asking the right questions.*

"Min," Ruth answered. "Min Liu hired us."

"I know that name," Anthony said absentmindedly, stirring his oatmeal.

"You should. Her name is on the side of this building."

Anthony paused for a moment as annoyance swirled around him. "No, it isn't. It said—"

"LIUYEN," Ruth interrupted. "Min Liu is the majority shareholder and current CEO of Liuyen, her father's tech company."

Realization dawned on Anthony. He looked over his shoulder, taking in the opulence around him with a fresher perspective.

"Congratulations," Ruth said. "You've been promoted."

Anthony's malice and hatred shifted and the smell and taste of pickles disappeared, replaced by the crisp and unmistakable fresh scent of fear. Then that disappeared too, smothered by something that felt like sandpaper rubbing against Ruth's skin.

He plucked a strawberry from the fruit bowl with trembling fingers. "So . . . I'm supposed to — so I go somewhere else now?"

Ruth locked eyes with the Companion briefly. It stood up from the couch and took a single step before appearing directly in front of Anthony. The Companion's hand gripped its cane firmly as it squatted in front of the boy until its eyes were level with his.

Anthony muttered to himself as he looked down at the strawberry he had just picked. Meanwhile, that feeling of dry, rough sandpaper wrapped around Ruth. It tightened and squeezed without mercy, billions of sharp edges pinching her skin and biting into her as time slowly inched forward. The back of Ruth's eyes stung and she sat up straight and bit her tongue in an effort to distract herself from the pain.

He's hopeless, the Companion remarked bluntly. It grunted as it stood back up. Then it bit loudly into its apple. *Panic attacks, right? God, those are just the most annoying thing for us, aren't they?*

"Obviously," Ruth muttered. *Crap.* Not out loud. She winced, the scraping feeling against her skin teetering on the edge of unbearable.

"Hey, Anthony," Vashti said, but her eyes were entirely fixed on Ruth.

"*Mmmm*, no—" Ruth tried to warn. *Don't tell him,* she wanted to say. *He doesn't need to know I can feel his panic, too.*

And then Anthony finally looked up. His face was pale and beads of sweat had blossomed on his brow and his hairline. "W-what now?" he managed to ask quietly, his fights clenched tightly to hide their trembling.

Well, this isn't going to work, the Companion complained, rolling his eyes.

Fuck this.

Ruth couldn't take it any longer. She grabbed the pitcher of water next to her and immediately tossed its contents at Anthony.

Anthony jumped. The moment his backside left the seat, Ruth exhaled, taking in as much air as she could. Ruth felt her skin *breathe* again; the prickly feeling of sandpaper disappeared. Meanwhile, Anthony sputtered in surprise at his freshly wet clothes.

The Companion's mouth opened and closed like a stunned fish. Then it frowned with pursed lips and tilted its head to the side. "I don't think that's what the textbooks meant when they recommended vagus nerve stimulation for panic attacks."

"Shut up," Ruth growled.

Vashti grabbed Anthony's arm. "You're not *going* anywhere else, Anthony. We're not with the arenas. This isn't a trade." She glanced at Ruth, eyes wide. A similar but much softer fear threatened to take over Vashti as well. "Right? There isn't . . .

that's not what's happening here." Vashti's words were pleading but hopeful.

"No," Ruth gasped. She sat up straight, placing the now-empty pitcher beside her. "No. I'm sorry, I should have been clearer. I . . . apologize. We have nothing to do with the arenas. And we have no intention of taking you back there."

Anthony nodded. Relief washed over him.

"So," Vashti said after a beat. "What . . . *are* we doing here?"

Anthony frowned at that. "Wait, so you don't know, either?" He grabbed the nearest cloth napkin and started patting himself dry.

Ruth summarized her conversation with Nina from the night before in very few words. There wasn't much to review, really. Someone was blackmailing Min. Their job was to eliminate the threat and keep said blackmail contained. She left out some of the less relevant but arguably more concerning details, though. Like LIUYEN's recent success in mapping the deviancy trait and their more active work in suppressing and inducing it. But she did mention Nina's comment about it being their last assignment.

Ruth wasn't used to experiencing Vashti's optimism. On Nina, optimism smelled like fresh rain and blooming flowers. But Vashti's optimism was feverishly hot and choking, like the sun's heat in the middle of a desert. It was uncomfortable, but almost worth it to see Vashti's feeble attempt to mask it. The corner of Vashti's lips quirked up and her brows jumped toward her hairline. But then she swallowed, cleared her throat, and straightened her spine to compose herself.

"Our last assignment?" Vashti asked. "For both of us. Nothing else after this."

"Nothing else. We'd be free to go."

Vashti nodded. But despite her poise, her blazing optimism flared. "Right. Well, let's not screw this one up, then."

Vashti had many questions. Ruth had few answers.

What's the big secret that Min doesn't want out?

"I don't know."

Who is blackmailing her?

"I don't know."

How bad is it?

"I don't know."

It was at this point that Vashti lost her patience.

"Well, what exactly *do* you know?" she finally asked, folding her arms across her chest.

"That in a moment Nina and Min will be here," Ruth announced. Vashti frowned, cocking her head to the side, likely sensing their own physical movements now that Ruth had brought it to her attention.

"They're both nervous," Ruth added, stirring her coffee.

"Nina is walking ahead of her. Barely. Smaller steps, though. She's trying to slow them down."

"Hallway negotiating," Ruth decided. "Nina still doesn't know everything. She's irritated. Min's anxious."

"Hmm." Vashti rose to her feet. "I guess we'll know more soon. Time to go."

Neither of them had the chance to explain themselves to Anthony, who was looking at them as if they'd each grown a second head. "How do you—"

"I'm here to collect you," Max said, having appeared seemingly by magic at the dining area entryway.

"We know," Vashti said with a smile and a wink. "Thanks for breakfast, Max. It was amazing, as always."

"I know," he retorted back with a smile. Max hurried the three of them into one of the many studies in the home. Today, he chose Ruth's favorite. It was a smaller room, in contrast to everything else in the penthouse suite, and fitted with a rustic vintage desk of mahogany and walls lined with books and eclectic artwork.

Anthony chose the chair directly in front of the writing desk. Ruth opted to stand.

"You're serious," Vashti said, standing beside her. "She promised this would be our last assignment? And you believe her? This isn't some sort of trick?"

"Not a trick," Ruth said. "Nina was telling the truth. Well, Nina at least *believes* she's telling the truth."

Vashti scoffed. "That doesn't exactly inspire confidence. Nina doesn't see straight when it comes to Min." Vashti's vitriol seeped out from every pore in her body, but her hopeful optimism remained. "Just because Nina is a lovesick idiot and believes whatever lies come out of that witch's mouth—"

"Then I suppose we'll find out the truth very soon," Ruth reassured her, shifting her attention to the boy.

Anthony was completely still save for the muscles in his upper arm. They moved in tandem with a consistent rhythm, flexing, relaxing as his fists opened, closed, then opened, closed. His breaths were even, nearly matching the flexing motion beat for beat in short quick inhales and exhales.

He was counting each short, measured breath in a desperate attempt to keep his rising panic at bay. But it wasn't working. And now Ruth was riding the growing sand dunes of panic along with him. Her vision darkened and she nearly lost her balance when she lifted herself from the wall and stumbled towards Anthony.

She put a gentle hand on his shoulder. "Slower," she instructed. Her thumb touched the base of his neck, just briefly and she rested her palm between his shoulder blades.

And suddenly *she* was the one drowning, sinking and choking in the dust storm of panic. It pricked at her skin and dug into the palms of her hand where she had touched him.

Ruth followed her own instruction. "Slower," she repeated. She imagined the base of her lungs filling with pristine air, then she held it there, allowing it the opportunity to purify before returning what was left of each breath back into the world. Inhaling and exhaling, encouraging the storm to cease.

When her vision cleared and she felt more confident in her tongue, she nodded. She was calm but very tired. "Good," she remarked before taking a step back.

The door unlocked with a soft click. A crushing wave of anxiety flooded through the study. But this time, Anthony and Vashti were prepared. Ruth felt everyone in the room brace for impact as the door opened and Min Liu stepped through, cup of coffee in hand, Nina at her heels.

Apprehension was Min's primary emotion this morning. She was tired, but nobody would have been able to tell just from looking at her. Her face was smooth, clean, and completely devoid of dark circles or any other clear indications of exhaustion. Her black dress and blazer were pressed and perfectly fitted. Each step she took carried her with confidence.

And of course, there was the rest of her.

From her completely shaved head to her toes, Min was covered in tattoos. And if an onlooker had the courage to stare for a few moments longer, they would notice that every tattoo on the left side of her body was perfectly mirrored on her right, save for a few central works of art on her sternum. The only part of her body that had been untouched by ink was her face. Floral patterns, ever-seeing eyes, animals in pairs, symbols, and phrases. Ruth estimated her body was covered in hundreds of individual and perfectly matched tattoos. Despite them, or perhaps because of them, Min was the physical embodiment of tailored and purposefully curated perfection.

"Good morning," Ruth said, smiling broadly. "Long night? Just wait until you hear about ours."

Min glanced at her but offered no other outward indication that she had any intention of addressing Ruth's concerns. Instead, she stepped behind the office desk and sat down, directly in front of Anthony. Nina opted for the chair beside Anthony.

Finally, Min smiled. She held Ruth's gaze. "How are you?" she asked, her voice as soft as wool and light as a feather.

Ruth sniffed. "Underpaid."

"We both know that's not true," Nina muttered.

"I'm sorry, I don't recall addressing you," Ruth said pointedly to Nina.

"I imagine introductions are in order," Min interrupted swiftly. "What's your name?"

He swallowed. "Anthony. Velázquez." He wasn't nervous, Ruth realized. In fact, this was the calmest she had seen him within the last twenty-four hours. Hierarchies were reassuring like that. Anthony had just been granted an audience with the only person who mattered. There was likely nothing he could say or do to change his situation; but still, there was probably a morbid sense of peace in knowing which set of hands held his life.

Min hummed. "And you're Gifted." It wasn't a question.

Anthony nodded once.

"Use your words."

Ruth nearly shuddered as Anthony's defiance washed over her as well. "Obviously," he answered back.

"Show me."

It took Ruth a moment for her to understand Min's question. But Anthony was a quick study. He took the cup of coffee that Min had set down a moment ago in his hands.

At first, nothing happened. Moments stretched into seconds. Anthony stared at Min, his eyes piercing and fierce, betraying his contempt and rage. The coffee cup stayed warm, liquid and unmoving as the water on the surface quietly evaporated.

Ruth shivered. This kid had a death wish.

Then Ruth shivered again.

The temperature in the room had plummeted over the course of just a few seconds. In front of her, where the coffee cup had once been, was a ring of condensed water that was beginning to freeze. Crystals appeared as Anthony froze the moisture in the surrounding air. Vashti shoved her hands under her armpits and scowled at Anthony.

"Asshole," Vashti grumbled. Ruth chuckled and the air that escaped her lips turned into a wispy cloud.

Anthony looked perfectly comfortable. He then slowly leaned across the conference table, and handed the coffee cup to Min, still hot and steaming.

"Well." Min said finally, standing up. "I believe you've made this room completely uninhabitable for a few hours." She raised her coffee cup slightly, as if making a toast. "Shall we?"

The four of them followed Min out of the office and into the common living area. Min and Nina made themselves comfortable on the L shaped couch while Vashti chose a singular reading chair. Ruth leaned back against the window and Anthony stood beside her.

Min kicked off her heels before tucking her feet underneath her. "My name is Min Liu. Do you know what I do for a living? I imagine keeping up with dalliances and exploits of corporate America and tech was a waste of time while you spent the last few years beating people within an inch of their life."

Anthony stiffened, but he said nothing.

"There was a question somewhere in there, Anthony," Min reminded him.

"You're the founder of LIUYEN."

"My father," she corrected, "and mother were the founders. Now they're dead and I own it. Do you know what it is we do here?"

"I don't know. There was some scandal about a data breach a few years ago. But like you said, I was too busy beating people within an inch of their life to keep up with LIUYEN's latest scandal."

Min rested her head on her hand, arm propped up by the back of the couch. "It's a tricky business, possessing data, respecting privacy laws and regulations."

She looked at Nina, rolling her neck towards the side to look at her lazily. "It's safe to assume they've all already canoodled and discussed the job offer without us?"

Nina leaned forward, running her hands through her blonde hair. "I'm sure they'd love to hear it from you directly."

"If you don't mind," Ruth said, with a broad smile and dead eyes.

"Understandable," Min replied. "It's as Nina said. Everyone in this room gets a clean slate and nothing but glowing recommendations for your LinkedIn profiles."

Vashti grimaced. "Please don't."

Min's laugh was drier than an overcooked chicken. "When you find the drive and return it to me, you will owe me absolutely nothing. This would be the end of our partnership and our time together. And, naturally, I'd pay each of you handsomely for a job well done."

Vashti raised an eyebrow. "How much?"

"Fifty million dollars. For each of you."

Surprise emanated from Anthony. Intrigue from Vashti. Ruth's sharp inhale betrayed her apprehension. "That's too much."

Min raised an eyebrow. "Oh?"

"That isn't payment," Ruth said, keeping her anger in

check. "That's a retainer fee. I thought you said you were letting us *go*."

Min tilted her head to the side. "If the problem is your inability to trust, I can have my lawyers draft up a more impressive contract with the appropriate amount of superfluous legalese. But I can assure you, that I have no intention of soliciting your services ever again, Ruth. Besides . . . one hundred and fifty million dollars is child's play for me. For *us*," gesturing towards Nina. "And you know it."

Ruth's eyes narrowed, and Min sighed, exasperated. "What do you want, exactly, Ruth? More? Fine. Less? Also fine. I really couldn't give a damn about the amount of money the three of you decide is appropriate. I'm offering it only as an incentive." Min's features tightened and her smile fell. "This isn't charity," she said bluntly. "I have a job and I need it done. And frankly, I needed it done *yesterday*. And what I *do* know, is that none of you have the freedom to refuse an assignment from me at this point in time anyway."

Min was met with silence. Ruth glared at her, but her shoulders relaxed slightly. She nodded at Min.

"So," Min said. "Shall we begin?"

Vashti

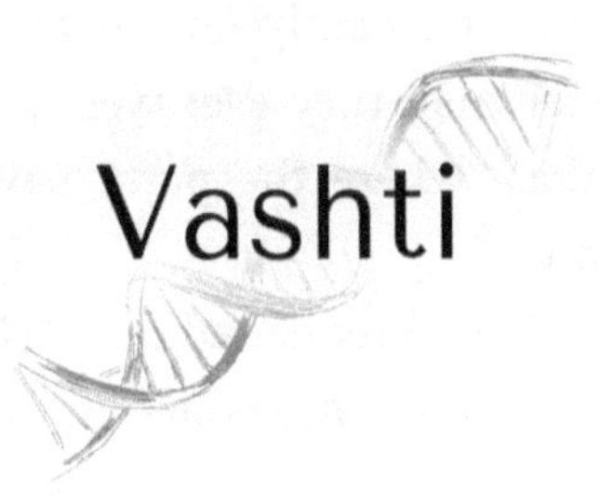

Vashti entered Anthony's room later that evening with a single knock to announce her presence before she barged in. She found him sitting on the bed upright, staring at his hands.

She tossed him the coat Max had so graciously and discreetly given her while Nina and Ruth schemed together in hushed whispers. Nina was entertaining at best and insufferable at her worst. But Nina and Ruth *together* . . . the two of them treated Vashti like she was their adopted child. Vashti was eighteen. She had long earned her seat at the big girl's table.

Well, fuck their table.

"Let's go," she instructed Anthony once he'd put the coat on.

After a thirty-minute train ride, during which the two of them exchanged approximately a dozen and a half words, Vashti and Anthony were eating tacos on the curb off Knox and

Henderson. It was late, nearly one in the morning, but the streets were livelier than they ever were during the day. This was Uptown Dallas, where the party never ended and the liquor flowed freely.

"Don't worry," Vashti reassured him. "No one's looking for you. And even if they were, they won't find you here."

Before Anthony could protest, a woman holding her high heels in her hands proceeded to projectile vomit into the street, just a few feet away from them.

Vashti took another bite of her taco. "What a champ," she marveled.

"How do you know they're not looking for me?" Anthony asked.

"You saw the place when we left," Vashti said with a noncommittal shrug. "It was a disaster. Can't host an arena with no arena. I'm sure your group relocated within the hour to distance themselves from the heat. Plus, now the entire location is burned, too. The managers are going to have to restructure the whole year's scheduling to make up for the loss."

Anthony hummed as he finished his fourth taco. "So . . . which arena were you with?" Anthony asked.

Vashti grunted. It wasn't like she had done a particularly good job keeping it a secret. *And it's not a secret*, she reminded herself. "Gamma. Two years."

Anthony nodded slowly. "I heard the Ivies were . . . intense."

Vashti nearly choked, a dry chuckle competing with the food in her mouth. "Sorry, I haven't heard that term in a while."

"I didn't mean—"

"It's fine," she said a little too quickly. The Ivy arenas were intense in the same way that Hurricane Katrina had just been a mild storm. Most arenas had a strong preference to keep their fighters alive; kidnapping Gifted was a dangerous, time-consuming enterprise, so it was just good business to keep their product functional for as long as possible. Not to mention the required months of training and hoping they didn't get maimed or mauled by someone with more fighting experience.

But the Ivies were built differently.

While most arena guests loved seeing familiar faces, patrons of the Ivy arenas showed up for bloody violence and excessive gore. And in the spirit of capitalism, the Ivies met that demand with supply.

Being traded or sent to an Ivy was the most terrifying thing that could happen to Gifted in the arenas. Anthony hadn't understood it when he'd first been 'recruited.' Until Arena Rho was pitted against Beta a few months later. Anthony hadn't even fought that day. His arena had benched him, knowing full well that he wasn't likely to make it out of the ring with all his limbs still attached. Ivy fighters had a habit of sending their opponents home in body bags.

And Vashti had survived them for two years.

"When did you get out?" Anthony asked.

"About two years ago." She swiped at her chin, catching a wayward splatter of adobo sauce.

"Wait." She watched the wheels in Anthony's head churn as he attempted to do the math. It looked painful.

"I was fifteen," she said quickly, saving him from an impending aneurysm. "I was fifteen when I was . . . when I joined Gamma."

"How did you get out?"

"Same way you did."

He hesitated as leaned back. "So, these people got you out only to make you a . . . what, a mercenary for hire?"

"Not for hire," Vashti said between loud slurps. "I have one boss. My only contract is with Min."

"Are these her usual gigs? Kidnapping and trying to get ahead of the next Ashley Madison data breach?"

Vashti glowered. "Sometimes. I go where Min and Nina tell me to go."

"What about Ruth?"

"I work *with* Ruth."

"Is that why you were assigned babysitting duty?"

Her eyes narrowed. She was going to kill him. This is what she got for trying to do something *nice*.

"What were your instructions this time, anyway," he continued, clearly irritated. "Jump into this hole in the middle of the night, blow the whole place up, but don't forget to bring Popsicle Boy with you on your way out? Collateral damage is irrelevant?"

Vashti groaned. "We *told* you. The explosion wasn't us."

"Even if you didn't cause the explosion, you still killed people!"

Vashti blinked. "You mean . . . your *handlers*? The people who kidnapped you in the first place?"

Anthony's cheeks flushed. "They weren't all *just* handlers. Some of them were different. Not everyone—"

"*Every* one of them," Vashti corrected. "Was a piece of shit that had it coming. And if I could go back, I'd do it again. Only next time, I'd do it more slowly." She paused looking straight at Anthony with an intensity that begged to be challenged.

Anthony sank a bit lower on the bench. "It wasn't all bad. Some of the handlers watched out for us."

Vashti sighed. "I brought you out here because I wanted to talk."

"Aren't we?"

"Yes, but — look, I'm not good at this, alright? But the four of us are about to steal some stupid encrypted data so the richest woman in the world doesn't get blasted on the next news cycle. And I don't understand why that would be such a big deal, but Min has promised that if we do this, we get to leave *all* of this behind. So I'm on board. But she's also a vindictive and unforgiving bitch. And if we fail, whatever future any of us think we have is immediately nonexistent." She hesitated. "And I've found that generally, these sorts of high-stake heists go a little smoother when there's a *tiny* bit of trust."

Anthony seemed unimpressed. "Is *that* why you brought me here? As a team building exercise?"

Well, I tried. Niceties and platitudes be damned. "I am here because you have been a panicked, anxious, on-the-edge-of-a-breakdown hot mess for the last twenty-four hours. And we do not have the luxury, funds, or time to donate to your current mental health crisis."

Anthony's face turned beet red. "I'm *fine.* I'm not — I've never had—"

"Do you know what Ruth's gift is? Have you figured it out yet?" The rest went unsaid but she hoped the infuriating look in her eyes communicated: *Or are you stupid?*

His brows furrowed. "I don't—"

Vashti spared him the mental energy. "She's an empath. She can sense your emotions."

"No," Anthony argued brazenly. "No, that would be a psychic gift. I thought psychic Gifted didn't exist."

"Obviously, they do. Look, I won't pretend to know the secrets that Min is hoarding from the rest of the world. But as far as I know, Ruth is the only psychic Gifted on the planet. And Min has taken *very* extreme measures to make sure no one knows."

Anthony hummed. He stuck his feet out far in front of him,

dipping low into the seat. "So Ruth feels other people's feelings."

"In her own way. And you've been . . . unstable to put it mildly."

"*Hey!*"

"Ruth can feel it and it's distracting. She's kind of the brains of the operation so you need to get your shit under control so *she's* under control. Got it?"

"Fine." Anthony folded his arms across his chest and stared at his shoes. "I'll handle it. Anything else?"

Vashti rubbed her eyes. "Look, I know the last day has been . . . a lot."

"*No shit,*" Anthony mumbled.

"I was in an arena for years. I *know* it's hell. And . . . and I know you're scared—"

"*Oh*, just don't," Anthony warned. He drew his hands over his face and sat up straight on the bench.

"And anxious. I had nightmares for months when I first got out and sometimes I still—"

"I don't care what the hell you have," Anthony interrupted, deep lines etched into his forehead. "I'm not interested in swapping war stories."

Vashti bit her lip and sighed. Her eyes burned and her vision was hazy. "Look, Anthony . . . I *really* need this to work, ok? This last job. So I can leave and just go home and—" Her voice cracked. "I just really need this to be over."

Anthony didn't say anything at first as he swung his legs back and forth beneath the bench.

"Where's home?" Anthony asked quietly.

She sighed. "I don't know. I don't think I have one. But the concept seems nice." After a moment, she dared ask. "Do you have one?"

Anthony's face contorted as if in pain, lips curling as his nostrils flared. "I . . . did, yeah."

And to Vashti's surprise, he told her about it.

IN THE EARLY hours of the next morning, Vashti found Ruth sitting at the dining table, a hoard of papers strewn on top of her laptop. She looked like she hadn't slept at all that night. There was an empty bottle of wine on the floor by her foot and she was holding a glass in her hand as she perused her notes. Ruth didn't acknowledge her until Vashti took the seat beside her.

"Light reading?" Vashti joked.

Ruth muttered something under her breath and set her glass of wine aside.

Vashti took it. "It's a bit early for this isn't it?" Vashti chastised before she took a snip.

"And you're a bit young for it, aren't you?"

Vashti nodded, as if conceding, and set the glass down. Vashti could never do this: see the big picture when provided with a mountain of details. Dozens of notes, blueprints, addresses, memos. It was all just chaos to Vashti. Ruth was able to create order out of raw information. Vashti was just a weapon.

"It was quiet last night," Ruth said, breaking the silence. "For me, at least. No nightmares from the boy." She looked up at Vashti. "I assume last night went well."

"Well enough," Vashti sighed. "Is . . . is *it* here? Right now?" Vashti asked carefully. *The Companion* was a touchy subject. And they never knew who was listening.

Ruth didn't even flinch. "When isn't *it* here?" she grumbled. Before Vashti could push her for more answers, Ruth lifted her laptop up and grabbed the piece of paper underneath. It was small, about the size of a postcard. She handed it to Vashti.

It was a photograph of a boy and a girl. The boy was wearing a button up blue shirt while the girl sported full graduation regalia. She was ecstatic, holding up her high school diploma above her head, mid-scream. She had thick brown hair that barely fit underneath her cap and flowed well past her shoulders. Her other hand was wrapped around the boy's neck. Were it not for the smile on the boy's face, you would have thought she was trying to strangle him.

The boy in the picture was Anthony.

Vashti flipped the photograph around to look at the back.

V & A. Graduation.

Vashti's head shot up and she stared at Ruth wide-eyed. "How did you get this?"

Ruth stared at her expectantly. "Her name is Vanessa. Anthony's sister."

"Is she Gifted as well?"

"Yes. But he didn't mention specifics about her Gift. They were close. Apparently, the day he was taken to the arenas . . . well, the handlers were supposed to take *her*. But he pissed them off so they changed their mind and took him instead."

"What did he do?"

"He disfigured one of the handlers. Froze half of his face off."

Ruth laughed, retrieving the photograph. "Min would have liked him. What about the girl?"

Vashti shrugged, noticing Ruth's odd phrasing. *Would have liked him?* "I didn't get a lot about her."

"And what about *him*?"

Vashti fidgeted in her seat. Certainly, Ruth could sense her nervousness now. "They're adopted. They call the man who cared for them Logan. He wasn't Gifted. He's the only family they ever knew. He seemed . . . nice."

"He's dead," Ruth said blankly, slipping the photograph back under her computer. "Complications from a gunshot wound six months after Anthony was taken."

Vashti's heart froze. Her own lungs felt heavy in her chest.

"What was that?" Ruth asked.

Vashti tried to steady her breathing. *Pull it together, Vashti.* "Nothing."

"What *is* that?" The question seemed desperate, falling out of Ruth's mouth like water from a faucet. "You're sad. For *him*? You don't even know him." She scowled at her, as if disappointed. "What on Earth is the matter with you?"

"You can't fault me for sympathizing," Vashti snapped. "Just because you're incapable of feeling anything at all until you steal it from somebody else—"

"You should think about your next words *very* carefully."

Vashti held Ruth's gaze, leaning towards the older woman and keeping her voice quiet. "These feelings," Vashti spat. "They're *mine*. I'm allowed to have them. But I am always on your side despite them. And you should already know that."

A few slow moments passed, but eventually Ruth relaxed, sitting back in her chair.

"You're right," Ruth said hurriedly. "I know."

Crisis averted. "So, who is she?" she asked. "This girl. Vanessa. Why does she matter?"

"Oh, right. Vanessa is the girl who stole Min's hard drive."

Vashti balked. "Wait . . . *her*? *Why*? How does she even know about it?"

"Nina thinks she's with one of those hacker groups. You know, free the people, don't use our data, hacktivist types. She clearly had some help getting in, but she put in a lot of the grunt work herself. She'd been working in the building as a janitor for the last several months, probably gathering intel on the layout and security protocols of the building."

"How did she know what to look for?"

"No idea," Ruth said. "Like I said, she probably had some help. She stole this drive from Min's *personal* office. But remember our primary objective is retrieving the data and keeping the information contained. By any means necessary."

Vashti thought about the young girl she had seen in the photograph. The year written on the back was from three years prior. Since then, Vanessa's brother had been stolen from her. Their father had died. And she had become the enemy of the most powerful woman in the world.

"These two really know how to get themselves wrapped up in the middle of it, don't they?" Vashti said.

"Vashti," Ruth said, carefully. "You can't tell him."

Vashti didn't hesitate. "I know."

"About his sister. Or about his father."

"I *know.*"

"He'll start to ask questions. Questions lead to answers, and he will not like these answers. For my sake at least, we need him fully operational."

"I. *Know.*"

Ruth nodded, leaning back a little. "Good. Whatever you did last night helped calm him down. He's going to need you. And clearly Min needs him for leverage, that much is obvious now. He may be a powerful Gifted but he's too raw to be useful. So please make sure he doesn't crack and become a liability."

Leverage. Liability. This was why they had taken Anthony, to add another leg on his journey of exploitation. They were going to find his sister and take that drive.

And then they were going to kill Vanessa.

If the last few years hadn't broken Anthony yet, the end of this assignment surely would.

"Vashti?"

Vashti willed herself into a calm acceptance and nodded. "Fully operational. No problem."

"Oh, and another thing," Ruth said. "Something Nina told me earlier — about Min, and the company. It's the reason Min cares so damn much about whatever secret is on that drive."

Vashti quirked an eyebrow, intrigued. "What did she say?"

Ruth pushed her laptop aside. "It's about the Gifted gene."

Ruth

They left for the airport that morning.

It had been surprisingly easy to rouse Anthony. The boy had showered and changed into a fresh set of clothes before Vashti had even left the comfort of her sheets. And yet, there was a sullen slowness in the way he moved. Bloodshot eyes and the dark circles around them betrayed his fatigue. He tried to hide each yawn in the crook of his elbow or the back of his hand and avoided eye contact with everyone for the entirety of the morning. Nightmares then, enough to stave off sleep and cause the redness in his eyes, but not disruptive enough to rouse Ruth from sleep as well.

Max drove them to the airport. Nina and Ruth sat in the middle row of the Bentley Bentayga while Vashti and Anthony occupied the rear.

"So who are we today?" Nina said. She had four sets of passports in her hands. "Hector Seville," Nina read, then handed it to Anthony. "How mature." She leafed through the next passport and frowned. "Nancy . . . Drew. Oh, Ruth, *really*."

Anthony and Vashti stifled their chuckles.

Ruth shrugged. "I suppose your wife does in fact have a sense of humor."

Anthony examined his new identification and plane ticket. "Do I need to have, I don't know, a backstory prepared or something?"

"It's a flight not an improv show," Vashti reminded him.

Ruth glanced at Anthony through the rearview mirror just in time to catch the tiniest hint of a blush. "Just wanted to make sure," he muttered.

"All the more reason to go over the plan one more time." Ruth rolled her shoulders back. "We arrive at DFW in less than an hour. After that, the next time we regroup, we'll be on the other side of the world. So, Anthony." She looked at him, ignoring the rising panic emanating from him. "Explain it to me."

Anthony sighed and patted the duffel bag beside him. "Change of clothes are in here. When we get to the airport, we change *first*. Then we go through security."

Ruth nodded. Ideally, they'd split up at the airport, but Anthony had never been to an airport. Expecting him to navigate the hellish experience that was TSA security *alone* was simply unrealistic. He would need a chaperone to walk him through the discombobulating experience — and Vashti had volunteered.

Well, she'd been volun-*told*.

"Ew," Vashti whined, holding up their plane tickets. She wrinkled her nose. "Economy?"

Nina tilted her head to the side and raised a brow. "What on Earth did you expect?"

"But you're both first class," Vashti grumbled, peeking over Nina's shoulder.

"And?"

"Baby-sitting duty wouldn't suck as much if we were first class."

Aren't they adorable? the Companion muttered from the passenger seat.

"Two barely legal adults in first class unsupervised would draw attention," Nina said. She let out a long breath, settled a bit deeper into her chair and closed her eyes.

"Continue, please," Ruth said to Anthony, massaging her temples. "Before I strangle you both."

Anthony folded his arms across his chest. "When we land, we make our way to the safe house. No stops, no detours," Anthony finished.

"And where's the safe house?"

Anthony's upper lip twitched in mild annoyance. "I don't know. Apparently, I can't be trusted with important information . . . like our destination."

Ruth scowled in mocking pity, her bottom lip quivering. "You don't need to know where the safe house is because your babysitter" — she motioned towards Vashti — "knows where it is."

"So don't fall behind," Vashti warned.

Ruth interjected. "Once we're across the pond, we can regroup and plot a course of action from there. According to the tracking information from Bio-Sec, the trail went cold somewhere just north of Manchester. So that's where we'll be going."

"Great, glad we're all on the same page," Nina said with a yawn. "Now, if you don't mind. We woke up at the ass crack of dawn, and I'm going to try and take a nap."

Ruth rolled her eyes, but obliged. She closed her eyes and rested her forehead against the cool glass, appreciating the silence. Nina was out like a light and in a matter of minutes, so was Vashti, lightly snoring with her head down, chin grazing her chest.

Anthony though, was wide awake for the rest of the drive.

The boy navigated his emotions like a soldier navigated a minefield, terrified that every step would be his last. The moment his mind touched something noxious — anxiety, doubt, fear — he retreated as if he'd been bitten. Usually, the rebound sent him flying directly into another equally pernicious feeling. He'd recoil and ricochet from one emotion to the next, spiraling so violently in the chaos of his own making until he buried his nails into his palm or pinched the back of his hands.

"You don't have to be so afraid of them," Ruth grumbled. She winced, immediately regretting her decision to speak for two reasons. First, she was off the clock. Dr. Ruth Doe wasn't working right now. Second, well, now the boy was panicking. Ruth had sounded terribly annoyed and now the boy was feeling self-conscious.

"Afraid of what?" he asked.

I guess the doctor is in, the Companion said with a snicker. It craned its neck so it could have a better view of the conversation. *He looks nervous. Good job.*

"Your emotions," Ruth said, remembering the first few weeks after Vashti's extraction from the arenas. Vashti had dealt with her emotions differently. Anthony pushed them away the moment they were within reach. But Vashti had set up an impenetrable wall of anger and disdain instead, shielding herself from anything else.

"The arenas are a scourge on society," Ruth said. "They are owned, created, and upheld by monsters. But the people forced to fight in them are *not* monsters."

"Why not?" Anthony countered. "We could have fought back. Or said no. I could have refused to do it."

"I have no doubt that you did," Ruth said. "At first. If you weren't stubborn enough to fight them back at first, then you wouldn't have been stubborn enough to survive. That's what it turned into eventually, didn't it? Survival out of spite?"

A heat wave of anger threatened to suffocate the air from Ruth's lungs.

The Companion recoiled. *Well, he didn't like that.*

"You don't know me," Anthony said, his fury flaring. "You don't know anything about me."

A scoff from the Companion. "No," Ruth said. "I don't. But what happened to you is *not* your fault."

"I'm not an idiot," Anthony spat. "I didn't kidnap myself. I know it's not my fault."

"So why are you so angry with yourself?"

Anthony hesitated. "I-I'm *not.*"

"You didn't get angry until I suggested something about you," Ruth said. "I just assumed something — that you survived out of spite. I'm not sure if you agree or disagree with that statement, but it resonated with you to some degree, and you didn't like that. Usually I'd give you a few weeks before we confront the source of this friction but we have twenty more minutes until Max pulls up at the airport so I'm hastening our progress. So, did you? Survive out of spite? Or do you wish you had?"

Vashti readjusted her position, rolling her head back until her occipital lobe hit the headrest, her mouth slightly ajar. She proceeded to snore.

The distraction had done something to the boy's anger, though: siphoned some of it until all that remained in Anthony's grasp were the remnants of his rage, most of it now replaced with despondency.

"I . . . wanted to leave, I did. I made plans . . ." His words were barely a soft whisper, as if he were trying to convince himself.

"You survived, Anthony."

His regret tasted like rotten fruit. Ruth's hardened exterior cracked. Not *that*.

You better get over it, her Companion warned. *You know what we're setting out to do.*

It was right. The boy was just another means to an end, an insurance policy to ensure his sister cooperated. Once they'd secured the hard-drive, they'd have to terminate Vanessa. And if Anthony regretted the arenas, regretted the things he'd done in order to survive them . . .

She wasn't sure he'd survive after this.

"Don't regret that," Ruth said, her vocal cords tight. "The things you did to survive."

Anthony didn't answer. But the taste of rotting fruit persisted on the back of Ruth's tongue until they finally arrived at DFW Airport.

Anthony

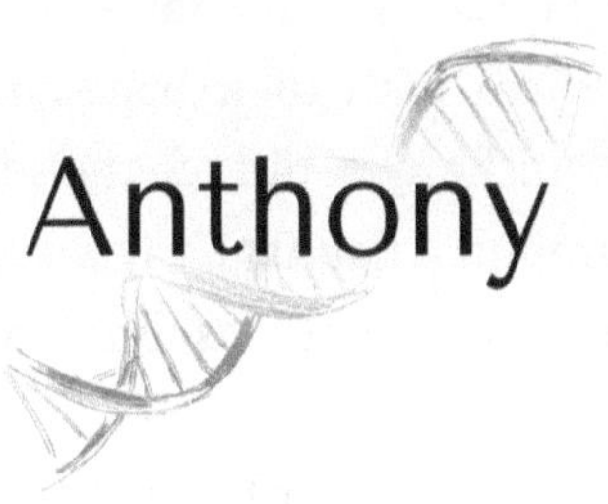

If all went according to plan, the next time Vashti and Anthony would see Ruth and Nina, they'd be on the other side of the globe. Which was perfectly fine in Anthony's opinion. Vashti was tolerable at best, but Nina's easy smile instilled immeasurable suspicion in him.

And then there was Ruth and her . . . invasive Gift. He understood that it wasn't Ruth's fault that she could sense his emotions, but God, hadn't he earned even a crumb of privacy at this point? It wasn't enough that for the last two years handlers had kept a close eye on him every waking moment and every fitful night of sleep? He had to be around someone like *that*?

"You and Ruth have been . . . working together for two years, right?" Anthony asked Vashti as they walked down the length of the drop-off area. Max had dropped off Nina and Ruth earlier so at least Anthony didn't have to worry about Ruth peering into his head at the moment.

It was early in the morning, only the barest of light peaking above the horizon. And yet, the airport was as lively as the arena on fight night. Cars were bumper to bumper and people ducked between them with their bags and children on their heels. And inside, Anthony could see the scurrying shadows of people rushing through what Anthony assumed was security.

Vashti didn't seem nearly as bothered by the crowds. "Yeah, two years. Why?"

"How do you get used to Ruth? Her being in your head?"

"She senses emotions, she doesn't read minds," Vashti explained. "And for the record, I'm pretty sure anyone can sense your emotions. You have a very expressive face."

He frowned as he became incredibly aware of his furrowed brow and the muscles around his eyes and mouth betraying his indignance. "Well, that's fair."

"Your shirt's buttoned wrong."

"No, it's—" Anthony looked down, then groaned. *Damn it.*

"Just fix it before we go inside," Vashti said, standing just beside a pair of automatic double doors.

Anthony undid the bottom three buttons quickly. "How much do you usually get paid to do this stuff?" Anthony asked. "Is it a flat fee for each job or something?"

"Actually, it's more of a base salary with commissions to promote productivity."

"Seriously?" He buttoned the last . . . wait. He rolled his eyes, realizing his mistake, and undid the three buttons again.

"No, you idiot."

"Well, how much *do* you get paid then?"

"That's none of your business."

Wait. Were there *extra* buttons on this damn thing? He was going to burn this place to the ground. Well, not really, he couldn't do that. But he could freeze it. Maybe freeze this shirt and then toss it at a wall so it shattered into a million pieces. "*Goddamn it.*"

Someone behind him stepped through the double doors.

Somehow, the soft whoosh of the sliding doors sounded like nails on chalkboard and Anthony gritted his teeth.

"Anthony, will you just calm down."

"That's not how that works, you can't just *tell people to calm down!*"

Oh, God, his hands were shaking. He hadn't even noticed. Of course, Vashti had noticed, though. Everybody here noticed *everything*, like his stupid fingers and thumbs getting in each other's way while he tried to button up his *stupid shirt.* The back of his eyes stung and his entire neck felt hot. Was he sweating?

Oh God he was going to cry. Over a *fucking shirt.*

Vashti shoved Anthony's own tremulous hands aside and took over, buttoning his shirt for him as if he were some sort of invalid. He desperately wanted to say something, to fill the silence with mindless chatter, or make some stupid joke that made Vashti roll her eyes at him again.

But she just buttoned his shirt. Like a damn professional.

Say something! He imagined thank you would be a good place to start. Or he could just *explain.* Tell the truth. That he hadn't worn clothes with buttons in years. It's not like arena fighters had anywhere important to be. His wardrobe consisted of shirts with holes and sweatshirts that had probably belonged to someone three times his size.

He'd also broken his right hand in thirty-four places a few weeks after his arrival. Holly had fixed most of it, but, apparently, there were a lot of bones in the hand, and Holly was good, but she wasn't a miracle worker. His hand was still functional, but a lot of fine motor skills were lost to him. He'd spent months secretly practicing how to write with his left hand but it still looked like chicken scratch. The arenas didn't provide a lot of school supplies either, like pen and paper.

Finally, after what seemed like eons, Vashti had his shirt buttoned up right. "There. See? You good?"

No, Anthony thought. He was far from good. He was a goddamn mess. But instead of saying that, he just nodded.

Vashti nodded back and led them into the terminal.

His panic returned.

Disorientation hit him like a freight train. The air was thick, choking and heavy with exhaustion as anxious travelers shuffled and ran through the terminal. There were huge groups of people — at least a hundred or so — clumped together, shuffling slowly towards metal detectors. Everyone kept their heads down or stared straight ahead, somehow completely ignorant of their surroundings and yet mindful enough to side-step anyone who happened to get in their way. Someone muffled announcements over an old intercom. Sensors beeped and shrieked. Babies yowled, kids screamed, men in security gear shouted at people to wait in line, no not *that* line, take that off, keep the line moving — *next!*

Next!

Next!

No, this wasn't the arena. They weren't announcing the next person in line to place their bets. They were . . . doing something else. They *had* to be doing something else.

God, this place was massive. And yet, there was hardly room between two people for single sheet of paper.

He needed to leave.

No, he reminded himself. He needed to get to security. That's what Ruth had said. He and Vashti were supposed to—

Wait — where was Vashti?

His breath caught in his throat and his heart stopped. He wasn't supposed to lose her. Now he was alone. Alone among a crushing sea of warm bodies.

It was so hot. And *loud.*

What was wrong with him? Crowds weren't new. He was an arena fighter. A champion. He'd fought in front of crowds far rowdier than this. Maybe some of the people at this station had even seen him fight.

A chilling thought burrowed into the back of his mind.

Is *this* what people did when they left the arenas every night? They hopped on a flight back home? Head back to college or go back home to their families who had no idea they'd gambled away thousands, sometimes *millions* of dollars?

How many of these people had seen him fight? Had frequented an arena and watched people like him attack and wrestle each other because it was a fun thing to do on a Saturday night? Placing bets and succumbing to such profound drunkenness they forgot their own names? They would forget the arena rules, too, the rules about *not* touching the merchandise and had to be reminded that the fighters were not for sale *or* for rent — even if it was just for an evening.

But somehow, if they wrote a check with just enough zeros at the end, the handlers would turn a blind eye and pretend they didn't notice.

Were those people here? Right now?

What if they recognized him — not just from the nights, but from . . .

He needed to leave.

But there were so many people. Pushing and shoving. *Touching.* Someone would find him and they would take him back. He'd never heard of someone who was taken back to an arena. But then again, he had never heard of anyone successfully escaping either.

No. No one would recognize him because he didn't matter. He was a nobody. He was just some Gifted. A deviant. An arena fighter. A number. A killer. And sometimes, just a pretty face.

He'd kill them if they tried to take him back.

A hand grabbed his wrist and yanked him to the side.

"Don't touch me!"

But Vashti didn't let go. She dragged him through the sea of sweating bodies and bad breath until they were back outside again. The grip around his arm was like a vice and for a terrifying second, he wondered if she was contemplating leaving him here.

Please don't, he thought. *Don't leave me here.*

But Vashti hadn't made any such threat. She just stared at him with a foreign softness in her eyes.

Anthony's throat felt rough and dry, as if he'd poured sand into it. So instead, he shook his head, glancing back into the gaping entrance of the airport. It seemed to swallow anyone who walked towards it.

"Ah-ah." Vashti grabbed Anthony by the jaw, forcing him to look back at her. "You'll get your chance for a re-match in a second, don't worry."

Anthony's reaction was immediate. He slapped Vashti's hands away from his face. *Don't touch me! Don't touch me, don't—*

She held her hands up as if in surrender. "Sorry."

Anthony blinked. A choked sound that was *supposed* to be a laugh escaped him. "Did . . . did you just apologize?" He leaned forward, his hand on bent knees as he caught his breath.

"I'm glad you noticed, actually. You won't be hearing an apology from me ever again, so I'd commit the moment to memory."

She wasn't laughing at him. They'd been at the airport for less than five minutes and he couldn't even make it five feet into the building. But she didn't seem angry with him.

"It's . . . overwhelming," Vashti said. "The airport. We should have warned you."

"I-I've travelled before," he said. It didn't sound very convincing.

"Traveling through a portal with your arena is stressful, but the airport is its own hell," Vashti said. "Also, don't panic, but I'm pretty sure we're being followed."

The hairs on Anthony's neck stood as if at attention, and he instinctively drew on his Gift. "Should we go back inside?" he asked, hating how his voice shook at the suggestion. "It'll be easier to lose them."

Vashti grabbed his arm and led them across the street and towards the parking lot.

"Vashti, I don't see—"

"They've been watching us since Max dropped us off," Vashti said, rushing down a flight of winding concrete steps. The narrow hall smelled of wet rain and urine. "I thought it was just coincidence but when we stepped out of the airport, they did, too."

Anthony took her word for it. Vashti broke into a sprint, rushing towards the other end of the parking lot. But the lot was crowded. Drivers searched for empty parking spaces and pedestrians hoarded their families and dragged their bags between cars. Vashti dodged pedestrians with the ease of flowing water. Her braid had fallen out of her loose bun and served as her shadow, trailing her every movement and quick turn. Anthony followed, but his feet weren't nearly as nimble or as graceful as hers. At one point, he was nearly run over by a car. A driver honked in protest and Anthony waved an apology. The further they ran, the broader the distance between Anthony and Vashti. He was going to lose her for the second time in less than five minutes.

Vashti dove to her left and down a flight of stairs towards the lower level of the parking garage. Anthony crashed into the wall in his attempt to change course. He grunted, grabbing his right arm as he stumbled forward, barely making it to the foot of the steps just as Vashti's braid disappeared around another corner.

His face exploded with pain.

Anthony landed on his back, gasping as air rushed out of his lungs. He sat up slowly and grabbed his jaw.

"What the hell!" he yelled at Vashti.

Vashti winced and clutched her hand. "Sorry. I thought you were the girl following us. Come on, let's—"

Anthony reached for his Gift. A thin shard of ice appeared as he focused and the moment it crystallized in his hand, he hurled it towards Vashti.

Vashti howled as the shard of ice pierced her leg. She reached for the shard but cut herself in the process, crimson staining the nearly invisible weapon.

"*Puta!*" she spat at him.

Suspicion confirmed. That was *not* Vashti.

Anthony inhaled and allowed his Gift to surge as he reached for the water that surrounded him. There was water everywhere, in the pipes hiding behind the concrete walls, the drinking fountain just behind him by the stairs, and in the air, heavy and thick from the Texas humidity.

That will do, Anthony thought. The water came to him in streams, slithering between the cracks in the ground.

The girl with Vashti's face didn't notice. The ice in her leg melted and joined forces with the surrounding small streams.

Anthony let his Gift swallow him whole, extending past his arms, his chest, and towards his face, until his skin was completely encased, frozen and hardened, but malleable to his every movement.

He saw Imposter-Vashti's features falter and she hesitated. Then, eyes darkening, the shapeshifter barreled towards him, weaving between Anthony's round of projectiles like an accomplished dancer. Ice plowed into two parked cars and the alarms immediately went off. Before she could throw himself at him, the imposter gasped, stumbling. Behind her, Vashti — the *real* Vashti — rushed towards them, hand outstretched. One of Vashti's smaller knives had found its home in the shapeshifter's other calf.

She yanked it out and threw it towards Vashti.

Vashti ducked. As she did, the end of Vashti's tight braid wrapped itself around the hilt of the knife before it could complete its course. Anthony summoned a wave of dirty street water and sent it careening into her face.

The imposter fell back, sputtering. They didn't give her a chance to recover. Vashti's braid moved, *again.* Anthony watched, eyes wide with intrigue, as the braid slowly wrapped itself around the shapeshifter's neck, once, twice and then again for a third time. The shapeshifter didn't seem to notice. She remained on the ground on all fours, hacking and coughing up dirty water as blood leaked from her wounds.

Then the braid tightened, and the woman's eyes bulged.

"How did you know it wasn't me?" Vashti asked, her eyes still fixed on the girl that stole her face.

Anthony couldn't peel his gaze away from Vashti's braid as his Gift receded. "Uh . . . she apologized. You said you'd never apologize."

"Huh," Vashti said flatly.

The shapeshifter was still tugging at Vashti's braid, desperately trying to free herself as she choked. Her lips were turning blue, eyes increasingly unfocused.

"She's going to pass out," Anthony pointed out dryly. "We can't ask her questions if she's unconscious." The basement was full of cars, which meant nobody was going in and out. But it was only a matter of time before someone came down to investigate the annoying symphony of car alarms.

Vashti grumbled, but the braid relaxed slightly. "Who are you?"

They allowed her a few moments to quite literally catch her breath. Then Vashti's braid tightened, just slightly, and the woman panicked again.

"Who are you?" Vashti repeated.

The girl snarled.

Vashti rolled her eyes, and slowly shrugged her shoulders, as if relaxing a tight knot of muscles. Then the shapeshifter was in the air, lifted only by Vashti's braid around her neck. Before Anthony could protest, her braid slammed the woman against the wall beside her.

"Hey!" Anthony said, quickly standing and holding out his hand to stop Vashti. "Are you crazy?"

But the girl with Vashti's face was back on her knees, the side of her face streaked with scratches where the brick had rubbed against her. Her eyes rolled like marbles in her head and her hands were at her throat, clawing at Vashti's hair.

Then the woman's face finally changed. And changed, and changed . . . it kept *changing*. Melting and re-modeling into all the people she had once been.

"We asked a question," Vashti seethed. "Who. Are. You."

"*Vashti*," Anthony warned.

Vashti cursed, but finally released her. The girl tumbled to the ground, and Vashti's braid fell with her.

The girl on the ground looked up.

She had short, black hair that fell in disorganized waves. Her nose was bleeding, her face dotted with freckles and littered with scratches and blood seeping from a gash on her head.

"My name's Jen," she said.

"And who sent you?" Vashti asked.

Jen ignored Vashti's question. Instead, she looked directly at *him*. "Are you Anthony?"

His eyes narrowed. "Who wants to know?"

Jen hesitated. "Simi."

Vashti's entire demeanor changed. Her back stiffened and she jumped towards the girl she'd just strangled for the better part of the two minutes. Vashti helped Jen to her feet. "Shit! *Why didn't you just say so?*"

"You . . . know each other?" Anthony asked.

"Is V *here*? She's not in London?"

Jen blinked. "Why the hell would she be in London?"

Vashti motioned towards Anthony. "Fuck. Jesus. We need to go. You too, Jen. Take us to the shop."

"Pretty sure we have a flight to catch," Anthony reminded her. His eyes darted between the two girls. "Seriously, what the hell is going on?"

Vashti turned to face Anthony. He'd only known her for a few days, but he'd never seen her look this worried.

"It's your sister, Anthony," Vashti said. "I think she's here."

Ruth

They're all lying to you, you know.

Ruth bit her tongue to keep herself from telling the Companion to shut the hell up. It used to be more useful, noting things that she missed: a twist in someone's lip that suggested contempt, an abrupt jerk that stemmed from fear rather than surprise. Plus, it was helpful to have someone around to talk through things. It made her Gift feel like a more collaborative experience.

Her companion was supposed to be *part* of her Gift, a personification of her powers. A tool.

It wasn't supposed to have its own damn personality.

She huffed, trying to remember her seat number. Was it twelve? Or thirteen?

They're all liars.

"Would you shut up," she muttered.

Liars. You can't trust them.

Of course they were all liars. She didn't choose to go into business with Min and Nina due to their moral values and highly ethical mission statement. Then again, it had never been much of a choice, had it?

"Excuse me," Ruth said to the woman already seated in 12A. "I believe you're in my seat."

"Oh," the woman looked surprised. She had a British accent. "I thought nobody had this one?"

Ruth blinked.

Kill her.

Jesus Christ, *calm the hell down.*

Ruth exhaled, her smile broad and sickly. She showed the woman her boarding pass. "I'm in this seat, see? So if you could just—"

"Oh, but would you mind terribly if I were here? And you took A11? I do much better by the window and I asked earlier and attendants said no one was in this seat so they didn't mind me taking it. And—"

"Leave." Ruth said. Ruth made sure to bathe the word in contempt as it left her lips. The woman stiffened, feeling terrified for her own safety just as Ruth had intended. She quickly grabbed her things and scurried out of her seat and across the aisle.

Ruth sat down and closed her eyes, exhaling slowly.

"Have you ever done that to me?"

Ruth sat up and whirled around. Nina was behind her, standing up so she could see over the seat. "Tell the truth now. You *made* her scared of you, didn't you? She ran off with her tail between her legs. You're not even that scary. Not usually, anyway."

Ruth sighed. "We're not supposed to be seen together."

"Do you do that a lot?" Nina continued, poking Ruth in the shoulder. "Influence other people's feelings? I mean, I know you *can* but you don't do that to *me*, do you? I thought you said changing emotions was difficult?"

Kill her, too.

Ruth ignored it. "It's been getting a bit easier," she finally admitted. "Tends to take it out of me, though. Would you like a demonstration?"

"No, not really," Nina said quickly.

"Go away," Ruth demanded. "I want to take a nap."

Nina pouted. "But then I'd be bored. And it's a long flight."

"Watch a movie."

"Oh, but irritating you is just *so* much more fun."

Ruth turned back around and settled in her seat again, but Nina was a dog with a bone. "I'm serious. *Have* you done that to me before?"

What was all this about, anyway? "What are you feeling now?"

Nina thought about it. "A little nervous."

"Good."

Nina scowled at her. "You're mean." But Nina fell back in her seat with finality.

She's lying, too.

Shut.

Up.

HALFWAY ACROSS THE ATLANTIC, Ruth was awoken by Nina violently shaking her shoulders.

The overhead lights were off and nearly everyone in first class was asleep. Outside, she spotted the wing of the plane, the only illuminated thing in the dense night sky.

"What is it?" Ruth grumbled. She'd better not be drunk. Nina liked to talk when she got drunk, and Ruth was *not* in the mood.

But Nina, for the first time since they'd embarked on this expedition, looked *very* worried.

"They're not here."

Ruth blinked.

She knew exactly what Nina meant. And yet she still had to ask, "What do you mean?"

"Your little *shadow*," Nina spat the last word as if vomiting up a bitter pill. "And the boy. I went back to check, just to make sure. I had a bad feeling. They're not there."

"Are you absolutely sure? You may not be familiar with the back of the plane but they like to pack them in there like sardines—"

"Ruth!" Nina interrupted, a wild look in her eyes. "They're not here. Jesus. The kids missed their flight."

Vashti

It took a little over an hour to get to the tattoo parlor. They had to get on a train, a bus, and then walk fifteen minutes along the side of the road since this part of town didn't have any sidewalks. It was still morning, but the streets were quiet, sleepy, as if fatigued. Townhomes, shop fronts, and tall wistful trees cast long shadows onto the winding streets. And those shadows provided the only cover from the relentless sun's heat, beating against the back of their necks.

But finally, they made it to the small tattoo parlor that stood between a noodle shop and a laundromat.

Jen and Vashti led Anthony behind the shop, towards the employee entrance. He followed silently, and Vashti found it unnerving. It had only been two days, but she'd somehow already grown used to his quiet scoffs when he disagreed and sarcastic quips in his desperate attempt to fill an awkward silence. She couldn't imagine what was going through his head at that moment, and so, perhaps unwisely, she left him to his own thoughts.

There was a surveillance camera a few feet to the left of the employee entrance. Vashti looked up and Jen waved.

The door lock clicked and Vashti's heart hit her throat in anxious anticipation. The door opened to a winding staircase that took them below ground. Jen went down first, then Vashti with Anthony trailing at the back. The path ahead was illuminated by the soft, patchy glow of cheap light bulbs, and as they approached the basement, they could hear the bustling activity of the rooms below. The noise grew and swelled with carefree laughter, endless chatter, and the occasional loud *thud* of a body being slammed into a foam mat.

And at the bottom of the concrete stairs, stood a familiar figure: a girl in a pair of worn, distressed jeans and a sleeveless undershirt. She was slightly taller than Vashti, which didn't say much given her own petite frame. But unlike Vashti, who was slim and lean, this girl was built like a boxer. Her light brown skin only further defined her toned muscles. She had two sleeves of tattoos along her arms: a series of geometric shadows, lines, curves, and negative space.

The moment she laid eyes on Vashti, the stern look in her eyes melted. But her jaw fell when she noticed Anthony, who was craning his neck, taking in his new surroundings.

"Anthony?"

He whirled around. Vashti held her breath. The entire basement grew silent.

Anthony frowned, frozen in place. But his eyes welled with an emotion that felt like daggers in Vashti's heart. The frown line above his brows deepened as he wrestled with disbelief. His voice cracked.

"*Vanessa?*"

His sister didn't hesitate. She ran to him, colliding into Anthony so ferociously she nearly knocked them both to the ground. She wrapped her arms around him until her knuckles went white, gripping the back of his shirt so fiercely — as if he may simply disappear. "You're . . . you're here," she muttered between desperate gasps. "Oh my God, you're here. You're really here."

Vashti could only watch as the girl convinced herself that this moment was real. That he was *here*. That she — Vashti of all people — had brought her brother to this hovel in the middle of nowhere. Vashti could barely breathe, suffocating on the tension in the room.

"Yeah." Anthony squeezed his sister back. A sad smile took over his face. "Yeah, I'm here."

"I'm sorry. I'm so sorry," Vanessa's voice trembled. "I couldn't find you. We were looking. I swear we were looking . . ."

"V, it . . . I—"

"I couldn't find you." She clawed at him desperately. "We — I couldn't *find you*. I'm sorry. *I'm so sorry*."

They held onto each other through sobs that rattled their chests.

"I know, V. I know . . . I *know* . . ."

Vashti left quietly, walking past the half dozen people who had gathered to watch the tearful reunion. She found a boy who was furthest from the pair and grabbed his shoulder. "Take me to Simi."

The boy pouted. "But—"

Vashti dug her nails into his shoulder and he whimpered. "*Now*."

Interlude II: Raahi

Dad was never the same after the robots came.

For three days, their father barely spoke to them. He had placed half a dozen locks on the basement doors so it was impossible for he or his sister to play Dragons (because, honestly, what was the point of pretending to be a Dragon if you couldn't do it in the *dungeon*?). Dad walked the two of them to school personally for the rest of the school year. Which was odd because they usually went with Anansi's mother. His eyes were always focused on something far ahead and he always double-checked the basement doors to make sure they hadn't opened on their own somehow. And then at the end of the day, when Raahi detailed his day's events during dinner, he noticed that most of the time, Dad wasn't even listening. He could tell because Dad wouldn't ask any questions or make his usual funny faces at all the right parts of his story. He just hummed and nodded.

Then, on the last day of school, Dad took Raahi and Ruth hundreds of miles from home to Sarovska, where their aunt lived. Sarovska was one of the largest cities in the world, located just outside of the Capitol.

Raahi was excited. He *loved* the Capitol. And this would be Ruth's first visit. He prepared himself for a fun weekend. He hoped they'd go to the aquarium to see all the sea creatures. Then after the aquarium, they could go to the Capitol and see the rooms where the Council met and look at all the Mirrors from past Sanctuaries. Raahi had read that in total there were six hundred and fifty-three Mirrors! And all of them were on display in the Capitol, complete with their histories.

But they hadn't seen the sea creatures or the Capitol or the Mirrors. Dad had enrolled them in boarding school for the rest of the year.

Then he had left them there.

Dad wrote him letters. He wrote one for Ruth, too. But she couldn't read yet. So Dad had told Raahi to read it to her. That didn't seem to help. Ruth cried because he couldn't read the letters in Dad's voice.

The next time he saw Dad, he looked sad.

The deep, dark circles under his eyes had dug crevices into his skin and when he tried to smile, his eyes remained narrow and dark.

Raahi didn't care. It was still his dad. And even if the robots made him sad, Raahi and Ruth could make Dad happy again.

Ruth had learned far too many words since the last time they'd seen each other and she was determined to use every single one of them to inform their father that their Aunt Hera was just ok, her cooking left much to be desired, and that she hoped they would never have to go back again. Raahi was largely in agreement with all these observations, so he said little. Instead, he found himself glancing up at his father's hollow eyes.

Was he in there?

Dad caught on to his nervous glances.

"What's the problem, Raahi?" he said, picking up Ruth under her arms. She squealed, waving her arms above her head like a ridiculous buffoon. He had learned that word earlier that week.

Raahi frowned. "Nothing."

Dad sighed but didn't ask again.

Their home looked exactly the same, but it smelled like stiff air and stale bread. Dad noticed Raahi's upturned nose and in response, he opened up all the curtains and shutters. The air moved, carrying dust and sediment as the fabric billowed and the fresh Nivean air rushed into the room like an inhale.

His sister squealed again, flapping her arms wildly as she reached for the windows that, in her eyes, had opened all by themselves. Dad didn't use his Talent often, so even Raahi found himself enamored as well.

Dad chuckled and when Raahi looked up, he saw his dad looking back at him and smiling.

Raahi released his dad's hand, pleased and immediately at ease.

What a silly thing, to have been worried at all.

Part III: A Long Way Down

Interlude III: Raahi

"Raahi!" Dad yelled.

Raahi didn't move. He was in his room, reading a book and Ruth was . . . well, she was not bothering him for once in her life. If he left his room now, his sister would remember he was around. And then he'd have absolutely no free time until it was time to go to bed. And he was just about to finish this chapter, too.

Maybe if he pretended to be asleep—

"*RAAHI.*"

He groaned, kicking off the sheets and making sure to stomp his feet as loudly as possible. His dad was sitting at the dining table, wearing one of his silly glasses — *magnifiers* — Raahi remembered the word. It made it far easier to see really small things, like the small metal thing in his father's hands.

Dad glanced up at him. "Go down to the basement and grab my needle nose pliers."

"I don't know what those are," Raahi said a little too quickly.

Dad didn't fall for it. "Chop, chop."

Raahi groaned but shuffled towards the basement. Maybe if he found the pliers quickly, he could finish the last chapter in his book before dinner.

It was odd, going down to the basement now. Raahi and his sister only went down when absolutely necessary. When Raahi and Ruth had first come back home, the basement had stayed locked for weeks. But then, Dad would go down to grab something and forget to lock it back up again. And when the robots didn't come back, Dad forgot to close it more frequently. Now, nearly a year and a half later, the door generally stayed open, the robots long forgotten.

Raahi and his sister had asked time and time again about the robots. Of course, now Raahi was old enough to know that there hadn't been any robots at all. But *something* had happened down there, and it had terrified their father. Raahi knew better than to ask his dad directly about details from That Day. But that didn't mean he wasn't curio—

"But my favorite story is about the Queen and the Cricket—"

Raahi rolled his eyes. Of course she'd snuck down here to play some game involving fifteen characters from her own imagination. The Queen and the Cricket wasn't even a real children's story. Their father had made it up one night, and every time he retold the story, Ruth would change the details.

"The Queen and the Cricket? What story is that?"

Raahi froze. Someone was downstairs with his sister, and he didn't recognize that voice.

Raahi rushed down the stairs, fear gripping his heart.

Ruth sat up on the tall workbench. Someone must have put her up there because it was far too tall for her to have climbed up herself. Two complete strangers with pale skin stood in front of her.

"Look!" Ruth pointed at them. "The robots, remember?"

The taller one, the man, gestured towards Raahi. He wore black trousers paired with a black shirt with buttons along the front. Raahi eventually plodded towards the man.

The woman next to him wore spectacles, round with a thin gold rim that balanced delicately on the edge of a flat nose. She was just as pale as the man, and wearing a similar ensemble of black trousers, but with a gray loose-fitting blouse. The man and the woman shared similar features: a flat nose, small lips, and a round face.

Oh my God. Raahi had been so stupid. They weren't robots.

They were *aliens*.

"Your sister's been keeping us entertained," the woman said with a stomach-curdling smile that stretched her skin and made Raahi's crawl. "Are you her brother? What's your name?"

Raahi didn't answer that question. "Are you aliens?" he asked instead.

The woman laughed, a staccato barking sound that surprised Raahi. The sound was also enough to alert their father, who came rushing down the stairs.

When he arrived, a familiar hollowness made its home in his eyes and all color left his cheeks.

"Get out," Dad said, sternly. Dad grabbed Raahi's sister, resting her on his hip. He yanked Raahi back by his upper arm. It hurt, but Raahi bit his lip and kept quiet.

"Oh, come now, Mr. Varo," the woman spoke again. "Let's set a good example for the kids, yes?"

"*GET OUT OF MY HOUSE!*" Dad bellowed. The house trembled. Boxes and tools on shelves fell from their resting space and the light fixture above them swung wildly, aggravated by Dad's Talent. Ruth buried her face in Dad's neck and Raahi cowered behind him, grabbing onto his leg like he was Ruth's age again.

The woman hardly moved. "Temper," she said softly, but it sounded like a warning.

"I've given you what I can," Dad said, taking small steps back. Raahi tried to match his pace, nearly tripping over his feet. "It won't help, though. That's not how the Mirror works. There are people here who can *help* you. They can help your people."

"What you gave us is invaluable," the woman said again. "I'm grateful. And if I'm to be honest, it's enough. We will manage, thanks to your generosity."

Raahi looked up at his dad. These people . . . suddenly everything fell into place. The Mirror. Their father was in possession of a *real* Mirror. And these people had come through it.

"If the Mirror is still open, then it is *not* enough," Dad warned. "We have people for this, entire departments dedicated to this. We can *help you*," Dad explained.

"I want to go outside," the woman said, blatantly ignoring Dad. She looked past them and directly towards the stairs.

"Yes! I can take you outside," Dad said, eagerly leading them towards that direction.

"Next time," she quickly amended. "First tell me about your, ah, what do you people call them? Talents? Gifts?"

Dad hesitated, but the lady only smiled. She gestured around her haphazardly. "We don't have those where I'm from. You gave us so much information last time. All helpful, but we can't use it. And imagine if we returned back home, talking about silly things like Doomsday and the End of the World. Our company wouldn't make it through the first news cycle. Stocks would plummet. And I have no intention of living through a Great Depression in my lifetime."

Raahi blinked. What was she talking about? Judging from

the look on his father's face, Dad was just as confused. Depression hardly sounded like a great thing.

"You are correct, the Mirror is still open," the woman continued. "But only because we haven't applied your technology quite yet. Despite all the data and material you so graciously shared, you made the most interesting assumption about us: that the people of Earth are also in possession of your very unique . . . Gifts."

The woman pulled a bench from under the table and sat down. The man, who had said very little up until this point, stood beside her, towards the head of the table.

The woman spoke again. "We will go outside some other time. But we want to know more about your talents. Your Gifts." She gestured towards the seat beside her. "Your daughter had already started telling us all about them. Telekinesis for you, isn't it? We'd love for you to fill in the gaps."

"Daddy?" Ruth's head turned to the side, realizing that she was the current topic of conversation.

"Raahi go upstairs. Take your sister with you."

"But, Dad—"

"*Now.*"

It was happening again. The distant look in Dad's eyes along with the panic. Dad would send them away.

Raahi nodded, his vision clouded as tears spilled and trailed down his cheek. But he took his sister's hand and led them back towards the stairs.

"Let them stay," the woman said with a sweetness that rivaled that of licorice. "We insist. She can sit with me." She held out her arms expectantly.

Ruth shook her head and held onto her brother. "I want to go to my room now," she told him.

The woman sighed, resting her empty hands in her lap. "The Gift emerges usually around puberty, yes?"

Dad nodded, but Raahi and his sister noticed their father's hands behind his back, waving violently as if he'd suddenly developed a tic. The message was clear. *Go.*

Raahi held onto his sister tightly and took a careful step backwards. The woman noticed. She looked at the man she'd come with, and nodded slightly.

The quiet man appeared behind his father, and wrapped a thin wire around Dad's neck. The wire dug into the skin, unyielding as their father clawed at the air. The pair fell to the ground, and their dad gasped — or *tried* to. Dad was making horrible sounds, his eyes wide as he flailed his arms.

Raahi screamed and leaped towards the man, battering him with closed fists. The man didn't even seem to notice. He pulled tighter, red beads collecting around the length of the wire.

But then Ruth screamed.

His sister's scream instilled terror in Raahi's heart, squeezing every ounce of breath and life that he had to offer until he was paralyzed with fear. The man felt it, too, and immediately released his nearly fatal grip on his father.

Raahi's legs felt cold and damp. He looked down. He had wet himself. He was too terrified to care. To even *move.*

The woman moved towards his sister, even as her companion stole short inhales and exhaled far too quickly, lost in panic. There were fresh tears in his sister's eyes and her bottom lip trembled. Snot dribbled past her nose and towards her chin as she cried.

"I looked through your notes," the woman said calmly. Somehow, she was the only one who hadn't been affected by that unexpected wave of terror. Where did it come from? "A lot of your devices require your Gifted people to operate them.

Unfortunately, we are completely devoid of this resource. But I was curious about Gift emergence. Utterly fascinated. Apparently, moments of intense stress can trigger the Gift a little early."

Then the woman rested both of her hands on Raahi's sister. Dad immediately attempted to scramble to his feet. But the man shoved Dad down back to his knees. He kept his hands on his shoulders, his nails digging into the space below his collarbone.

"How old is she?"

Dad didn't answer. He just glared at the woman. The room shook again, dust shifting as shelves and boxes and tools trembled.

"We'll take her."

"*No!*" the garbled noise coming from their father sounded inhuman.

The woman made good on her unspoken threat and the space between her hands and Ruth's neck shrank. "*Yes,*" she stated plainly. "We'll bring her back. And in exchange you will find us more. Like this one here. Do you understand?"

A pulse of energy surged from their father's fingers and the Mirror lifted away from the walls, yanked from their screws and nails, and fell forward.

It didn't matter. The Mirror would not break. Dad knew it. Raahi knew it, too. Mirrors were indestructible and only outsiders could walk through them freely. Niveans, like Dad and Raahi, could only traverse the twisting paths of the Mirror if they were traveling with an outsider. It was a security measure enacted billions of years ago to prevent something Raahi's textbooks called *colonialism.*

If this woman took his sister through that Mirror, there was no way for Raahi or Dad to follow. She'd be lost to them, unless they kept their promise and brought her back.

Then the man with the wire punched Dad. He slumped to the ground in a heap, unconscious.

"Dad!" Raahi rushed to him, shaking him with both hands. "Dad . . . *Daddy* . . ."

The other man knelt down on the ground so he was able to look directly at Raahi. "Do you understand what my wife has said?" he asked. His voice was flat, though the accent was similar.

Still shaking his father, but now with less fervor, Raahi nodded.

The man hummed, then stood up. And when he did, Raahi watched the woman walk through the mirror.

She held his sister in her arms. Ruth continued to cry, mumbling nonsense and the name of her brother through exhausted and frantic breaths. Her arms were outstretched towards her brother.

"*Raahi!*" Ruth screamed before she, too, was swallowed by the Mirror.

Then Raahi was alone, with only four years' worth of memories of his only sister, and an unconscious father who would do anything to see her again.

Vanessa

"It took you two years to own your own tattoo shop," Anthony said, a smirk tightening the corner of his lips. "Always the overachiever."

Vanessa nodded, her heart swelling with pride. She'd imagined showing him this place countless times. And here he was, standing right next to her, taking it all in. "After I left school, I started working here," Vanessa explained. "Technically, I just manage day to day operations while the owner backpacks across Europe."

The parlor's storefront was on the smaller side, only large enough to comfortably accommodate three tattoo artists and three customers. But the two floors beneath had become a haven for Gifted. A safe place for Gifted who just needed a place to crash for the night or a place to get away from difficulties and prejudices of daily life. The lowest level was home to six bedrooms, each outfitted with a pair of bunk beds. The floor right below the storefront served as a common area, complete with stained couches and rickety futons, dusty bookshelves that housed old gaming consoles, and a blinking television. The rug between the couches was so thoroughly stained, Vanessa wasn't certain if the original color had been cream or yellow.

Downstairs, in the common area, Steve had his headphones on and was fast asleep on the futon. Someone had left a pile of books and two laptops unattended on one of the tables behind the couch. Maddie and Roshan were seated at one of the tables, pretending they were invested in their card game, but they couldn't tear their gaze away as they watched Vanessa give her long lost brother the tour of the place.

Her heart lurched. Her *brother*. He was *here*.

He smelled like the floorboards of the parlor, old and damp. He didn't slouch anymore, either. She used to make fun of his posture, joking that he was well on his way to becoming a hunchback. In response, he'd flip her off and slouch even more.

He'd surpassed Vanessa in height ever since he turned thirteen, but he was so much bigger now. He must have put on nearly thirty pounds of pure muscle, and he seemed completely unaware of his own size — he'd run into the corner of a table half a dozen times in just as many minutes. And his *hair*. It was longer. *Very* long, and he had it tied up in a messy bun that rivaled that of a sorority girl's.

And then there were the scars, raised and lacking in pigmentation like shards of ice embedded into his skin. They were everywhere: the back of his hands, the right side of his neck just below his earlobe, his forearms. Earlier she'd noticed a pair of concentric circles around both of his wrists.

Anthony didn't notice her staring, though. He was too distracted by everything around him.

Eventually, Vanessa led the two of them towards the room at the far end of the hallway. There were too many eyes on them in the common area. Anthony didn't seem bothered by it;

she supposed he'd become used to the gawking as an arena fighter. She made brief eye contact with Maddie, glaring at her as she tugged at her Gift, just enough for her eyes to glow.

God, all this staring was driving her mad.

"Come on," she muttered. At least the back room had a door that locked.

And, thankfully, it was empty. And quiet. She leaned against the doorframe and tried to ignore the sound of her own heart, pounding behind her sternum. What if she breathed too loudly? Moved or spoke and the illusion shattered? She knew it was ridiculous . . . but maybe, if she didn't move, if she didn't breathe, if she kept her eyes on him and didn't even blink, he wouldn't disappear. He'd still be here because he had never been taken. He'd always been here. He was safe. And Logan—

Oh *God*.

Did he know about Logan?

Vanessa had become intimately familiar with grief over the years. Guilt that had held her hostage. Hopelessness had become her constant companion.

But she hadn't prepared herself for the day she would finally experience relief.

Vashti

Simi had found a comfortable position in her oversized office chair. Her left leg dangled off the edge in front of her while her right hooked over the chair's armrest as she thumbed over her console. And her large over-the-ear headphones meant she probably hadn't heard Vashti come in.

Although, in her defense, most people never heard Vashti when she entered a room.

Simi's computer workspace was set up along the edge of the wall with four computer monitors atop a large walnut desk. Two of the monitors were in some computer code she didn't understand. Probably some college students' homework that she agreed to do for a couple hundred bucks. One monitor was idle. The fourth monitor displayed her current run of Minecraft.

"Can we talk?" Vashti asked.

Simi spun around. Her hair was put up in an afro puff at the back of her head and she wore a tight-fitting graphic shirt that read "ERROR 404."

"Shit, Vashti. You scared me."

Vashti fingers twitched around the door knob. "Can we talk?"

Simi followed Vashti into the supply closet next door. Simi shoved an empty bucket aside to make room for her feet. "Cozy," she noted.

Vashti released a heavy breath. "You sent that shifter after us."

Simi ignored the accusation. "Was it him? Her brother?"

Vashti nodded. "How did you find him?"

"How did *you* find him?"

"We pulled him from the arena," Vashti said, leaning back against the door frame. "Ruth and I got hired to find him."

"And where's Ruth now?"

"On a plane about to cross the Atlantic Ocean."

"Hmm," Simi hummed, her gaze hardening. Vashti's toes clenched in an effort to conceal her own discomfort. It was odd. Vashti didn't cower when Min shot her one of her threatening glares or when Ruth scolded her for being too emotional. But Simi, staring at her through dark brown, nearly black eyes peppered with flecks of gold and hazel . . . Vashti felt as if she were being scrutinized within an inch of her life.

And Simi didn't even have a Gift.

"You're sure your keepers aren't in Dallas still? You didn't lead them straight to us?"

"I'm not an idiot."

"You're going to get everyone here killed," Simi said simply.

Vashti's back stiffened. "I'm careful."

"You work with a goddamn empath and billionaire megalomaniac," Simi chastised. "You'll bring hell down on this place and get everyone killed, and it's going to be an accident. I don't care if your reflexes are superhuman. You can't watch *all* your blind spots."

Vashti swallowed and looked away. "You know I can't just *leave*."

Simi sighed and Vashti winced at the sound, as if her exhale had pushed her further away.

"It's just . . . you have to keep us posted, Vashti," Simi whispered. The accusatory tone in her voice had disappeared, replaced with quiet understanding. "I don't doubt your intentions at all."

Vashti arched a brow.

Simi held up her hands. "Alright, fine. At first, I thought you were a Trojan Horse, but that was a *long* time ago. You keep things too close to the chest. You have to let us know if you need help."

"And how am I supposed to get a message to you?" Vashti asked. Her throat was raw as she held back tears. "When Ruth and Nina are breathing down my neck? Ruth showed me Vanessa's picture and I'm lucky my surprise was more obvious than my fear. If she suspected that I knew her, or knew that I . . . that I . . ."

Simi closed the space between them and wrapped her arms around her. "It's alright, you're alright."

Of course, I'm alright, she wanted to say. But instead, a choked, harrowed breath caught in the back of her throat.

"You're here now, yeah?" Simi said, squeezing her tight. "You're safe now, too. Ruth isn't here."

Vashti sniffed. "I . . . I know."

"You did good, Vashti. You brought him here."

"No, I didn't," Vashti said, her voice cracking. "I nearly took him to the other side of the world. I thought that's where Vanessa was going to be. She's going to hate me, Simi. She's going to—"

"*No.*" Simi stepped back and gripped Vashti's shoulder as

she looked at her. "No, V doesn't hate you. You know this. She loves you."

Vashti shook her head as silent tears tumbled down her cheeks. For the last six months, she'd guarded her heart, monitored and scrutinized her own emotions until she could control when they emerged. It was exhausting to supervise her own emotions like an owner training a reactive dog.

Everything she'd felt over the last several months came spilling out of her. And she couldn't stop it. She couldn't stop the tears, her racing heart, her lungs pushing out oxygen faster than she could breathe it back in.

"V would have hated you a lot more if you died on her," Simi said. "You stayed alive. And despite everything, you still managed to bring her brother back here. Let's talk to Vanessa, alright? Get the two of you up to speed on everything that's been going on."

Vanessa's chest tightened. "Right now? They just found each other, maybe we should give them some time . . ."

"Nonsense," Simi said, opening the door and leading Vashti back to the office. "I'm sure Anthony's going to have a lot of questions, too. Like how the hell you know his sister."

Every time Vashti returned to the tattoo parlor, she sat down and completed a thorough debrief of sorts with Vanessa and Simi. Every assignment, every detail, every notable conversation. She recounted everything. And despite her radical honesty, Vashti had a strong, sneaking suspicion that the distrust between her and the rest of the parlor crew worsened anyway.

But Vanessa believed her. Always.

Vashti told them about Anthony's retrieval and rescue from the arenas. That Ruth had told her where to be and nothing more. She told them about Min's assignment and Ruth's mistake: sharing a photograph, and with it, the motive behind Anthony's rescue.

"She plans to use Anthony as bait," Vashti said after nearly an hour. "They want to draw out Vanessa and take back the drive. What is that thing anyway? And why do you even have it?"

Vanessa looked away, but didn't answer.

Vashti sighed and continued. "I think there's someone else after Anthony, though."

Simi and Vanessa answered simultaneously. "Who?"

"I don't know. There was some sort of explosion in Chicago before the arena got to Dallas. And then another one at Old Red. It made Anthony's extraction . . . complicated."

Vanessa groaned, massaging her forehead with her fingers. "That was *us*," Vanessa said. "We pinned down Anthony's arena a few months ago and caught wind they were coming to Dallas. We planned on infiltrating."

Vashti gasped. The explosions must have been Vanessa's fire. *She* had caused the explosions in Chicago and Dallas. They'd all been so close, just meters away from each other, and they hadn't even realized it.

"We got all the Gifted out of the arena," Simi added. "Some of them went their separate ways, but a few have been staying here, at the parlor. They had nowhere else to go. We tore that arena *apart* looking for Anthony, but he was the *only* one we couldn't find."

Nausea shredded Vashti's insides apart. She looked up to meet Vanessa's gaze, but Vanessa wasn't even looking at her. Instead, her eyes were fixed on a stain on the carpet. She couldn't even imagine how Vanessa felt in that moment, so close to finding her brother, so certain he'd be there. Only for it to be another dead end.

This had been Vanessa's *only* mission for the last two years: find her brother. She and Simi had spent years following leads and breadcrumbs that led to dead ends. They'd swindled their way into nearly a dozen arena fights over the years and had managed to free a handful of Gifted in each one. And if what Simi was telling her was true, Arena Rho was the first time they freed *every* Gifted.

Every Gifted . . . except for one.

Vashti cleared her throat. "Do you have the hard drive, Vanessa?"

Vanessa didn't hesitate. "Obviously."

"Min promised to terminate our contracts if we get it back for her."

"That's generous," Simi muttered as she sat in front of her computer.

Vanessa crossed her arms over her chest. "And you expect me to give it back?"

"Not yet," Vashti said quickly. "Not until we know what's on it."

"Why don't you come take a look, then," Simi said as the monitors on her desk lit up.

Everyone clamored towards the other side of the room to look at Simi's computer screen. Vashti stayed furthest back next to Vanessa. She smelled like burned hair and smoke. Of lavender and cinnamon.

Then Vanessa's warm hand found Vashti's coarse palm. She wove her fingers between Vashti's and squeezed. And Vashti's heart pounded so forcefully in her chest she was sure everyone else could hear it.

"We can't open the data without the key," Simi explained, pulling up what Vashti assumed was a list of files available on the stolen hard drive. Vashti couldn't be sure. For starters, everything was in Mandarin. Vashti couldn't help but notice that Anthony's attention was on the screen displaying Minecraft. A pair of creepers were headed towards Simi's character. Anthony looked concerned.

The monitor displaying Minecraft went black and Anthony fidgeted, startled, then glanced at Simi. She narrowed her eyes at him, but her attempt to silently chastise him was undercut by the burgeoning half-smile dancing at her lips. She cleared her throat. "Focus," she warned. Anthony blushed.

"Min thinks this drive is in Europe," Vashti said. "That's why she sent us there."

"I tampered with the geo-positioning," Simi said. "To Min and everyone else, it looks like the drive is somewhere in London. Couldn't have her track the thing down to our location, now could I?"

"Why did you even take this?" Anthony asked his sister.

All heads turned to Vanessa, whose cheeks were now a stunning shade of red. She cleared her throat. "I was angry."

Vashti stood up. "Are you joking?"

"I wanted to find dirt on Min," Vanessa said quickly. "We've been at this for two *years*. You have another three years on your contract and you've nearly died a dozen times . . ."

Vashti wasn't sure if she wanted to kiss her or scream. She turned to Simi. "And you just *let* her break into Min's office?"

"Are *you* joking?" Simi scoffed. "You think I knew about her little plan ahead of time? You think she'd tell me her insane plan and I wouldn't immediately handcuff her to the bed?"

"I'd burn the goddamn bed for starters," Vanessa grumbled.

"What the *hell* is wrong with you?" Anthony's anger was quiet, like the aftermath of a destructive storm. He didn't raise his voice. In fact, it was barely above a whisper. But his brown eyes were dark and piercing. He gripped Simi's chair so tightly, his knuckles turned white. "If you'd been caught . . . Min . . . she would have *killed* you."

"Obviously getting caught wasn't part of the plan."

"Oh my God, V. You can't just run hot and jump headfirst into things like you have some kind of death wish!"

Vanessa tilted her head. "Um, you just got here, Popsicle. I'm not taking a lecture from you. You don't even know Min. You've met her *once*."

"Yes, and once was enough!" Anthony's tone ratcheted up an octave. "It's the only useful skill I've learned the last two years."

"And what's that?"

"Knowing when someone is capable of killing you! There's a . . . " He paused. "You get good at reading people, knowing the difference between what someone's *capable* of doing and what they *plan* on doing."

"You think I don't know what Min's capable of?" Vanessa shot back. "After listening to Vashti tell me *every* detail of *every* day working for that woman? Both of you have spent the last two years putting yourselves in danger every day."

"Not by choice!" Anthony countered.

"Well, *I* had one!" Vanessa said. "I had a choice when I saw Min's floor was hiring for a janitorial position. And I took it. And I don't regret it."

Vashti groaned. She understood Vanessa's desperation, and she understood the hopelessness of feeling like there was nothing you could do to change anything. For years she'd watched Vanessa hunt down her brother, and up until a few days ago, that's all Vashti could do: Watch and offer nothing in return.

If Vashti had been in Vanessa's shoes, Vashti was certain she would have done the exact same thing.

And yet . . . "Vanessa, that was *reckless*," she said.

"I don't care!"

"Fine!" Simi interjected. She turned to Vanessa and let out a measured breath. "V, I said it two weeks ago when you walked in here with this drive in your hands, and I'll say it again. What you did was . . . incredibly dumb. I literally just gave Vashti a piece of my mind for making moves without letting the rest of us know. But we're all here now. By some miracle, we all did it. But moving forward? *This* is the inner circle. No secret missions. We work together. Deal?"

The others exchanged hesitant glances. Vanessa spoke up first. "Look . . . I'm sorry. I still don't regret it, and I know *nobody* wants to hear that. But I promise, moving forward, I'll be upfront about what I'm thinking, alright?"

Anthony's shoulders fell in quiet acceptance. "Fine."

Vashti massaged her temples. "Alright, so what's in it? The drive? What did you take that has Min completely beside herself?"

Simi reached for a stray potato chip on the table and popped it into her mouth before answering. "Initially, a whole lot of nothing. Some information that strongly insinuates that they haven't taken the last three data breaches seriously. Tons of privacy violations. Blah, blah, blah."

Simi clicked on a folder that looked completely identical to every other folder on the screen. Then she turned around and faced them, hands crossed just above her stomach.

Vashti's eyes narrowed. "What is it?"

Simi pointed at her computer with her thumb. "This won't open without Min's DNA. That's what's wild is *this* folder right here is the *only* thing protected by Bio-Security Tech. Everything else is just regular encryptions. So, whatever is in *here* is the mother load. We might not be able to open it yet, but I had some free time on my hands. I made a model of the code needed to decrypt the folder."

When nobody said anything in response, Simi groaned and pouted, clearly disappointed.

"Okay, look. This file is encrypted, and the cipher is a biological key. Without Min's biological data — basically, her DNA straight from the source — I can't open it. Biologically encrypted data can't be read or hacked by any normal computer because computers can only read *binary* code. Well, unless you have a twin, I guess, but that's not really a hack, is it? More of a loophole."

"So even if you make a model of the key, that folder won't understand what you're saying anyway?" Anthony asked.

Simi pointed at him. "Exactly. To get into this folder, we need Min's DNA — fingerprint *and* blood by the way — and a Bio-Scanner, which usually go for half a million dollars a pop."

"Where do we find a scanner?" Vashti asked.

"How do we get Min's *blood?*" Anthony retorted.

"Great questions," Simi praised. "Ok, now remember what I just said. The model I created is of the DNA sequence required to open up the hard drive. Which means I've successfully mapped Min's entire DNA. I can't use it to open the file. But I have a model of her *entire* DNA."

"Okay . . ."

"And I double-checked," Simi added quickly. "Triple-checked. I don't know what's on the drive yet, but guys . . . Min's DNA? It's going to rock this world."

"Simi," Vanessa seethed. "Just *tell* them."

But before Simi begrudgingly spelled out the big secret, Anthony's eyes shimmered with quiet understanding.

"Min is Gifted," he said. "Isn't she?"

Simi sucked her lips between her teeth and nodded. "It's written *all* over her DNA."

Vanessa

They ordered noodles from the shop across the street. Simi had gone home and Vashti had opted to eats hers in one of the rooms downstairs, so Vanessa and Anthony had retreated to the main shop upstairs, in an effort to avoid roaming, curious eyes and never-ending questions.

"You still eat like an animal," Vanessa said, snapping her chopsticks at him.

"You want that?" Anthony asked, his eyes gazing at Vanessa's food with abject longing.

"Here." She pushed her bowl towards him. "Not very hungry."

"You sure?" he said as he reached for the bowl.

"Knock yourself out."

He grinned and did precisely that. "I see you finally got tatted up."

She looked down at her arms. When Gifted reached for their powers, a glowing, iridescent pattern lifted up from just under the skin: a hidden tattoo across the upper back, neck, and arms. Each Gifted had their own unique pattern, like a fingerprint, and Vanessa, who had been unable to commit to any form of art on her body for most of her life, was now covered in ink, lines, and swirls layered atop her own pattern.

"Just my arms and back," she explained, holding them out for Anthony to see. "When my pattern appears, the tattoos disappear."

"Clever."

Anthony shifted in his seat. "Uh, what does . . . what did Logan say about it?"

Vanessa's heart hit her throat. Guilt crawled into her chest, displacing the very air she breathed. Her lips parted, hoping the right words would find her when she needed them most. They didn't come.

But Anthony was still waiting for her answer, head down, eyes transfixed by his sister's soggy noodles. He poked and prodded at them with his chopsticks, but couldn't even feign interest in them anymore.

He already knew. "How?" Vanessa stuttered.

"You haven't mentioned him at all yet," Anthony said, clearing his throat. "When . . . when did he . . ."

"A year ago," Vanessa said. "Complications with his leg after he got shot that night. He was in and out of the hospital a lot. They said a clot made it to his lungs . . ." Her voice trailed off as her vision blurred. It never got easier. "He was asleep when it happened. I couldn't wake him up the next day."

Ear-splitting silence filled the space between them.

Vanessa leaned back, her hands locked together in an attempt to compose herself. But the grief had returned. Why was it like this, even now? Denial, anger, bargaining, depression, acceptance. They made it sound like some sort of staircase towards further enlightenment. But grief was this messy, chaotic expedition with a destination that only seemed to extend further into the future as time passed her by. Sometimes, she thought it was better, that *she* was better. Sometimes, for a while, for weeks at a time, it didn't hurt as much.

Then the grief return. And it was as if she'd made no progress at all.

"I'm sorry I couldn't find you in time," she whispered. "I swear, I tried. *We* tried . . ."

"I know," Anthony assured her. "It's not your fault." He looked up briefly from his bowl, eyes red-rimmed. "None of this is your fault."

She nodded, weaving her hand through her hair before inspecting her splitting ends. "I think your hair is even longer than mine," she said, desperate to change the subject.

Vanessa didn't think it was possible, but somehow his face fell even more. The muscle in his lower jaw twitched and he hesitated, before hiding his face behind his bowl of noodles again.

He gnawed at his bottom lip. "They didn't let me cut it. I was a crowd favorite. Apparently, the women liked *my look*." The last words dripped with venomous hate. And their implication made Vanessa's skin crawl and her core blaze with fire.

"What does that mean?"

He shrugged, a futile attempt at nonchalance. "They studied the guests pretty well. They said people would bet more money on me when my hair was longer. So, I wasn't allowed to cut it." He let out a dry laugh. "Gave me a nickname and everything. Called me *Sampson*."

She'd heard stories about the brutality in the arenas from dozens of other Gifted who had managed to escape, aged out, or on very rare occasions, had fulfilled their contracts. Vashti had told her about the ruthlessness of the Ivies and had endlessly reassured her that most of them weren't like that. As if that was supposed to make a difference. One of the fighters from Arena Rho, a powerful Gifted with shockingly white hair, had told her that his last fight had been with Anthony, and that it had been particularly difficult for both of them. But he hadn't gone into any further details.

"Do you . . . want to talk about it?" Vanessa asked.

Anthony shook his head. He continued to swirl his noodles around with his chopsticks.

She probably wouldn't have wanted to talk about it either.

But then Anthony surprised her. "It wasn't all bad," he admitted, cheeks flushed, his voice breaking like shards of glass beneath a heel. Painful. Piercing. "The other Gifted . . . it's not their fault. *Our* fault. They're good people. We have to fight each other but it's not personal. Not usually. Holly did a pretty good job healing us most of the time. And the staff—"

Vanessa saw red. "Staff?" *You mean those psychopaths that came for me but took you instead?* She gripped the edge of her chair and swallowed the words before they could spill over. "Sorry," she said quickly. He was talking and there she went, with her big mouth and her hot head. "Sorry, I didn't mean to—"

Anthony's cheek flushed red. "No, it . . . it's what — you know, never mind."

Vanessa panicked. She was such an idiot. Was this going to be every conversation? Accidentally stepping on land mines because she was too dense, too *fucking* insensitive, to watch where she was going? "No, I didn't mean — I'm sorry. I *want* to know. But only if you want to tell me. I don't want you to—"

"It's where I lived, V, alright?" he said, his irritation squirreling out of him. "I know they're not *staff*. They're not — they weren't my friends. And I know it wasn't a job. I was . . . I'm just a victim like everybody else. And I got trafficked just like everybody else. But it was my life and it was normal and-and — I can't—" Her brother's eyes bulged and his head bobbed up and down as he struggled to find air. "I can't—"

I can't breathe.

Vanessa reached for his hand. Her fingers had barely grazed his when he lurched to his feet. The bowl of noodles toppled over, spilling broth onto the tile floor.

"Don't touch me!" he yelled. He shoved his hands beneath his armpits, his palms pressed against the sides of his chest.

It took everything in her power to stay away. She gripped the edges of the table, occupying her hands so she didn't defy his only request. *Don't touch me.* She bit her tongue and could only watch, helplessly, as Anthony stood there and tried to remember how to breathe.

Minutes crept by. But with each agonizing moment and faltering breath, the panic slowly subsided. Finally, he found his voice again. "It keeps happening," he said. His voice was soft, more akin to a helpless whine.

"What does?" she asked.

He stared at the floor. "*This.* When I . . . can't breathe."

Vanessa swallowed. "The panic attacks?"

His brow stiffened and the corners of his eyes twitched. "It never happened in the arena. And now every time I talk about it, I just . . . I can't. It wasn't even that bad. I mean, it's harder at the beginning. But they have to make it hard, otherwise you'll spend the whole time thinking about trying to find a way out. It's just hazing. Like . . . fraternity shit."

Vanessa was absolutely certain none of it was anything as simple as *hazing.* But she held her tongue.

"There was this one kid, Asha. They let him off too early. He cried a lot, I guess. Made the staff nervous."

That word again. *Staff.*

"When he got the green light to fight, we did our best, you know? He was always first in line to see the healer, and we helped him out with sparring and technique. We really tried.

And then one day I went to go get him for breakfast and he was swinging from a ceiling fan."

Jesus Christ.

"But it only happened one time," Anthony added. "So it wasn't that bad." He shoved his hands in his pockets. "It *wasn't.*"

Vanessa waited. She wanted to make sure he had nothing left to say. After a few long moments she pushed herself away from the table and walked up to one of the tattoo stations. She felt Anthony's eyes burrowing holes into the back of her head as she rummaged through her things.

When she found what she was looking for, she glanced over her shoulder and nodded at the chair at her side. Reluctantly, Anthony shuffled over and sat down.

"I picked up a side gig cutting hair in college," Vanessa said as she plugged in the clippers. "I'm no barber, but I think I can work with this. What do you think?"

Anthony's eyes briefly settled on his own reflection before darting up to look at Vanessa instead.

Please, she thought to myself. *Let me help.*

She shouldn't have worried. Anthony's nod was immediate. "Yes," he said. "Yes, please."

Vanessa

The haircut Vanessa had given her brother wasn't her finest work, but Anthony didn't seem to mind. When she was all done, he was practically beaming. He looked more like *Anthony* again, the brother who had taken her place.

Then they sat on the floor and talked.

She told him she'd dropped out of college, how losing him had shattered her naive, doe-eyed optimism until all she had left were its broken fragments, each one shaped like vengeance. She told him about the nights she'd spent in jail, picking fights with anyone who dared to even *look* at her wrong, and how disappointed Logan looked every time he bailed her out. About the months Simi and her family took her in after Logan died and she had nowhere to go. How she threw herself into work at the tattoo shop until the owner handed her the keys and then how she and Simi came up with the idea to transform this place into something else.

"I met Vashti after Min had hired her straight out of the

arena. I guess Min goes every now and then to scout for new spies to keep on retainer."

"How did you run into her?" Anthony asked.

Vanessa chuckled. "You're not going to believe this."

"Try me."

She folded her arms over her chest. "At McDonald's."

His eyes narrowed. "No . . ."

Vanessa shrugged. "She picked up the wrong order. I ran across the street to trade because I *really* wanted my McChicken. I'd been thinking about it all week."

"A McChicken? Really? That's a shit order, V."

"*Anyway*." Vanessa scowled at his interruption. "I think she thought I was following her or something—"

"I mean, you *were* . . ."

"Because she threw me on my ass the second I tapped her on the shoulder. Which sent both of our orders flying. We both had to walk back and place our orders again."

"That's it? But how did—"

"I slipped my phone number in her to-go bag."

Anthony burst into tearful laughter. Two years ago, she probably would have attempted to strangle him for laughing at her. But today, his laughter — even if it was at her own expense — was the most pleasant thing she'd heard in years.

She suspected it would get old pretty soon though.

In turn, Anthony didn't share much about the arenas. He didn't talk about the fights or the "staff" that had taken him. But he did talk about the white-haired boy Vanessa had already met, Wyatt. Apparently, Wyatt had been "recruited" months before Anthony, and the two quickly became close friends, relying on each other for the strength to crawl out of bed every morning. Joking around and pranking the other kids in an attempt to forget how they'd all ended up there in the first place.

She'd have to find Wyatt later and thank him for keeping her brother alive.

After that, Anthony claimed one of the available bedrooms and passed out for the rest of the day. Which meant Vanessa had one more conversation left before she could call it a night.

When she opened the second door on the right — the room that she always ensured would be ready for Vashti whenever she returned — Vanessa found her girlfriend, sitting cross-legged on the bed. Clearly, she'd sensed her arrival and had sat up the moment the door had moved.

Vashti said nothing, her eyes wide and hopeful.

Fuck it.

Vanessa slammed the door behind her and closed the space between them in a matter of footsteps. Her lips crashed against Vashti's and immediately, in an instant, she was home. Vanessa held Vashti's face in her hands as she kissed her, falling deeper into her, feeling more secure in the familiar feeling of it all.

Vashti pulled away first, just barely. Her lips brushed against Vanessa's. "I'm sorry," Vashti whispered. "I'm so sorry I didn't know you were here, I should have—"

Vanessa pulled a bit further back, looking into her dark and brooding eyes. "You found my brother. And you brought him back."

But Vashti shook her head. "I almost didn't. Simi and Jen found me first."

Right. *Simi.* She'd been spying on the city cameras, hoping for Anthony to appear when they didn't find him two nights ago. And when Simi *had* found him, she'd sent Jen to retrieve her without telling Vanessa first. Logically, Vanessa understood why she'd done it — after they'd failed to find Anthony at Arena Rho, she probably didn't want to give Vanessa any more false hope.

Besides, Vanessa had done the exact same thing just a few weeks earlier when she'd hidden her own plan to rob Min.

Vanessa sat down on the twin bed with Vashti. "When we lost Anthony at the arena bust downtown, Simi ran a facial recognition program on local cameras. But we couldn't find him anywhere. It made no sense. Everyone at the arena swore up and down that Anthony was supposed to be there. We checked to make sure there wasn't a body—"

"Vanessa . . ."

Vanessa moved on quickly, remembering that feeling of grieving, *again*. "I talked to Simi. She said she caught Anthony *and* Ruth on cams leaving downtown just this morning. She put two and two together, figured they were coming after the drive in London, so international flight. DFW. It was a *long* shot. Jen lives in the area so she had Jen tail you at the terminal. Nobody caught *you* on cams, though. If Simi had, she probably could have given Jen a heads up."

"I'd die before I get caught on cams," Vashti scowled. "Jen could have just *talked* to us. She tailed us and then pretended to be *me*."

"Jen thought you finally went turncoat. She thought you were taking Anthony *away* from us. On purpose."

Vashti looked away. "I'd never do that."

"Jen doesn't know you like I do. Like *Simi* knows you."

All the Gifted who frequented the parlor knew who Vashti was, and knew who she worked for when she wasn't standing next to Vanessa. But some of them — well, *most* of them — were still suspicious. This place was supposed to be a haven for any Gifted who found their way here, but Vashti never really felt welcome.

"I need to get back to Ruth," Vashti whispered.

Vanessa blinked, sitting up again. "What, right now? You can't be serious."

"Not now, but soon. It'll be suspicious if I don't touch base with her."

"I thought you two got separated."

"We did," Vashti said as she brought her knees up to her chest. "But we have a system. There's a safe house that we use in case we get separated during a job. Ruth will go there as soon as she can. I need to get there." She rested the side of her face on her knees and looked up at Vanessa. "And we need to give the data back to Min."

Vanessa tucked rogue strands of Vashti's hair behind her ears. She wanted Vashti to stay here, so they could whisper sweet nothings into each other's ear like a pair of lovesick, star-crossed lovers. Then they'd fall asleep in the other's embrace, tangled in a bed that was far too small for both of them. The next morning, Vanessa would have to get up early to open the shop upstairs, but she would hope for cancellations so she could come downstairs and be with Vashti.

Was it so horrible to want something so mundane?

"Stay here," Vanessa said. Begged. *Pleaded.* "Just stay."

"Ruth would find me."

"We could take her."

Vashti's abrupt chuckle riled something feral within Vanessa's gut. "You want me to give Min my two weeks notice? People have tried. They're not around anymore to tell us how it went."

"Yeah, well, they're not us."

"Yes, they *are.* The rumors don't hold a candle to this woman, V. And now, Simi's saying she's *Gifted.*"

Vashti took Vanessa's hand in hers and squeezed. She held Vanessa's hand up against her cheek, her lips barely grazing the back of her hand. "I don't know what Min's Gift is," Vashti whispered. "And the fact that I've never known and couldn't tell terrifies me. Ruth certainly doesn't know either."

Vashti looked up, eyes wide as some terrible realization dawned on her.

"What is it?"

"I didn't even think . . . Ruth told me something about Min just before we left. I should have said it earlier, but I wasn't thinking. *God*, I'm so stupid."

"Vashti, breathe . . . slow down." Vanessa drew small circles across the back of Vashti's hands. "What happened?"

"Min's company has been working on mutating Regulars. She wants to make a statement and announce the project in a couple of months. They've only successfully done it with animals but Min is trying to *make* Gifted. That's why she even gives a shit about the information on this drive getting out. There's some secret on the drive that she wants buried. That's why she hired us to find the hard drive."

Vanessa leaned back until her spine was flush against the wall. "Manufacturing Gifted. *That's* their play."

If it wasn't so fucking infuriating, it was almost funny.

What would this brave new world look like, where the people in charge could create Gifted in their own image?

Perhaps, LIUYEN would do the noble thing, create a steady stream of Gifted healers so the world never knew pain and suffering again. More likely, they'd create an entire arsenal of strongmen and sell them off to the Army by the dozen. They'd create spies who could walk through walls and living nuclear warheads to ensure different groups of people behaved accordingly. The world would clamor for a piece of the very thing they had shunned and isolated for the last twenty years. Vanessa had no doubt that the original Gifted, those born with their Gifts and persecuted for it, would grow increasingly irate that they'd never received this sort of preferential treatment. And with rising civil unrest, came government involvement to "keep the peace."

And Gifted would just have to accept that all the propaganda and fear mongering had never been about protecting the general public from an unpredictable group of powered people. The problem hadn't been that their powers had been dangerous, or that these powers existed at all.

The problem was that *they* had always wanted it.

Two years ago, Vanessa would have been absolutely furious at the gall of it all.

But then, her brother was taken. Her father, the only family she had ever known, had died. Simi, her best friend during her very short stint at university, never left her side and the two of them saw an opportunity when this nearly dilapidated and run-down tattoo shop became theirs. Together, they created a place of employment for Vanessa and a safe haven for Gifted.

Vanessa had made a new life and even made some friends. She kept her ear to the ground, listening for any whispers that her brother was still alive. She met the most beautiful girl she'd ever known with dark black hair and deep chestnut skin who had also lost someone to the arenas. And for the first time in years, Vanessa felt something other than grief and hopelessness.

But the more she learned about Vashti's past, the people she'd lost, and the ones who currently held her hostage, the more Vanessa's own virulent anger spiraled.

And now she had another missions: save Vashti and her brother before it was too late.

Her brother was back. Vashti was here. But neither of them was free.

"If I go back," Vashti said slowly, "and give Min the harddrive, then that's the end. This could *really* be the end. And I can come here for good."

"What about Anthony and I?" Vanessa reminded her. "They know I'm the one who took it. I'm on her shit-list which means Anthony is, too. And Min isn't the type to let bygones be bygones."

Vashti's jaw tightened. "God, Vanessa, why did you take that thing anyway? Why would you do something so *stupid!*"

Angry hot tears welled in Vanessa's eyes. "Because the last time I didn't do anything, I lost my entire family."

"You know that's different—"

"It doesn't feel different when you're the one who gets left behind," Vanessa said. "I'm not losing anyone else."

Vashti sighed and leaned forward, gently resting her forehead on Vanessa's. "You won't lose me."

Vanessa closed her eyes. "I *know*. Because we're going to get you out."

Vanessa didn't get much sleep. She tossed and turned for another two hours before she decided she'd had enough and finally got up.

It was barely seven in the morning, and Simi was already in their shared office. Seeing her sent a rush of relief rolling through Vanessa. Simi had a cup of coffee in her hand, which she promptly handed to Vanessa.

"You look like shit," Simi said.

"Kind of you to notice."

Simi shrugged and turned on her computer. "So what's the plan?"

"What makes you think I have a plan?"

"Because you look like shit," Simi said, gesturing vaguely towards her. "That's what you look like when you've been thinking. It generally takes a lot out of you."

Vanessa scoffed and rolled her eyes. "Shut up."

Simi grinned.

"I don't have a plan. I've just been going through our

options," Vanessa said, her voice low and solemn. "Even if Vashti returns the drive, Min will still want my head. Or, most likely, she'll just get suspicious and hurt Vashti. The only way we all walk out of this unscathed is to open that file and expose whatever Min's hiding. Which means we need Min's fingerprint, a bit of her blood, and a five-hundred-thousand-dollar scanner. But . . . I don't know how."

Vanessa looked up and allowed her mask to fall. "You're right. It was impulsive. I . . . stole that hard-drive, but I didn't know what we'd need to open it. If I'd just slowed down and come up with a real plan first—"

"Then maybe you would have missed the opportunity entirely," Simi interrupted. "Or maybe you would have stuck around for too long and gotten caught. Or a thousand other things. But we're all together right now. You, me, your brother, *and* Vashti. We'll figure it out *together*."

Vanessa shoulders slumped. She nodded.

"Besides, I've already come up with a way to get our hands on one of those fancy scanners. I'll need Anthony but we can handle it."

"And Min's blood? The fingerprint?"

Simi's fingernails tapped against the lid of her coffee cup. "Vashti's the only one who can get close enough."

Vanessa shook her head. "Absolutely not. The whole point of this is to get her out. Not throw her back in."

"I can do it."

Vashti's voice surprised them both and Simi nearly jumped out of her chair. "*Jesus*, Vashti, stop doing that!"

Vashti's eyes were bloodshot. "Simi's right. I'm the only one who can get close enough to Min. Fingerprints are easy enough. We can lift that off something she's touched, right?"

"And the blood?" Vanessa asked. "Fresh, unoxidized blood?"

"What about a blood sample? From a lab?"

"Labs don't keep people's blood indefinitely," Simi said. "Unless Min's had her yearly checkup done within the last three days, that blood sample is as good as gone."

"Min has private doctors, Simi," Vashti said. "And if she's really Gifted, I don't think she's shipping her blood off for testing. It's probably all done in house. Maybe some of it *is* stored. Or we convince her doctor to get more blood. Say they need to do . . . I don't know, do additional tests or something."

"Convince?" Simi narrowed her eyes. "You mean *threaten*."

Vashti shrugged. "If that's what it takes."

"If you can get me the name of her private doctor I can start digging," Simi said. "Find something you can use."

Vashti glanced at Vanessa. "So . . . one last job?"

God, she hoped so. Vanessa offered a slight nod. "One last job."

Anthony

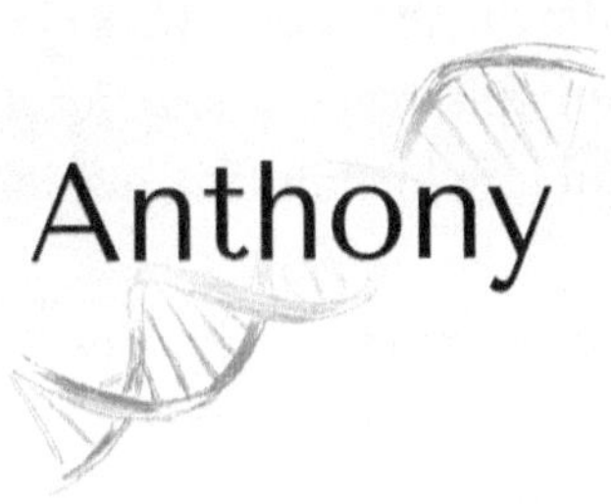

Anthony slept soundly and without interruption for the first time in two years. But when he woke up, panic threatened to choke him out.

Where am I? Where am I? Where am I?

The same question echoed in his mind every morning when he woke up in the arenas. They traveled so frequently it was difficult to keep track of where they were — even though it hardly mattered where they were if he couldn't leave the grounds unattended. So what if they were in Los Angeles? Albuquerque? Portland? The fighters would only see the four walls of the building that contained them.

Where am I? Where am I?

Habits were hard to break.

Where am I? Where am I?

Eventually, he'd remember the important parts. That he was in the arena. That he would never see Logan or his sister again. That his new friends lived here with him, too. That he was a fighter.

But this morning was different. It wasn't as loud. Usually

by the crack of dawn, the arena was already bursting with rowdy activity. But this place was quiet. He could make out some muffled rumbling just outside his door, but otherwise it was silent.

Anthony stood up, rubbing the sleep out of his eyes. He wasn't in the arenas or Min's condo. He was at the tattoo parlor. Vanessa's tattoo parlor.

He opened the door and remembered he was *home*.

He was equipped with a change of clothes and toiletries, courtesy of the bags he'd brought for his trip to London. Once he'd showered and changed, he padded up a floor to find the others.

"*Anthony?*"

He scanned the room in search of the voice he'd recognized and found Wyatt and Ender, beaming at him from the couch.

They jumped over the sides and top of the settee in an effort to rush towards them. Ender hugged him so tightly it knocked the wind out of Anthony's lungs.

"We thought you died!" Ender yelled a *little* too loudly as his Gift rode the coattails of his excitement. Anthony winced.

"Inside voice, man," Wyatt chided with a broad grin. "But, hey, we're glad you didn't die! I figured you ditched to find your family when everything went to shit. Since we'd just talked about how that was a *really* bad idea."

That conversation seemed like a lifetime ago.

"Where's everyone else?" Anthony asked.

Wyatt shrugged. "Lots of people took their chances and went back home. Or to wherever home was last. Your sister and the people here . . ." The glint in his eye flashed for a moment and his smile faltered for the first time. "They . . . took care of the staff that was left. Made sure nobody was coming after us."

It took a moment for the meaning behind those words to

register. *She killed them.* Vashti and Ruth may have eliminated anyone who was in their way, but Vanessa and whoever she'd brought with her that night had finished the job.

He tried to reconcile that knowledge. He knew his sister was a girl who loved school, wanted to work in a lab, loved art and tattooing but was secretly terrified of needles. But over the years, she'd changed, too. She hunted down human trafficking rings. She dated assassins.

She killed people.

The door to the back office opened, and Vanessa stepped out. "Glad to see you're finally up, Popsicle. And good, you bathed. Now get in here. Simi brought donuts."

Wyatt wrinkled his nose. "Is she always this bossy?"

"Yes," Vanessa and Anthony said at the same time.

"Hurry up, Popsicle."

Anthony sucked his teeth. "I hate it when she calls me that," he groaned, before joining the others in the office across the hall.

Ruth

Ruth couldn't believe she'd *lost* them.

After a moment of panic and a litany of curses on the plane, Nina had subsequently put on her headphones and resumed her in-flight movie of choice, *Moulin Rouge*. Meanwhile, Ruth had spent the remaining four and half hours cycling between fury, irritation, and concern. It was a miracle she hadn't accidentally induced mass panic and hysteria on the plane.

This assignment had gone sideways so quickly.

Ruth couldn't have been any less interested in the boy. Despite Min's fascination with him and his family, she was sure they could recover the drive without him. But Min insisted on blackmail as leverage which meant the boy was part of the deal, too.

But Vashti was *her* responsibility, and for all Ruth knew, she was missing because the boy had screwed something up.

She can handle herself, the Companion said. *But what's this one up to, though?*

Ruth glanced up at Nina. After they'd landed, they'd

dropped their bags off at the hotel and Nina had insisted on stopping by a nearby pub to touch base with her contact. Ruth watched from a nearby booth as Nina chatted with the bartender. Finally, after a few minutes, Nina gestured for Ruth to join her.

The bartender remained at his post while Nina led Ruth towards the back of the pub. The swinging doors opened to a narrow stairwell and they followed the stairs down to a storage area filled with crates of wine and liquors.

The man waiting for them was a tall and burly gentleman built like a WWE wrestler. Ruth couldn't help but wonder how he'd made it down the narrow stairwell in the first place. A pair of round glasses sat on the bridge of a flat nose.

He greeted Nina with a warm smile and full, gruff baritone voice. But apprehension evaporated off his skin. He tried to hide it though, arms folded across his chest as he leaned against the table in the middle of the room. "Nina," he greeted. "Six months and not even a Christmas card?"

"I missed you too, Harlan," Nina said as she inched towards him. Her fingers lingered along the edges of a closed spiral notebook on the table. She opened it up and began leafing through the pages. "And how are your boys? Peter and . . . is it John? Jack? Eldest should be twelve now, yes?"

The man's face fell as faint wisps of fear surrounded him in a hazy aura. His smile tightened and he swallowed. "They're . . . fine," he said, but the familiarity in his demeanor had already slipped.

"Wonderful. Well, now that the pleasantries are out of the way, let's cut to the chase. My friend and I need a ride."

"Where do you need to go?"

Nina cocked her head to the side, in a mock display of confusion. She approached him with deadly intention. "Well, aren't you eager? Usually, we do the '*that's not how it works, Nina*' bit first."

"I thought we already wrapped up pleasantries. Remember?"

Nina took another step and Harlan mirrored her movement with careful steps in the opposite direction until his back was flush against the shelves. He was a constellation of emotions. Fear and anxiety overpowered the room's nascent scent of rotting wood and empty bottles of beer and spirits.

Nina shrugged. "Fair enough."

Harlan cleared his throat. He was nearly three times Nina's size, and yet the foul smell of terror wafting from him was overwhelming.

Without warning, Nina grabbed a bottle of Pimm's by the neck and smashed it against the table. The bottle exploded and wine splattered all over the walls. She pointed the jagged end of the bottle towards Harlan with a maddening smile and rabid eyes. "*Why* are you trying to rush me out of here?"

Wait . . .

Ruth flinched, realizing her mistake. It hadn't been Harlan's fear she picked up on.

It was Nina's.

How had she missed it? The only thing emanating from Harlan was anxiety. But that ugly stench of fear? That was coming from Nina alone.

Pay attention her companion sang again directly into her ear.

"Nina," Ruth muttered in a low voice. She tip-toed around the table until she was behind her partner. She tried to target her fear, relax her instead.

Nina rested a gentle hand on hers. "I'd *really* rather you didn't," she said.

Suddenly Ruth became completely still, paralyzed in space

with one hand resting on the table and the other shoved into her pocket. Her throat was swollen and she felt as if she were breathing out of a straw.

Nina wore a sheepish but unapologetic smirk on her face. "Ruth, I love you, but I need you to sit this one out. I can't exactly have you playing with my feelings like you did with that poor woman on the plane."

Terror gripped Ruth. She could barely see the color of Nina's eyes. Her pupils refused to focus. She couldn't move; she couldn't even blink.

She couldn't even see the Companion. But she could hear it. *Ruth.* It sounded scared. *Ruth, what's happening?*

"Nina?" Harlan's voice broke through. "What are you—"

"Ah-ah!" Nina whirled around and covered her own mouth and nose with her hand.

Harlan mirrored the behavior perfectly, his palm flush against his lips, his fingers closing off his nostrils to prevent him from breathing. Slowly, Nina released her hand from her face but Harlan remained utterly statuesque. She rolled her shoulders and stretched her arms forward, like a cat who had just woken up from a long, restful nap. Harlan's face went from pale to pink to tomato red. But his mouth stayed closed and his fingers held his nostrils shut.

Ruth willed herself to scream, but no sound escaped her lips. Hysteria twisted in her gut. How was Nina doing this? This was well beyond Nina's usual Gift of healing injuries and breaking bones.

This was control.

Nina faced Harlan. "Sorry. This is all a bit dramatic, I know. But I need you to understand that I'm really, *really* serious. Because my friend and I really screwed the pooch on this one." She leaned back on the wall beside Harlan, still holding the broken bottle top in her left hand. "You've heard of my wife, yes?"

Nina dropped the broken bottle in her left hand and its remnant shattered on impact. She reached for an open wine bottle on the table in front of her and helped herself to a tasting straight from the bottle. Nina's nose was bleeding, but she didn't seem to notice.

"My wife," Nina continued, "is a peach. I love her to death; I'd do anything for her. So, Harlan, I need a guaranteed, expeditious ride out of this depressing city two weeks from now. Can you do that?"

Harlan's eyes fluttered.

Nina's back straightened. "Oh, damn it!" She waved her hand and Harlan's hand fell from his face. He collapsed to the floor on his hands and knees, wheezing and hacking. Ruth sensed Nina's contempt falling from her like acid rain, seeping into everything around her.

Gradually, Nina released Ruth from her control as well. Her muscles relaxed in concert, allowing her to reclaim her body with more grace and poise than Harlan, but she still had to grip the table ledge to keep herself from falling.

Nina met Harlan on the ground, one knee touching the wet and slippery floor.

"A ride, Harlan," Nina said. "Can you do that for me?"

Harlan glared at Nina with bloodshot eyes. Ruth sensed his contempt. Indignation. *Defiance.* Unadulterated hatred. But through the haze of anger. Something sweet like honey, yet fiery and hot like a ghost pepper.

Harlan wanted to kill her. But, of course, he couldn't because he had a family. Children.

That was what Ruth sensed through the muddled catastrophe of emotion that surged from Harlan: *love.*

"Yes," Harlan growled. "I can get you a ride."

Nina turned and looked at Ruth in search of confirmation.

Ruth nodded. He was telling the truth. He could do it.

Nina smiled. "Excellent. We'll need details, if you don't mind." Then, finally noticing her own blood dripping onto the murky floor, she wiped her nose with the back of her hand. "Sorry for the mess, Harlan. Going off script tends to take it out of me."

~

THE COMPANION WAS MUCH MORE talkative that evening. Its thoughts drowned out her own, humming like a hoard of bees.

Well, that was embarrassing.

She did that to you.

Paralyzed you.

Took away your power. Threatened you.

And you let her.

We let her.

Since when did we let people do that sort of shit, anyhow?

It's that girl. Making you soft.

Vashti.

Picking up strays.

Because you've gone soft.

Like a peach.

Little peach. A soft fuzzy peach.

"Yoo-hoo," Nina whistled, snapping her fingers in front of Ruth's face. Ruth blinked in surprise and stumbled, her foot catching on a loose cobblestone.

Ruth groaned. "Why haven't these people ripped these roads apart and replaced them with something functional."

Nina held her right hand in the air, then loudly proclaimed, "For the history!"

Ruth rolled her eyes and cursed. "Stop that."

Nina pouted. "Are you mad at me?"

"Of course not, you maniacal, impulsive little sh—"

"Here we are!" She grabbed Ruth's arm and dragged her up the stone steps towards their hotel. Ruth wrinkled her nose. Nina's euphoria smelled like cinnamon.

Naturally, they were staying at an unnecessarily luxurious hotel, with decorative pillars made of marble and deep red, curtains drawn over the floor to ceiling windows. A man wearing a tuxedo played the piano in the lobby, and despite the late hour, the bar hosted a lively, but demure crowd. Visitors and guests nursed dark amber drinks around round tables, offering light chortles and punctuated laughs when someone said something mildly interesting.

Ruth rolled her eyes. Most of them smelled bored.

"Oh!" Nina rested a hand against Ruth's shoulder. "Bring up a bottle of champagne when you have the chance? We're celebrating,"

"Of course," the concierge said. He handed them the bags they'd dropped off earlier that day.

Nina grinned. "My little peach," she said in an obnoxious baby voice, snuggling Ruth like a lovesick teenager at the movies.

Yes — this was *definitely* the drug.

Soft like a little peach, the Companion reminded her.

Ruth stiffened.

Finally, they made their way up to their room. It was lavish and *quiet*. Nina opted to shower first, leaving Ruth alone with her thoughts. And it. Their thoughts. Her thoughts? It was getting harder and harder to tease them apart.

Nina had paralyzed her. She'd taken her to a pub to meet a man Ruth didn't know existed. And in that strange place, Nina used her Gift on her and paralyzed her.

For as long as she could remember, she had only ever been

someone else's property. First, she belonged to a lab, until Min killed its keepers and absorbed all of its research. Min had awarded her the opportunity to pursue higher education, but it had come with a price. Her current contract bound Ruth to Min for the next forty years.

And then this week, when Min had offered this final opportunity . . . a way out? A means for her to *finally* be her own person? She'd known it was too good to be true. Min didn't release her personal projects into the world. Min craved control. She would never freely relinquish it. Besides, Ruth's ledger was so profoundly stained with red, Ruth wasn't sure if she deserved it.

But Vashti was still a child. Her ledger didn't count. Not yet.

Nina was so thoroughly trapped among the vines of Min's authority she'd long forgotten the scent of love. She was a product of her environment. She didn't know better . . .

No, her companion seethed. *You're a fucking psychiatrist. You're the one who should have known better.*

A loud *pop*. The champagne was here. Nina had opened it. Her hair was wet, her face barren and completely free of the heavy eyeliner she usually wore. She looked younger without it.

Had she finished showering already? How long had it been?

"How did you do that?" Ruth asked, her voice flat despite the chaos in her mind.

"Do what?" Nina asked.

"At the pub. You . . . froze me somehow."

Nina pulled a small, opaque bottle from her purse and tossed it to Ruth. "A little something the R&D department's been working on. It boosts my Gift, but just a little bit. And it only lasts fifteen minutes or so."

Ruth shook the bottle. It was half-full.

"You want to try some?"

Ruth glared at Nina. "Why? Why did you use this?"

"Why did I employ an intimidation tactic against a man who was four times my size?" Nina asked. "Because Harlan likes to haggle and I wasn't in the mood."

"He was terrified when you mentioned his kids. That was enough!"

"His ex-wife has full custody and he sees them three times a year. He may not want to see them dead, but they're not the most reliable bargaining chip. Harlan's favorite person is himself, so it makes sense to threaten him directly."

"But you didn't just *threaten* him." Ruth's voice cracked. "You used me."

Nina sniffed, nostrils flaring and chin jutting out slightly. "I was making a point."

"You *paralyzed* me!"

"Alright, fine. Next time, I'll warn you if that makes you feel better."

Ruth saw red. *Next time?*

She did that to you. Paralyzed you. Took away your power. Threatened you.

And you let her.

We let her.

"Anyway, I did let you play, too," Nina said. "You were involved, remember?"

"When did—"

"At the end," Nina said plainly, taking a swig of champagne right out of the bottle. "I checked in with you. To see if he was telling the truth.

"And that's supposed to make up for what you did to me?"

"I'm the blunt instrument," Nina pointed at herself. Then motioned towards Ruth. "You're a bit more precise. That's how we work together so well, isn't it? I needed him to know we were serious. And you confirmed the information we received was accurate. Some may go as far as calling it teamwork."

"That—" Ruth pointed at the door. "*That* wasn't teamwork. You didn't tell me what you were planning. Instead, you paralyzed me and used me as a pawn to intimidate someone else. Someone who *probably* would have done whatever the hell you wanted anyway!"

"Well, I like to be certain. It's simple risk minimization. I threatened his kids, then I threatened him directly."

"Why did you use me to do it?"

"Because you would have stopped me!"

Ruth scoffed. "You don't know that."

"You *would* have, actually. Because you're just about the worst type of mercenary. You have a moral code."

"I have *boundaries*," Ruth corrected. "Lines I'd rather not cross."

"Yes, well, those are *your* boundaries, aren't they?" Nina corrected. "Not mine. I care about my family and that's it. *You* project humanity onto the people you believe have earned it. That arena handler you stabbed in the car two weeks ago doesn't deserve to live because you despise the arenas. You decided he was lacking a soul before you even stepped into his car. But Harlan has *children*. So he can live, yes?"

"That's not—"

"Harlan *beat* his children. He nearly sent his ex-wife home in a body bag. *That's* why he lost custody. He thinks he loves them, thinks he cares, but he's a monster, too. But *you* didn't know that."

"You could have told me that," Ruth yelled. "You just said we're a team. But instead of telling me anything, you paralyzed me. You did not need to do that. *You did not need my body!*"

"Honestly, Ruth, I think you're overreacting."

Ruth's pulse pounded against her temple. "*What?*"

"I froze you for twenty seconds. You're *absolutely* over-reacting."

She's going to do it again, the Companion said.

"No," Ruth whispered. To Nina. To the Companion. "No—"

"No, what?" Nina scoffed.

She's going to do it again, it said, its eyes wide and pupils blown. Its shirt was untucked and it stood behind Nina. *She's going to do it again, isn't she?* It wrung its hands together. Where had its cane gone? *She'll do it again. We have to stop it. Get rid of her!*

Ruth clenched her hands. "No—"

"Shut up!" Ruth screamed, glaring at it. It was out of bounds, completely out of line. It didn't make the rules, either. It wasn't its job to tell her what to do. *"Shut up!"*

"Ruth?"

Nina glanced over her shoulder. "Ruth, I didn't—"

"No, shut up!" Ruth barked at Nina. "Shut the hell up; I'm not fucking overreacting!"

"Ruth . . ." Nina lowered herself on the bed, slowly, as if Ruth may pounce at any sudden movement. "Go to bed, Ruth. Look, I'm sorry, alright? You're worked up. Sleep it off. We'll talk about it in the morning." She yanked the chain on the lamp beside her, and smothered the room in a soft darkness.

"*Sleep it off?*" Ruth's words were quiet. Angry. Vibrating with the power of a thousand storms. Because now she finally saw, *finally* realized, that she'd been right all along. Nina was nothing like Min. She was so much worse.

At least Min *knew* she was a monster, she had made it abundantly clear from the jump. But Nina was the monster lurking in the shadows. She was the demon that held the knife while claiming someone else had swung. She feigned innocence. She pretended to have no agency or control. She cosplayed defeat.

Nina liked to believe that Min had taken Nina's independence from her, just like she'd taken Vashti's and Ruth's. But Nina wasn't bound by a contract. She was bound by her own twisted perception of what it meant to love. And she wielded that love not like a protective shield, but a deadly poison aerosolized by the winds of selfish regard. It was a love that stank of rot and mold.

They were not a team. Vashti and Ruth were a team. To Nina, they were expendable pawns. Bodies to be readjusted to suit her needs and further her own twisted agenda. Nina could claim until the end of days that she did it all for Min, but Nina's eyes had come *alight* when she'd taken Ruth's body.

She'd loved it.

She'll do it again, the Companion said. *To you, to Vashti . . .*

Nina's soft snores awakened something primal in Ruth: the primitive rage of an animal backed into a corner, the chronic resentment of a caged beast, and the fulminant influx of memories of a time when she'd been both.

She remembered an entire childhood, during which she'd been isolated and kept for study. For years, she had been pushed further and further because people were simply *curious*.

Ruth, the only girl in the entire world who could peek into minds. Could the girl make people feel sad? Angry? What about more complicated things like love? And hate? And despair? What about depression?

One by one, she infiltrated the minds of countless people. For decades. For science. *For them.*

"We want this man to cry. Can you make him cry?"

No, but she could make him very sad. That would make him cry.

"Can you make this man hit that woman?"

No, but she could make him angry. So angry that maybe he

would do something he didn't think he'd been capable of before.

"Can you make this man kill that woman?"

No, she really didn't want to make him that angry.

"What about himself? Can you make him do it to himself?"

That was around the time her companion showed up. It tried to help with the harder tasks. The ones that gave Ruth the nightmares and made it hard to sleep at night. It had taken the nightmares, too, swallowed the memories whenever they threatened to surface.

But not this time.

No, it said. *They won't do it again. This is our body. Your body. And you've forgotten a time when it wasn't.*

She left Nina's side, crawled into her own strange bed, and let the memories bury her alive.

Anthony

Anthony wore a black suit paired with a blue tie. It was Simi's brother's suit, and even though her brother was in his early twenties, the suit fit Anthony surprisingly well. And for the sake of today's performance, his short hair had been slicked back with enough product to suffocate a small animal.

"I feel like an idiot," he groused.

"You look smashing," Simi teased. She wore a gray blazer and pencil skirt. She'd changed her hair earlier this week and now sported faux locs. A pair of thin-rimmed, circular glasses rested on her flat-bridged nose. She had to keep pushing the glasses up on her face. It didn't seem like she realized how frequently she was doing it either. Whenever they slipped, she'd sniff and wiggle her nose up before realizing the issue.

"Your brother just *let* you borrow his suit?"

"He knows what I do on the weekends. He doesn't care about the suit."

Anthony's eyes narrowed. "He knows you hang out with a

rowdy group of deviants and have joined their ranks to engage in corporate espionage?"

Simi fumbled, stumbling over her words. With a slight shrug and tilt of her head, she said, "I may have left out the details."

"What details? That was the summary."

Simi harrumphed, readjusting her feet in her heels before the pedestrian light turned green. "God, I should have worn the other pair but I really wanted to break these in."

It was surreal being able to walk about in public, in broad daylight, unsupervised while the girl he was with complained about her choice of footwear. He could pretend they were two perfectly normal people . . . on their way to steal a Bio-Security scanner.

Just your average Saturday, really.

The light turned. "Remember the plan?" Simi asked.

Anthony nodded. It *seemed* simple enough. He just had to stand there and grunt when addressed. Simi was the one carrying the whole operation, which was good, considering nearly every step to her plan had been her idea.

She took the time to summarize his role, just in case. "You just stand there and look pretty."

He blushed.

Once they'd made it past the crosswalk, she led them towards the edge of the sidewalk. She grabbed Anthony's face with the patience and grace of a two-year-old mastering fine motor skills. "Hold still," she instructed, then touched his right temple before releasing him.

He massaged his jaw. "What was that?" he reached for the side of his head.

Simi slapped his hand away. "Don't touch it!" She sucked her teeth, exasperated.

"Well, what did you do?"

She touched her own forehead. "De-identifier," she explained. "Scrambles our faces so we don't get caught on security cameras."

"Sounds illegal."

Simi smiled. She had dimples, he realized. "We're stealing a bio-scanner. Prioritize your crimes."

"Are you *sure* about this?" Anthony asked again, trying to distract himself from the fact that he had noticed she had dimples. "I can't believe Bio-Sec's security would be so—"

"Embarrassing?" Simi said with a roll of her eyes. "I mean honestly, a *phishing* scam? I have half a dozen Bio-Sec employee IDs, passwords, high school mascots, and names of first pets because I sent an email saying their password expired."

The pair slowed down as they approached one of the taller buildings on Elm Street. The words *Bio-Security, Inc.* were scrawled on the side of the building in large block letters.

"You ready?" Simi had one hand on the metal bar, ready to open the door.

Anthony stood up tall, allowing the muscles in his shoulder to relax as he invited a deep breath of air into his lungs. "Ready."

It was good enough for her.

The moment she crossed the threshold, Simi's countenance and stance transformed. Her back straightened and the arm holding her leather bag stiffened, swaying less freely. The heels that she had complained about just moments ago, carried her so gracefully Anthony would have believed they were made of clouds. He trailed behind her, matching her determined gait while discreetly taking in their surroundings.

Anthony thought the building would have been emptier; this wasn't a tech company that bothered to market to the masses, anyway. But the lobby of Bio-Sec was a massive showroom. Each of Bio-Sec's recent releases and security upgrades were on display, available for guest interaction, like Bio-Sec's first home security system and their first model of Bio-Sec safes and eye scans.

Anthony forced himself to focus on Simi. His job was simple, and he wouldn't be the reason they failed.

They continued past all of the displays, towards the back of the open atrium. Eventually, they were greeted by an employee wearing a gray shirt with the word "STAFF" printed on the front. He looked like he'd just left lacrosse practice with his friends.

He grinned. Simi did not.

Before the employee could give his standard greeting, Simi announced, "I have an appointment."

STAFF's grin did not falter. "Absolutely. Are you here to pick up an order? I'm going to need the confirmation number and your ID."

She gave him both.

"Is this gentleman with you?" he asked as he looked something up on his computer.

"Yes."

"Does he have an ID?"

"No."

The employee hesitated and glanced at Anthony, brows furrowing, although his overeager smile was still very much present. Anthony didn't even address him. He just stared, seemingly bored. That's what the staff — his *handlers* — did back at the arena during fight nights. The handlers may have played Uno with the fighters the night before, but on Fight Nights, their eyes were dark and they never seemed to be focusing on anything in particular. Somehow looking at nothing but seeing everything.

The employee cleared his throat, then looked back down at

his computer. "Ah . . . alright. You're here for Mrs. Vinayesh's pick up order. Right this way, Ms. Stone."

Thanks to Simi's phishing scam, she'd been able to snag a list of several employee's login information and with that, the names of everyone who had placed an order with Bio-Sec in the last three years. Their ticket into the building was with the recent order of Ms. Shruti Vinayesh, current CEO of Valant, a tech company in India who was spending time in Dallas for a conference. A few weeks ago, she placed an order for a Bio-Sec scanner, and she'd sent her assistant to pick it up for her.

Her assistant's name was Lorynn Stone.

The employee led the pair of them further away from the atrium and towards a door in the back clearly labeled "EMPLOYEES ONLY" and locked with a 5-digit keypad. Once opened, he gestured for the pair to enter the designated space comprising a handful of offices and twice as many cubicles.

As soon as Anthony walked through the door, the alarm screeched. A few hidden Bio-Sec employees poked their heads from their tiny offices, similarly startled and concerned.

A litany of choice curses rushed through Anthony's mind, but he kept his mouth shut and his Gift in check.

"Sorry," the employee said nervously. He pressed a few buttons on the keypad and the wailing alarm stopped. "Is he a . . ."

Anthony's tongue was fixed to the roof of his mouth and Simi looked as if she was ready to strangle the part-time employee with her bare hands. Simi refused to help him finish his sentence.

The employee sighed, glancing between the two of them nervously. "I'm sorry we don't allow Gifted back here."

"I'm not Gifted," Simi said.

He pointed at Anthony. "But he's—"

"Ms. Lorynn Stone?"

Simi turned quickly, meeting the eyes of whoever had called her — or, rather, her alias's — name. A bulky, middle-aged man in dress pants and a button down approached them. He squeezed between the cubicles, taking up nearly all the remaining space in the hallway.

"Ms. Stone," he held out his hand and took Simi's in his. "I apologize for Rich, he's new . . . and young. My name is Glenn and I'll be taking care of you today."

Simi hummed. Anthony noticed her eyes take in the sheer size of the man in front of them. "Not a problem and I don't care. I just need to catch the next flight back and get this delivered so my boss doesn't fire me."

"Of course, right this way." The older man glowered at the employee who nodded and nearly stumbled over his own feet to escape.

Glenn led the pair of them through the meandering cubicles. "I apologize for the alarm system," the man said. "We're in the process of reconfiguring them. We find that most people who purchase our security products tend to prefer Gifted security detail over Regulars — for obvious reasons. And since all of our high-profile transactions take place in private, the screening systems are pointless."

"Reassuring," Simi said as he adjusted her glasses.

Anthony tried to keep track of the corridors but lost count at the third — or was it the fourth? — turn. Every hallway, corridor, and cubicle looked exactly the same.

Was this hell?

Finally, Glenn led them to an office — *his* office, complete with a nameplate on the door: Glenn Armstrong. His office was the size of a bedroom, complete with floor to ceiling privacy windows. They were still on the ground floor, and pedestrians outside walked past them without a second glance. There was a wet bar by the window and there, waiting patiently on Glenn's table, was their bio-scanner.

Well, Ms. Vinayesh's scanner. It was in a discreet, gray box. No stickers, no picture of the device on the box. Not even a ribbon.

That's it? Anthony nearly said the words aloud but caught himself just in time. Glenn seemed to catch the questioning look in his eye.

As if he'd read Anthony's mind, Glenn opened the box, revealing the thin piece of metal encased safely inside. He gestured towards the two chairs in front of his desk as he sat. Simi took the seat on the left, closer to the window.

Anthony stood.

"It's my understanding Ms. Vinayesh will be activating this at a later date?"

"Precisely," Simi said.

Glenn pulled out a stack of papers from a drawer behind the desk. "Perfect. I'll just need—"

Then his phone rang.

Glenn thumbed through the pages as he reached for the landline. He tucked the phone between his ear and shoulder. "This is Mr. Armstrong," he answered, half-paying attention.

Simi's eyes were focused on the scanner in front of them, so she didn't notice Glenn's eyes darken, his spine straighten and his eyes dart between his two guests just before he uttered, "No that can't be right. Have security detain her. I'm already seeing to the transfer of Ms. Vinayesh's scanner as we speak."

Simi's nose crinkled, as if she had smelled something foul, and she slipped her glasses a bit further up her face again.

"Fuck," she muttered.

Anthony reached for the wet bar with the tendrils of his Gift. The decanter shattered as the liquid within it burst from confinement. The liquid straightened, froze, and sliced through the cord that connected the phone to the cradle.

Simi dove for the scanner. She grabbed it, and leaped out of the chair and over the table. Her bare feet made contact with Glenn's chest, shoes abandoned beneath the table. In an instant, Simi stood behind Glenn, a ballpoint pen flush against his jugular. "The only people who know we're here are you and the nervous kid from the front desk. Your security systems are running a de-identifier on both of us and every camera we've passed in the last 4 minutes will be playing a loop for the next half hour. So what if, instead of pressing that panic button, you just let us take the scanner and go, yeah? Trust me, they're not paying you enough."

Glenn didn't even struggle or pretend to be concerned. Instead, he just stood up. Slowly.

Simi was much smaller than Glenn, but her grip around his neck should have at least made the transition to his feet uncomfortable. Instead, Glenn rose with the grace of a seasoned ballerina and Simi moved with him, unyielding in her grip and her stubbornness. Her feet scrambled for purchase and when he had stood up fully, she tried to wrap her legs around his torso.

Glenn reached above and over his head with one arm, grabbing Simi by her collar before tossing her across the room as if she were a rag doll. She rolled and hit her head against the opposite wall.

Apparently, Biosecurity, Inc preferred to hire Gifted for their security detail as well.

Glenn glared at Anthony. *You're next.*

And immediately, Anthony was in the arena. His heart sank, panic settled into his chest. Then he did precisely what he had done every single time he had been placed in the arena with an opponent. Anthony didn't simply *reach* for his Gift.

He allowed it to consume him.

He felt the push and pull of the water around him — in the air, on his skin, sinking deeper into the ground from the spilled Scotch — and there, in the walls. The pipes.

Anthony *squeezed* and the room exploded.

Water burst from every pipe in the walls around them. Glass from the window shattered. Water spilled and rushed towards him from every direction: the ceiling, the walls, the floor. The water swirled around the three of them, creating a hurricane of Anthony's own making. Glenn looked up and around, wide-eyed and a little nervous.

The first time Anthony had seen that nervous look in his opponent, he had felt a rush of excitement, something almost akin to glee. Anthony felt that excitement now, the urge to release the pressure of hundreds of gallons of water directly into Glenn's face and his body. Strongman or not, that much pressure would kill him.

But this wasn't the arena.

With a desperate cry, Anthony pushed the flood of water towards Glenn, but without the added power of his control. Glenn fell back, overpowered and caught in the water's tide, but not crushed and certainly not dead. Anthony and Simi seized the opportunity and fled out a broken window.

A crowd had started to gather around the building as distant sirens rapidly approached. The commotion was enough for the two of them to slip through the crowds unseen and into a nearby alley.

"*Shit,*" Simi complained once they'd put a fair amount of distance between themselves and the building they'd just robbed.

Anthony's heart dropped. "What is it? Did we forget the scanner?"

Simi stared at him, mortified. "What? No." She held up her shoes, dripping wet and soaked all the way through.

Anthony blinked. "You're joking."

"These are *Manolos*," Simi complained as if that meant anything at all to him. "And they're not even mine. They're my mom's. She's going to kill me."

Anthony felt his brain short-circuit. Then, he kicked off his shoes and gestured towards them. Simi frowned, crossing her arms in front of her before shoving her feet into his shoes.

"Thanks," she mumbled.

"Yeah." Anthony curled his toes in his mismatched socks. "No worries. Sorry about your . . . Malolos."

"*Manolos.*"

"That's what I said."

She rolled her eyes. "Come on, let's get that thing back to the parlor.

Nina

Nina had always loved with an intensity that terrified her. It was a love that hurt and blessed and left nothing but destruction and an insatiable craving for more. Her brain on love drowned in dopamine; laying waste to every other need, every other desire.

The trick though, was to find someone who could love her back.

She had squandered her chances at love already. She had a family once, before Min. She'd been adopted into a family who had promised to love her and care for her despite her genetic deformities. At that time, only her healing powers had manifested, and Nina was praised by her parents for her Gift. She fixed paper cuts, sprains, and broken bones.

But she was still a deviant. She had to be counted in the evenings and registered with the county, state, and US Government. Her Gifted status was marked clearly on her driver's license and passport. But despite all of this and because her parents had the money, she went to private school with other children her age. She performed above and beyond on her entrance exams.

And her parents were proud. But it wasn't a love that would last. All they had to offer was a broken love. It was all *anyone* ever had to offer.

Until she met Min. And years later, Min was still here.

If she had any reason to suspect that anyone was, in any sense, plotting the demise of the love of her life, then Nina would break them until they were nothing but ash and bone.

After the little *incident* at Harlan's pub, the following weeks had been tense. If Nina was to be completely honest with herself, she did regret taking control of Ruth's body. But the Gift enhancer inflated her ego, made her feel unstoppable, like a shot of tequila before she rushed to the dance floor. The right thing would have been for Nina to warn Ruth against interfering with her interrogation *beforehand*.

Nina had tried to apologize countless times already — or, rather, three and a half times. While Ruth said she forgave her, she'd maintained a cold distance. Her answers and responses to Nina's questions were clipped and short. She didn't laugh or roll her eyes at any of Nina's inappropriate jokes or join Nina in complaining about the horrors of English cuisine.

What Nina *had* noticed, though, was Ruth's tendency to talk to herself.

Ruth kept such an apathetic countenance at her baseline, that noticing any emotion beyond mild annoyance was a welcome treat. But recently, ever since that moment in Harlan's, Nina would find Ruth muttering to herself incessantly, brows furrowed, concentrating intensely as if she was having a conversation with someone. Two nights ago, when Nina had woken up in the middle of the night to go pee, she'd caught Ruth cutting her toenails on the floor, talking to . . . well, *someone*. Ruth's back had been facing the door and Nina had been careful not to draw attention to herself. She couldn't hear exactly what Ruth was saying, but the cadence of her voice rose and fell at all the right intervals, as if she were having an open dialogue.

And when their journey to find that stupid hard-drive led them to a dead-end, Ruth didn't even seem surprised. In fact, she was so unbothered, Nina had half a mind to believe she was behind their failure. But Ruth wouldn't sabotage this mission, not when Vashti's freedom was also on the line.

Now, they were returning home empty-handed. Their last hope was that Vashti had acquired some new information and had been able to acquire the hard-drive before them somehow. Perhaps that was why she'd missed their flight. Maybe she knew something Nina and Ruth didn't.

At least Harlan had held up his half the bargain. He had been honest and straightforward in their dealings and had arranged their transport to meet them at a coffee shop. Harlan was quite good at finding people.

In fact, finding Gifted people happened to be his Gift.

"*Oi.* You Nina?"

Nina looked up from her latte art. She arched a suspicious brow. "And *you're* our ride?" She lowered her sunglasses so she could inspect him further.

The boy grinned, revealing a missing incisor. A missing *baby tooth.* He hopped up onto the high stool. He was barely four feet tall and wore worn jeans, expensive sneakers, and a jacket that was three times too big.

"How old are you?" Nina asked.

"Old enough. You need a license to drive, don't need one to travel. And last I checked beggars can't be choosers." He pointed behind her and right at Ruth. "Can one of you get me one of them lemon biscuits up front?"

"Allow me," Ruth grumbled, rising to her feet.

Nina leaned back in her chair and gestured at the boy. "So you're our ride then, Oliver Twist?"

"I feel like I'm more of a Dodger archetype, actually."

"What?"

"You Americans don't read very often, do you?"

Nina breathed through the unexpected but very strong desire to snap his arm in half. "Can you get us stateside or not?"

"Yeah, sure. When do you want to go," he finally asked, tone shifting into something a bit more serious. "Right now?"

"Sooner rather than later would be ideal."

"No problem. I just need coordinates."

That was a first. "Like . . . longitude, latitude? You don't need an address? That's . . . different."

He shrugged. "So are you interested or not?"

"Yes. But *first*, we need to get to this address." She dug into her pocket and pulled out the address Ruth had scribbled for her. The safe house she and Vashti had decided on prior to this absolute shit show of a mission.

The boy's button nose crinkled. "This isn't a relay race. Harlan said all you needed was a one-way trip."

"Can you do it?"

"Nah, sorry," the boy said, ready to take his leave.

"Seriously?"

"I'm not a black cab service. I'm not playing hop-scotch with you lot."

"I'll pay double."

He hesitated. *Perfect.* "I don't do stops," he said, almost pleading. "That's how you get caught. I only do one-way trips. If I get caught it's an international incident. They'd call it human trafficking. And I'll be tried as an adult because I used my Gift. They'll send me off to a labor camp. I mean, look at me. I'm adorable. I wouldn't last half a day in a labor camp."

"I work for *very* powerful people. You won't get caught. And if you did, we'd take care of it."

He rolled his eyes. "How would—"

"Look me up. Right now. Nina Markov-Liu."

The boy narrowed his eyes but pulled out his phone and ran a search for her name, misspelling her name *Makrov*.

It didn't matter. Photos of her with Min Liu, the richest woman on the planet, estimated to be worth seven billion dollars and majority shareholder of her family's company, *LIUYEN Industries*.

Luckily for Nina, being married to Min did not award her a similar amount of immediate recognition. It was common pop culture knowledge that Min was married to a woman. But nobody was particularly interested in *who* she was. This was excellent for Nina, since she preferred to serve at Liu's company in this current capacity: espionage and general tomfoolery.

It was certainly more fun than attending stuffy board meetings.

"You're protected," Nina said. The boy looked back at her with eyes as round as globes. "You don't have to worry about the police. So . . . you said double your rates, yes?"

He nodded slowly.

"And if you ever need anything," — she took the boy's phone from him and saved her own personal number — "emergencies only. If you share this with your friends or you call asking for McDonald's money, I'll block you."

"Yeah, yeah."

"Great. Now, when we get to this first location . . . things are going to get a bit messy. So I'm going to need you to listen to me, *very* carefully."

Anthony

A week after Anthony had reunited with his sister, Vashti left.

Vanessa said this is how it had been for years: quick visits separated by months apart, even though a mere thirty miles separated the tattoo parlor from the apartment Vashti shared with Ruth. And while Vanessa claimed she was used to it, that it wasn't a big deal, he could tell from the pained look in his sister's eyes and the curl of her lip as she held back tears that she was lying. It didn't matter that they were practiced in the language of goodbyes. It still didn't make Vashti's leaving any easier.

Besides, this time was different. They had a plan to expose Min and if everything went according to plan, Vashti would never have to go back to them again.

If things *didn't* go to plan, they'd probably never see Vashti again.

"Didn't expect you to see me off," Vashti joked, her duffel bag slung over her shoulder. Holly waited in a corner, ready to open a tear to take Vashti to her next location.

Anthony frowned. "You brought me to my sister," he said.

"I almost didn't," Vashti said. "I almost took you to London."

"Yeah, but that's only because you thought she was there," Anthony corrected. "I owe you. For the rest of my life, I'll owe you."

"You don't—"

"I mean it." His voice cracked. It should have been embarrassing, but he didn't care. "I was planning something very stupid when you showed up. If you hadn't been there—"

"Don't give me too much credit, Anthony," Vashti said. Her brown eyes refused to meet his. "If I hadn't been there at all, Vanessa would have found you herself."

"Min sent you *and* Ruth to get me that night," Anthony reminded her. "If you hadn't been there, Ruth would have taken me anyway. And if Vanessa had gotten in Ruth's way, Ruth would have killed her, or maybe taken her straight to Min. But you *were* there. You found me first. The only reason my sister's even alive right now is because you were there. You . . . you know that . . . right?"

The change in Vashti was immediate. She inhaled, as if it were her first breath after an eternity below the waves of a violent sea. And finally, she looked up at him.

This was his first time seeing her, he realized, without guilt clouding her eyes.

"I owe you, Vashti," Anthony said. His eyes stung. He didn't care. "I mean it."

She let out a laugh that was wet with unshed tears. "Yeah, well, you can pay up when I get back."

Two weeks inched by.

Two weeks shouldn't have been so nerve-wracking. And

yet, the parlor seemed thick with choking angst and trepidation. The scrape of a chair or a drawn-out sigh felt like lightning fracturing the peace. There was no rest, no easy slumber. Peace was suspect, chaos expected. But the days passed and the signal they were all waiting on, never came.

So everyone kept themselves busy.

There were usually up to a dozen Gifted residing in the basement of the parlor. The frequent flyers, Ender, Wyatt, and Grace, a Gifted with the ability to walk through objects, seemed to live here permanently. Ender and Wyatt had nowhere else to go, and Grace was another tattoo artist who worked upstairs. When she wasn't working, she was down here, studying for her GMAT.

Otherwise, Gifted flowed freely in and out of the space, sometimes stopping by for snacks, to chat about their lives, or simply to escape whatever hell awaited them at their own version of home.

For Vanessa, this *was* home.

Which meant this was home for Anthony, too.

He fell into a quiet routine. The arenas had drilled their own routine into his skull and at first, Anthony relished the opportunity to replace theirs with his own.

He got out of bed at five thirty. It didn't matter when he'd gone to bed; he woke up every morning at the same time. Sometimes, he woke up even earlier, when the nightmares tore through his subconscious like a jagged knife. If he worked out in the morning, it helped force the remnants of sleep out of his eyes. Then showers. Breakfast. Sparring. Schedule announcements. Bathroom breaks. Sparring. Lunch . . .

No.

That was *their* routine. His old routine. He was supposed to be making his own. But there was so much free time now, and he didn't know how to fill it.

Talking helped. He filled the emptiness with endless conversation. With Wyatt and Ender. With Vanessa. With Simi. With strangers upstairs, where Vanessa worked. He answered the phones while Vanessa had her head down and focused on the artwork she was creating on someone else's skin.

Vanessa ate every meal with him, sure to bring him something new from a shop nearby or a convenience store. Sometimes other Gifted joined them.

Eventually, Anthony found a new routine. And he liked it.

Until one Saturday evening, the shop upstairs closed early, and the crowd downstairs grew and bubbled over until the rowdiness rivaled that of a fraternity house. Anthony squeezed past people he'd never seen before who paid him no mind. There had to be at least fifty people here.

Simi found him first. She grinned. "You ready?"

Anthony blinked. "Ready? Ready for what?"

Before Simi could answer, Vanessa tapped Simi on the shoulder. "Hey, can you find Holly? We need to open a tear."

Simi shrugged and disappeared into the crowd.

"V, what's going on?"

Vanessa wavered. "Look, you—"

"What the hell is happening, V?" Anthony's voice strained as he held back his burgeoning terror. This wasn't the routine. This was different. This was wrong. He had a routine. *A system.* Everything was different and he didn't know why. When routines changed, that meant something bad was going to happen. "Are we going somewhere, I just need to know—"

"No, *God,* no," Vanessa said quickly. "No, it's . . . it's just sparring night."

Anthony blinked. "Sparring night?"

"I'm sorry, I should have told you earlier. I didn't know how you'd take it with the arena. I just—"

"No, it's fine." Anthony shoved his hands in his pockets, hiding his trembling fingers. Sparring night. He understood sparring. It was part of a routine. That's what they used to do at the arenas. Fight night. Sparring night.

An awkward silence ballooned between the two of them before Anthony finally asked, "So, what exactly is sparring night?"

Just then Simi's head peaked from behind Vanessa's shoulder. "Great question," she said brightly. She held up a pair of metal bracelets. "I like to think of them as morale boosting, team-building exercises."

Vanessa rolled her eyes. "We'll show you; it'll be easier."

The entire tattoo parlor erupted in applause that reverberated through the walls. Simi grinned and dashed ahead. Anthony and Vanessa followed.

At the end of the hallway, Holly was yelling, although Anthony couldn't hear her at all. She waved her arms and made a pushing motion, gesturing that everyone should step aside. The crowd obeyed and Holly used the open space to create a portal against the wall.

She gave no further instruction. Everyone leaped into Holly's tear, one after the other without hesitation. Wyatt and Ender were one of the first to hop through, but Vanessa and Anthony lingered until they and Holly were the final three.

Vanessa cleared her throat. "Look, you don't have to come if—"

Anthony pushed her through the portal before she could finish the sentence, then jumped in after her. They stepped into an abandoned underground subway station. The curved walls were littered with graffiti and dilapidated, illegible signage. The air was hot and sticky.

The other Gifted seemed familiar with the grounds. Someone was passing out snacks of potato chips, popcorn, and sour candies. A group of boys Anthony had never seen before sat on the floor and passed around a flask and a box of cookies. A girl in her early teens attempted to balance on the metal rods of the defunct train tracks. Her tongue peeked out the side of her mouth as she focused.

Anthony didn't realize he stood at the edge of the platform, and he nearly fell head first onto the tracks. Simi grabbed him just in time and yanked him back onto his unsteady feet. But instead of letting him go, she pulled him further *into* the chaotic mosh pit ahead. He must have looked nervous, because Simi grinned, her wide, beautiful smile showed off her teeth and her one dimple.

They wove in and out of the crowd. Anthony tossed casual apologies at whoever happened to hear as they bumped into people and stepped on toes. Nobody seemed to care.

Simi stopped in front of an upturned metal trash can. Vanessa was leaning next to it, distracted by the dancing flames in her hand. The flames wormed their way around her wrists and between her fingers, sometimes slinking back into itself and moving in reverse. When she saw Simi, she stopped and patted the upside-down trash can, as if it were some sort of gift.

Simi climbed on top of it and then proceeded to yell.

Anthony could have told her that wasn't going to work. The station may have been loud when they'd first flooded in, but after just a few minutes, Anthony could hardly hear himself think.

"EVERYONE, SHUT UP."

Ender's booming voice rose above the fray. The group quieted and everyone's attention shifted to Simi and Ender, who had an arm leaning against the can. He waved.

Simi nodded, impressed. Someone handed Simi a megaphone. The feedback nearly toppled Simi over, but after an awkward test and cough, she continued.

"Alright, Gifted," she started. "If you ever want to learn how to handle yourself *without* your Gift you know where to find me. I'm down at the parlor most Tuesday and Thursday afternoons. But *today* . . ." She paused, megaphone still up over her mouth while the cavern rumbled with anticipation.

Then, she continued. "But *today* . . . is *MOTHER-FUCKING TOURNAMENT DAY!*"

The tunnel rumbled as Gifted cheered in response.

"For the new kids, let's go over the rules." She glanced at Anthony, a wicked glint in her eyes. "Tournament Day is the thirteenth of every month. The only people who can sanction a competitor to fight in the tournament are Vanessa and myself. *If* you want to compete, then you must beat *me* in hand-to-hand combat without the use of your Gift or come close. The only person who can override my decision is our supreme leader, Vanessa Velázquez. Once you have been approved, you will be entered for the next season of the Tournament. There are *no exceptions!*"

The words left her lips with ease. Clearly, this was a scripted announcement that she repeated at every single one of these events, or "tournaments." Her voice rose and fell as if she were reading the fine print of a verbal contract and the crowd seemed familiar with this tradition, too. Anthony felt that same anticipation and excitement from earlier swell as she neared the end.

"What do you lose if you lose a fight in the tournament?" Simi yelled into the megaphone.

The response was immediate. Nearly everyone in the crowd yelled back, *"YOUR DIGNITY!"*

"What do you gain if you win a fight in the tournament?"

"BRAGGING RIGHTS!"

"Awesome. I'm glad we're all on the same page now." Simi pulled out a scrap piece of paper from her back pocket. "We have . . . Amari Yinka and Emir Mustafa putting in their application for next season's tournament. You two, meet me up here. The rest of you MAKE SOME ROOM!"

The space shuddered with frenzied enthusiasm as the crowd fell away from the tracks and everyone was pressed against the tunnel walls. Simi jumped down from the can and led Anthony in the opposite direction, towards the tracks.

"Not you, Frosty," Simi said. "You get a front row seat."

Vanessa frowned, but before Vanessa could challenge Simi, two Gifted stepped forward.

Simi beamed. "Oh, great, Emir, Amari. Which one of you is going first? Or are we rolling for it? Dude, how old are you?"

They all looked at Emir, who looked like he hadn't even hit puberty yet. Emir frowned and puffed out his chest as he stood up straight. "Twelve."

Simi's eyes narrowed. "You're lucky we don't ID at these things."

"I don't have an ID. I'm twelve."

"Alright, smart-mouth." Simi crossed her arms over her chest. "How about *you* go first, then."

Simi handed him a pair of bracelets, the same slim, silver bracelets that she'd shown Anthony on their way out of the tattoo parlor earlier. Emir seemed familiar and immediately slipped them on each of his wrists. As soon as he did, the bracelets came to life, lighting up with a fluorescent glow. Anthony recognized them — suppressors, but a newer model.

"Well?" Simi asked, expectantly.

Emir looked down at his hands and wiggled his fingers. He shook his head. "Nothing."

Simi seemed content with that answer. "Great. What's your Gift?"

"Telekinesis."

"Nifty. Let's go."

Simi walked up the stairs. Which was odd, as there had been no stairs just a few moments ago. But now, a set of translucent stairs led them towards the tracks and *up*. Further and higher until they were ten feet above the tracks, standing on a transparent platform that seemed as sturdy as the ground beneath their feet.

"Priya does our force field work," Vanessa explained and nodded to their left. A girl in blue jeans and a tank top sat cross-legged on a bench, eating chicken tenders. There was no indication that she was creating this fighting ring platform except for her Pattern, marking her body and casting her in an eerie glow.

Up on the platform, Simi held a staff in her hands and leaned against it, her backside facing Anthony and the rest of the group. From this vantage point, Anthony couldn't help but notice and appreciate the view.

"It's wild, isn't it?" Wyatt stood next to him, his hand fist deep in a paper bag full of trail mix. Anthony nearly jumped out of his skin at Wyatt's sudden appearance, and Anthony felt a rising heat in his neck and cheeks.

"What's wild?" Anthony asked.

"You know . . . doesn't all of this remind you of something?"

Anthony reached into his friend's bag and helped himself. He understood why his sister had been so uncertain about him coming to this tonight. It was a reasonable conclusion that he would have a less than open mind about unlicensed fighting between Gifted. But the freedom to choose was the chasm that separated the arenas from . . . what had Simi called it? Morale boosting team-building exercises?

Anthony sighed. "Honestly, it really doesn't remind me of the arena at all."

"Yeah," Wyatt agreed. "That's the weird part, isn't it?"

The crowd roared to life and Anthony's head shot up.

There had been no announcement, no warning. Simi and Emir were staff to rod, locked into the first fight of the evening. And Emir was on the offensive.

He struck at Simi repeatedly, coming towards her head on. Simi's staff met his, stroke for stroke, beat for beat. When he realized he wasn't getting anywhere, Emir switched tactics, and tried to come in from the side.

Just moments ago, they had seemed friendly. Now, Emir was coming for her jugular.

Simi danced around Emir on a floor that didn't even exist. She dodged his first few attacks before parrying a wild attack from her left. She said something to him as she parried another attack and Emir nodded, backing up slightly.

Was she giving him pointers?

Simi, on the other hand, grabbed her staff and rushed towards him with abandon. She quickly swung to the left before Emir could adjust his stance and the blow connected, nearly sending him flying off the platform. Just before his feet could lead him off the edge, the platform extended, preventing his fall.

"That's a neat trick," Wyatt noted, more focused on Priya. Her body continued to glow as she watched and munched on her hot dog.

Simi charged forward once Emir was back on his feet again. She ducked as Emir swung, and his momentum flung him towards Simi, giving her the opportunity to throw him onto his back as he rolled over her. He managed to make it to his knees before she struck him for the last time. Her staff connected with his cheek and he fell face down on the raised platform.

Gifted groaned and winced everywhere, feeling his pain.

Emir slowly rolled onto his back and shook his head. The crowd whined, a united *"Awwwww"* bubbling from the group as Simi helped him up to his feet and down the transparent stairs. Anthony managed to catch a glimpse of Holly rushing towards him, her pattern glowing as she started to heal him.

Then Amari took his place, picking up the staff Emir had left behind.

The fight started just as suddenly but it was clear that Simi had to step up her game. Amari had also opted for the offensive from the jump. But Simi stayed on the defensive, mostly because she didn't have much of a choice.

Amari moved with a speed that rivaled Simi's. She barreled forward, backing Simi into a corner with a rush of quick attacks with her staff from the left, then below, then back to the left and right again. Amari struck Simi's shin and Simi fell to her knees. Amari brought her staff down towards Simi's head but Simi held it off at the last moment, still down on one knee, hands outstretched with her staff held up as she tried to push up.

The group below was rowdy, yelling and cheering. *Amari! Amari! Amari!*

Simi's left shoulder dropped, and Amari lurched forward, now off balance. Amari swung her staff wildly but Simi blocked each of her frenzied strikes with ease. But on Amari's last strike, Simi parried with a two-handed strike that knocked Amari onto her knees. Before she could rise, Simi was behind her, her arm hooked under Amari's throat and staff abandoned on the ground.

The hold was loose, and Amari noticed. She brought the pair of them down to the ground, hurtling forwards until Simi's back was on the floor. Amari stood above her panting.

Simi grabbed her staff and swept the rod beneath Amari's

leg. Before Amari could recover, Simi was above her again. This time, the end of her staff was aimed directly at Amari's throat.

"Amari! Amari! Amari!"

Wyatt tapped the shoulder of the boy beside them "Hey, didn't she lose?"

The boy made a face. "I mean, yeah, technically? But no one ever wins against Simi."

"Wait, then how does anyone make it to the tournament?"

"You don't have to *beat* her. Nobody's ever beaten her except for Vashti. You just need to make her tired. And she looks pretty tired."

Anthony *did* look. Simi took long and purposeful breaths but even as she swayed on her feet, the crowd cheered. After a few moments, she threw the staff to the ground, then held out her hand to hoist Amari up.

The crowd went ballistic.

The rest of the evening rushed past Anthony. There had been five fights, each one of them between two Gifted. Anthony lost track of the winners and the losers but the energy remained palpable until Vanessa announced the two Gifted who would be advancing to the finals: Ravina and Emilia.

Holly transported everyone back to the dingy basement where congratulations were in order for the finalists. Then, slowly and over the course of many hours, the Gifted finally dispersed.

Vanessa

Unlike the other Gifted who visited this place, Vanessa's place of retreat was the tattoo parlor upstairs.

"They said I could find you up here," Anthony said.

Vanessa turned to see him throw a piece of popcorn in the air before he catching it in his mouth.

Vanessa kicked a stool on wobbly wheels toward him. Anthony accepted the invitation.

"What are you working on anyway?"

She shook her head. *Nothing.* The pen was in her hand, but the paper in front of her was empty. She was *supposed* to be designing, coming up with new images that she could etch into someone else's skin. But her muse was missing in action.

Anthony spun around in his stool. He'd likely already forgotten why he'd come looking for her in the first place. Or perhaps he'd come up with no intentions at all. Usually people needed or wanted something when they visited her. But family was different, wasn't it? Or it was supposed to be different.

Family came into your room for no other reason than to mildly irritate you and steal an article of clothing.

"I liked the games," he said. "The tournament."

Vanessa's breath caught in her throat and she found herself wincing. "You don't have to—"

"It was fun to watch," he said with a slight smile. She frowned. He wasn't just saying this to appease her feelings of guilt, was he?

He *really* liked them.

"Why didn't you think I'd like them?" he asked.

"I . . . assumed a re-enactment of the last few years of your life wouldn't be a particularly fun event for you. Not when there are so many other activities we could have participated in on a Saturday night. Say . . . plucking every hair on your head with a pair of tweezers?"

"That is a very tempting alternative. I might have been more pissed off had I known that offer was on the table."

"Vashti hates them."

"Sparring night?"

She nodded. "She told me what it was like at the arenas. Sounds like hell."

"If she was at the Ivies, she had a harder go of it than me," he said, pushing against the floor so stool rolled a bit closer to her. "Trust me."

Vanessa hugged her own arms and folded forward with a long exhale. "Can I ask you something?"

"Sure."

"What . . . was it like at the arena. For *you*?"

Anthony exhaled loudly. "It . . . sucked."

She immediately wanted to take it back. Change her mind and say the right thing. *It's ok you don't have to talk about it if you don't want to. Don't worry about it. Never mind. Let's go watch a movie.*

"The beginning was the worst," Anthony said. "They wear you out. They do it on purpose, so you don't have enough energy to try and leave. And if you don't perform well on fight nights, you can get traded and sent to an Ivy. They moved us around so often, so it was impossible for anyone to find you. And they're right. You *know* they're right, because some of the recruits there have been there for years."

Anthony's spinning slowed. "So you get sad and depressed for a while. But eventually you just kind of accept it and realize it's not all that bad. The other Gifted are nice. I made friends. Sometimes the handlers brought back Burger King and that was cool. And then you remember that bringing back Burger King is the least they could do since they kidnapped you in the first place. And then you feel sad again. Because if this is all that's left, then what's the point of waking up tomorrow and doing it again ..."

Never mind. She didn't want to hear this. She didn't want to hear this *at all*.

She remembered what he'd said about the boy, Asha. As much as everyone tried to shield and protect him, they couldn't keep the hopelessness at bay.

"The night Vashti found me, I was planning on trying to make a run for it," Anthony said. "Which would have been *very* dumb."

"That's not dumb ..."

"It's *incredibly* dumb, V. I came up with this plan that I thought was genius and at the last minute Holly and Wyatt warned me about it. Said it was crazy and I'd get myself killed. And I would have. It was stupid. But I didn't care. I figured I'd either figure it out and get out, or I wasn't going back. I *knew* I wasn't going back. When I think about it now, it scares me, you know? That I was ok with those two outcomes. So . . . I think what I'm trying to say is, I'm really happy you blew that place up and Vashti found me first."

Vanessa rested her elbow against the table and propped her head up with her fist. "I'm glad you didn't do anything stupid, too, Popsicle."

"And Vashti's going to be fine," he added. "We're going to get Vashti out, and then . . ."

"And then we'll get everyone else out," Vanessa said. "We're going to find all the other arenas and we'll get every last one of us out."

Min Liu

The longest Min had gone without hearing from Nina was four months. It had been undercover work. Dangerous, but with a payout that had made it all worth it. Nina had taken the risk for the sake of the bigger picture. For the company. *Always* for the company.

Min loved Nina. Exponentially more than she loved the company. But Nina didn't believe that at all. She believed that Min was incapable of loving anything — or anyone — more than the company. And it saddened her to know that Nina still chose to be with her, anyway. Selfishly, Min never pushed this issue. Because she *did* love Nina. And if Nina was willing to accept this perceived after-thought of a love that Min had to offer, Min would run with it.

Nina and her two most effective operatives had been incommunicado for two weeks. And while this wasn't the lengthiest absence and it certainly wasn't concerning, Min felt her stomach drop deeper and deeper into the ground with each passing day. The three of them had never butchered an assignment. There was no reason to believe that the trio had any plans to set a new precedent.

But *so much* was riding on this one. And the worst part of it all, the reason why every day felt like she was marching through a fog that grew thicker and hotter with each passing day, was that nobody else knew why.

So, to keep the panic at bay, Min relied on routine.

Min showered twice a day, without fail. Once in the morning, to start fresh. And again every evening, to wash away the filth of existence. She scrubbed her skin violently and when she got out of the shower, she'd find patches of her skin that were flushed and pink from her assault. She had to be clean. It was important. She had to be untouched, unscathed, and perfect. Only then, could she climb into bed, a space also devoid of the murkiness of humanity and existence, and finally hold Nina. The only person who mattered.

But on day fifteen, she stepped out of the shower and wrapped herself in a white robe made of Egyptian cotton. But just as she opened her moisturizer, she heard a crash — a loud one coming from the kitchen. Glass shattered and she heard the faint shuffling of footsteps and scuffing of rubber soles against marble tile floors.

She thought about reaching for her phone just beside her and dialing 9-1-1. But she changed her mind just as her fingers touched the phone's smooth surface. Instead, she left the bathroom and found the Glock she kept next to her bed. Min knew she wouldn't need it, but that didn't matter. Presentation was everything.

She was not at all prepared for the scene in her living room.

Ruth was sitting in a dining table chair and she looked like she had survived a marathon through hell. She was bleeding from an injury to the right side of her head and had a piece of fabric tied around her face and between her teeth. Her feet were tied to the front of each chair leg and her hands zip-tied behind her. Despite the fire in her eyes, her head bobbed and her eyelids slowly closed and shot open again.

Nina stood behind her, looking a little worse for wear, but equally enraged. Her hand rested against Vashti's shoulder, and her grip was tight.

Of the three of them, Vashti was generally the most unreadable. Min never could tell if Vashti felt any emotion towards her other than hatred. But today, there was no mistaking the panic that had made its home in Vashti's eyes.

Min's voice was unassuming and flat when she finally asked, "What happened?"

Nina dug her fingers deeper into Vashti's shoulder. The younger girl winced, attempting to twist away. Nina didn't release her grip. With her free hand, Nina aggressively wiped away the blood on her lip, smearing it across her cheek.

"Your star pupil," Nina spat, spittle mixed with blood, "Is fucking *mental*."

Min twitched and her heart jumped.

Calm.

Min rested the gun on the console table beside her. "Go to my private study," she instructed. "Now."

Nina hesitated.

"Take Vashti with you."

Nina clearly still wasn't comfortable with that arrangement. But she nodded anyway, leading the girl away. Min waited until Nina and Vashti were out of earshot before she approached the broken woman in front of her. Min bowed slightly so her face was inches from Ruth's, but Ruth refused to look at her, her eyes unfocused in defiance and blinded by rage.

It didn't matter.

"Look at me," she said plainly.

Ruth did not.

Min sighed. This would come with consequences. So she did the rare thing and repeated herself.

Look at me.

Ruth pupils widened, then constricted again as every neuron in her body bypassed Ruth's will in order to fulfill Min's command.

Ruth looked at her.

Do not move from this position until I tell you otherwise.

It was a horrible instruction. Min's words were law. She had never encountered a person who had been able to resist in even the most minute of ways. She had learned quickly that her words had to be chosen with thought and care. "Do not leave" was too vague and could be generalized. "Do not leave this chair" said nothing about the location of both Ruth *and* her chair. And she was certain Ruth could be creative enough to bring that chair along if she decided she had places to be.

"Do not move" was cruel. But necessary.

Within minutes, Ruth would start to feel the tight cramping in her spinal muscles. Within the hour, she would feel as if she had run a marathon. By the end of the day, the muscle breakdown would be so intense, she would likely have a mild kidney injury.

She could *not* forget Ruth was here.

In twenty-five minutes, yell and remind me that you are here.

That should be an appropriate safeguard. But just in case, she added, *You can blink.*

Interlude IV: Raahi

For two decades, the Mirror opened. Sometimes multiple times in a month. Raahi's father found children without issue, usually street urchins and young children who had been abandoned at hospitals, sanctuaries, orphanages, and foster homes. Kids that nobody would notice were missing. *Always* young kids — no older than three or four. Thousands of kids must have traversed that Mirror and yet, his people didn't notice.

That angered Raahi even more.

The Visitors accepted each child. Dozens at first. Then hundreds. His father wasted away as food, water, and even life became less interesting to him.

Raahi's Talent revealed itself in a few years. He had accidentally cut himself while chopping peppers for dinner. The wound closed before he could find a clean washcloth. Initially, he thought this was the solution. The next time the visitors came, he'd fight them. And they couldn't hurt him back. He'd fight them with every fiber in his being until they couldn't hurt him anymore. And he'd force them to bring back his sister.

But hope blossomed for only a moment. His Talent was invincibility. He was *not* a healer. Fighting back would only put his father and his sister at risk. It was the same reason his father did not use his Gift to threaten the visitors.

Raahi immediately told his father when he suspected his Gift had surfaced. His father had warned him swiftly. "Don't let them know, do you understand?"

He had kept that promise.

But one week became one year. A year became a decade. Then a decade more.

Once a year the visitors brought a single still: a photograph. That's what the visitors called them. Photographs taken by *cameras*. It was how they watched Ruth grow. She was never looking at the camera, sometimes she wasn't even in focus. The photographs were clearly created without Ruth's knowledge leaving Raahi and his father with so many questions. Where was she? Was she safe? Hurt? Did she know where she was? What was she doing?

Did she remember them?

In one — only one — of the photographs, Ruth was smiling. She would have been twenty-four. Her smile was so broad and unexpected that her eyes were closed. She had dimples. Her hair was long and in chunky braids, half up, half down. Her skin hadn't darkened much over the many years; she was still several shades lighter than Raahi and their father.

It was the last photograph they ever received and the last time the visitors returned to their world.

Every month, Raahi's father waited at the top of the steps of the basement, waiting for the ominous hum of the Mirror to signal another demand: more lives, more children. But each month passed and the Mirror lay dormant. At first, they thought it was a good thing. Maybe, the next time they came, they would come with *her*.

But time pressed on. A month became two. Until a full year had passed and the visitors still had not come.

Later that year, Raahi received a phone call from the Security Department of his district. Raahi was over two thousand miles away, and at his very first position at the Council, working as a translator. They told him his father left a note.

Raahi,

I'm sorry I couldn't find her.

You are wonderful. You will do things that will shake this world and many others. And I love you.
Forgive me.

He was excused from his post at the Council and immediately transported home. He discovered a pile of rubble and ash instead. His father had been found underneath it, buried under the hell that had been the last twenty years. He'd brought down parts of the adjacent buildings, too, but it didn't matter. These homes had long been abandoned as citizens moved closer and closer to the city over the years. It had made their exploits — *kidnapping*, that's what it was — easier to manage. Nobody had been around to ask questions.

"We've already extracted his body," the officer explained. "He left a few things for you."

Raahi picked up a rock on the ground. He tossed it up and caught it, testing the weight. "What could possibly be left?" His voice was dark, even, and unyielding.

The officer motioned to his right, at a small, organized pile of effects.

Raahi's heart dropped.

"Apologies, we had to search this before you arrived—"

"I understand." Raahi's mouth was dry as bone and his voice warbled like a bird's. "I assume it wasn't until you found his body and identified him you realized this was . . . self-inflicted."

The officer shifted, visibly uncomfortable. "And the note. It was in the messenger bag. Paperwork, documents . . . and then this."

Raahi approached what was left of his childhood. The largest item was the trunk. When he opened it, he found several piles of documents and his sister's old toys, like the stuffed dragon she used to play with. Important documents like his father's birth certificate and identification documents were all in the messenger bag. But what seemed benign to this officer, and what made Raahi's head spin, was the tall, full-length Mirror. Unscathed and haunting.

"An heirloom?" the officer asked after a lengthy period of silence.

Raahi clenched his teeth. He held his hands behind his back and pushed the small, rough-edged pebble he'd found earlier into the palm of his hand before dragging it across. Back and forth until a familiar warmth slid past his fingers.

His heart slowed, finding peace in the visceral, more superficial pain in his hand.

"Sir?"

"Yes," Raahi answered this time. "An heirloom." He relaxed his fingers and looked down at the pebble. His hand was perfect and blemish free and the rock dirty and bloody.

Raahi tossed the rock towards the rest of the rubble. "Can you have all of this delivered to my residence near the Capitol?"

"Absolutely."

"Is there anything else you need from me in the meantime?"

The officer shook his head solemnly. "Not here. You'll be asked to identify him before arrangements can be made. But from us, nothing else, sir."

"You'll have to excuse me, then. I . . . I'd like some time alone."

"Would you like transport? We can—"

"I'll walk."

The officer started. "The nearest station is two miles from here. And—"

"*Please.*"

He nodded curtly. "I'm sorry for your loss, Mr. Varo."

Raahi nodded as his throat closed. He waited until he had walked at least half a mile, past dozens of empty homes and decrepit shops that sold nothing but ale and tobacco. He waited for the long light of sunset to settle into dusk before he sank to his knees. His vision blurred as tears fell from the corner of his eyes, and nausea gripped his stomach. He moaned, bringing his head closer to the ground and wrapped his hands over the back of his head. Now Raahi was truly alone.

Part IV: Blood, Sweat, & Tears

Interlude V: Raahi

When Min Liu walked through the Mirror for the first time in her life, she felt at home. But this place wasn't *her* home. It had never been her home. She had never been *taken* — not like the others. Yet somehow, coming here felt like she was returning to something familiar.

She'd stepped into someone's home, high above a sprawling city. Outside, two suns chased the horizon and ribbons of sunlight cascaded into the room.

"You're *very* late."

She spun on her heels and found herself face to face with a dark-skinned man with thick brows and dark brown eyes. *This* must be the boy her parents had talked about. He was a man now, well into his twenties.

Raahi.

He looked so much like his sister.

"When were you expecting me?" Min asked in return. Even her voice sounded different here.

"About a decade ago," Raahi said. His voice flowed like thick honey, drawing her in with every spilled word as he examined her like a rare specimen. "You're new. Where are the other two?"

He must have been talking about her parents. "They're dead."

Raahi hummed, then wandered towards the pristine couch and collapsed into it with a heavy sigh. He closed his eyes and massaged his temples. "So what is it that you want?"

The elevator pitch Min had memorized disappeared from her mind. "I . . . I just wanted to see it. See more . . ."

Christ, what *was* she doing here? This was a mistake. She shouldn't have come here.

He laughed showing off dimples on each cheek. "Really? You want *more*? You animals haven't taken enough?"

Oh, he meant—

No, that's not what she wanted. *At all.*

"How many?" she queried. "How many did my parents take from here?"

He rubbed his eyes. "Hundreds. Thousands. I have no idea. I don't remember."

Anger swelled behind Min's sternum. "They came through *your home*! How can you not remember *thousands* of children disappearing from *your* home!"

But the man was unimpressed by her show of irritation. "Is that what you're here for? After two decades of stealing children followed by years of silence. You're here for what exactly? Collect *more?* Have you run out already on your disgusting, molding, *dying* rock of a planet?"

Her vision blurred. No, she wasn't here to continue the horrors her own parents had started. "No. I . . . I just wanted to understand."

"And you're not here to bring them back, either?"

"I can't do that. They don't know anything about this place. Earth is all they've ever known."

"What of my sister?" he asked. "They promised to return her when they were finished."

"After twenty years, you want her to come back here? She doesn't know this place anymore."

"But *you* know her, don't you?" Raahi sounded deflated and empty. "You — the product of monsters — know my sister better than I ever will."

Min wasn't used to this — feeling small and out of place. People stepped aside when they walked past her and only spoke to her if they had something of value to say. Her colleagues respected her, her knives — Ruth and Vashti — feared her.

But Raahi — it didn't even seem like he hated her. Her parents, perhaps. But there was no envy in his tone, no malice in his words, and no hope in his empty eyes. He had lived a life of loss, and now that Min was here, he had nothing left to give.

She approached him slowly, then sat on the chair facing the window, just beside the settee. "Your sister is . . . stubborn. She works with me, and although I'm technically her boss, she takes no issue questioning me and my methods."

She paused and waited for some sort of reaction from Raahi. But he didn't budge, didn't so much as lift a brow. So she continued. "There's a girl, about a decade younger than her. Your sister has taken her under her wing. Ruth is incredibly protective of her. She has more of a maternal instinct than she suspected, and I think that scares her sometimes."

Raahi readjusted his sitting position, but continued to stare straight ahead. Min waited for him to speak, but again, he remained silent.

"She's a . . . healer of sorts. Of the mind."

"I thought her Talent was—"

"She's an empath, yes. But in regards to her vocation, she studied to become a type of healer."

Raahi didn't need to hear about the tests and the experiments. That it had been her own parents who had run those endless experiments on her in an effort to understand her Gift.

What good would that do?

Min cleared her throat as if swallowing her guilt. "The Mirror. How does it work? My parents traveled back and forth so many times, but nobody ever came after them. Are there more?"

"There are thousands of Mirrors," Raahi said with a sigh.

"But why could they only travel *here*? My parents tried to dismantle the one on their end, but they couldn't figure out how it worked. How do you control it?"

At first, Raahi didn't answer. He just stared at her in shock and disbelief.

Then he grinned bitterly and laughed.

"What?"

Raahi was still laughing when he answered. "You are all *absolute idiots*. That Mirror isn't a means of transportation."

"Then what—"

Raahi shook his head and rose to his feet. He pointed at the Mirror. "Get out."

Min scoffed. "Absolutely not."

"Get the hell out of my house."

"Just tell me what this thing is! I have to know why they . . . they did this to—" Min's voice broke before she could finish, snapping like a rubber band.

The man stopped. "What do you mean? What did they do to you?"

Min inhaled sharply. *That* wasn't important. There was nothing she could do about the past. "What are the Mirrors for?" she asked again, desperately. She was entirely at his mercy and they both knew it. He had no reason to pity her. Not after what her parents had done to him, to her, to so many people.

But, for whatever reason, Raahi Varo explained anyway. "The Mirrors only open when the world is dying. They're not for travel. They're an exit strategy."

Min frowned. "I don't—"

"My father tried to explain it to your parents so many times. When the Mirror opens, our Council helps. That's how it works. But instead of allowing us to carry out our duty, your family stole from us. They stole *people* from us. They doomed your entire planet. We tried to warn your people about your planet dying but they didn't care."

Min traced the edges of the Mirror, and the surface rippled as if she'd touched the edge of standing water. "You have to understand, Mr. Varo. Where I'm from, my people . . . we are bombarded with constant reminders of our impending doom. The people on my planet are shortsighted. We've known the end is coming for decades. Ozone depletion, overpopulation, pollution, famines, plagues, the looming threat of nuclear war. The question we often ask ourselves isn't how life on Earth ends, but when."

Raahi frowned. "And your people don't . . . care?"

"It's a learned helplessness," Min explained. "But the things you have accomplished here on your planet are extraordinary. Terraforming, geo-engineering, dyson spheres. Mechanisms that can reverse ecological change on a massive scale. But it wouldn't have been possible without your Gifts . . . what you call Talents. Meanwhile, we still burn the bones of long extinct animals so we can keep the lights on."

The man cocked his head to the side. "What did they do to the other children?"

Min flinched, then forced the knot in her throat to relax.

"Your scientific achievements would have been impossible without your Gifts. The children they took were nothing more than a resource. One that *we* lacked."

Raahi inhaled sharply. "We are not *resources*. We do not farm our own people here like livestock"

"That's because nature happened to work in your favor. We were not so lucky."

She looked over her shoulder. "I'm sorry, Mr. Varo. About what my parents did to your family. For what they did to your people. Truly, I am."

"What did they do to them?" Raahi asked again. His voice was soft and broken and Min felt compelled to answer.

"It's like you said. They farmed them," she whispered. "Like livestock."

Then she stepped through the Mirror and left.

Vashti

Vashti was no stranger to fear.

Over the last several years, Vashti had learned to command it herself. She found refuge in shadows and comfort in knowing the place terrified others. The unknown became her constant, and over time, she had learned to revel in it.

But now fear held her hostage and she was wholly at its mercy.

Even Min had looked at her strangely, not quite knowing what to do or what to think about this changed version of her most effective tool. It was as if she realized Vashti was damaged beyond repair and she couldn't decide if she was worth the effort of a refurbishment.

Nina shoved Vashti onto the couch. She fell onto it, adjusting her position as she closely tracked every living thing around her. Ruth's breathing, somehow steady, stuck in the hallway. Min's heart rate, quick like a rabbit.

But Nina terrified her. Her fingers twitched. The hairs on her arm raised and on high alert. Nina was unpredictable.

Min closed off the living area with a glass divider, finally separating the three of them from Ruth.

"Is that a good idea?" Nina asked.

"What. Happened."

Nina looked at Vashti expectantly. Vashti would have scowled if her mood had been any brighter. They had both been there. Why did Vashti have to tell the story?

When Nina maintained her silence, Vashti opened her mouth and did her best.

And as she told her story, she hugged herself, hiding her trembling hands in her pocket until she found the panic button Simi had given her before she left.

Vashti pressed the button.

TWO WEEKS AGO

Calling these spaces of reprieve "safe houses" was an over-statement. Usually, they were hotel rooms or Airbnb's that had been rented out under someone else's name. The safe house was just a place Ruth and Vashti agreed to meet in case they were separated. The only required characteristic of a chosen safe house was privacy.

This time, it was the corner room of the Motel 8 in a small town in the middle of east Texas.

Holly had transported her a few blocks away. When Vashti arrived, she scanned the room for any recording devices, microphones, or cameras. Then she'd closed the blinds and curtains, kicked off her shoes, and curled up on the bed, working through the plan in her head.

Now the real work began: preparing her statements for Ruth.

She always practiced before seeing Ruth again. She couldn't lie to her. Ruth would be able to tell immediately. But that didn't mean she had to tell the *whole* truth.

Vashti sat on the bed and practiced her breathing, slowing her heart rate, then speeding it back up on command. She listened as her body tensed and the hairs on the back of her neck stood when she held her breath and released it half a second too quickly. She held her breath, closing off her epiglottis, and practiced even and shallow breaths. She couldn't do anything about her pupils. But Ruth didn't really pay attention to that anyway. She only sensed the feelings.

Emotions were fleeting and ephemeral. They were muscles that could be flexed and relaxed at will. It just took practice and control.

Well, a *lot* of practice.

Vashti called the parlor every night for an update. Simi did find the name of Min's private doctor: Mike Thompson, an Ivy League grad. His mom's maiden name was Kelso, his high school mascot was the eagle, and the last four digits of his social was 2763. But even more importantly, Dr. Thompson reported directly to a slew of researchers and physicians that were technically part of LIUYEN's bioengineering and research division.

And *they* stored Min's blood in storage beneath LIUYEN headquarters. All Vashti needed to do was figure out a way in.

Vashti was studying the blueprints Simi had sent her when she heard a loud crash come from the bathroom. Vashti shoved the tablet behind the couch and jumped to her feet. *Finally.* Ruth had returned.

"Interesting point of entry," Vashti started as she opened the bathroom door. Then she froze.

"We need to talk," Nina said, maneuvering herself out of the bathtub.

Vashti blinked, then looked at the bathtub. A boy half her size was lying in the tub, tangled in old shower curtain. He looked up at Vashti, clearly surprised to see her.

"Who the hell is this?" Vashti spat, fuming at Nina. "And where's Ruth?"

"In Morocco."

"*What—*"

Nina grabbed Vashti's shoulder, forcing her to look directly at her. Her grip was like a vice and her eyes were as wide as moons. "We need to talk about Ruth."

"Where is—"

"Shut *up!*" Nina yelled, loud enough to cause the paper-thin walls to quiver. Just as Nina yelled, Vashti's humerus — *both* of them — snapped, under Nina's grip.

It was sudden and quick, and for the split second she thought she'd imagined hearing that *snap*. Then a wave of agony ricocheted up to her neck and down to her fingertips as if she'd been speared with a lancet. Vashti's mouth opened but her own shock silenced her scream. All that managed to slip past was an inhuman grunt as her knees buckled.

"Shit, *shit!*" Nina muttered as Vashti collapsed. Nina's hand was on her back, leading her towards the bed. Vashti heard a stream of apologies leave Nina's lips but she registered only a handful.

"*Shit*, I'm so sorry — *shit!*"

Nina was a mess. Hot and frustrated tears stained her cheeks and her fingers shook like leaves in the wind. "This will take a while," Nina said, rubbing her eyes with the back of her hand and inhaling deeply. "A few hours at least. Which frankly, should give you enough time to explain what the hell is going on with Ruth."

The boy — Vashti had nearly forgotten he was there —

shrieked. "*Hours*? I'm not leaving your psycho friend with my family for hours."

"She's not psycho!" Nina said angrily, focusing her Gift on Vashti's left arm. "And she won't hurt them."

"You don't sound so sure," the boy muttered.

"Nina," Vashti interrupted through clenched teeth. "I swear to God—"

"Okay, okay. This is Dodger—"

"It's actually Ashlin," the boy said.

"And he's helping us out. We made it to London, but the trail for the drive went cold. We figured maybe you knew something we didn't but ever since we lost you, Ruth . . . Ruth's just been — wait, where's the kid?"

"Present," the young boy said.

Nina glared at him over her shoulder. "No, not *you*!"

"Anthony? I lost him."

Nina's pattern dimmed and the pain in Vashti's arm returned in full force. "*Nina, come on!*"

Another litany of apologies and Nina drew on her Gift again, focusing on the task at hand while keeping a trained eye on Vashti's face.

"How did you lose him?"

"Oh, absolutely *not*," Vashti seethed. "You first. Where's Ruth? She must have told you about this place? Where is she? Is she ok?"

Nina grunted, the softness and concern evaporating from her face. "Ruth is *fine*. And you're right. We should talk about Ruth first."

"What about Ruth?"

"When did you plan on telling me that Ruth is losing her *god-damned mind*."

Vashti's mouth went dry.

Oh.

Crap.

Nina

Nina hated being the last to know.

When she learned her Gift was double-pronged — healing *and* harm — she hadn't known about it. Her adopted parents fostered the more productive part of her Gift and discouraged any negative emotion that may trigger the other. They must have picked up that happiness healed while anger broke. But at nine years old, Nina hadn't quite picked up on the distinction. Then one day, her parents brought home their daughter — born after years of fertility treatments. For the first time in her life, Nina experienced an entirely innocent jealousy at the realization that she was going to have to *share* her parents. The feeling was brief, but fatal. The moment her mother placed the baby in her arms, every bone in her newborn sister's body shattered.

When her parents had put her back up for adoption, she hadn't known. Her teachers had known but they'd said nothing. Her parents simply left her at boarding school, kissed her goodbye, and said they would see her at the next break.

They never returned. Instead, a stranger arrived to take her to her next foster home. Nina locked herself in a utility closet to prevent herself from making another fatal mistake.

But with Min, she was never the last to know. Min said that being the last to know could be fatal. She was Nina's confidant and partner.

Well, that wasn't quite true, was it? Because Min was still keeping one secret from her. But it was fine because Nina *knew* the secret existed. Min knew best. It would be fine.

When Vashti revealed the extent of Ruth's fractured mind, it took everything in Nina to not snap Vashti's legs as well.

"So, apparently, Ruth's Gift goes both ways," Nina summarized. "She can influence other people's feelings *and* she can pick up other people's feelings and craziness, too. Like the damn flu."

"*No*," Vashti said, rage glowing in her dark eyes. "It's *not* contagious."

"Unless you're a Gifted empath," Nina countered. "Capable of influencing *other* people's emotions, then yeah, I'd say it's fucking contagious."

Vashti focused her attention on Min. "Being paranoid is a necessity in our line of work. She's no more paranoid than the rest of us! And having hallucinations *isn't* an emotion!"

Min raised an eyebrow. "She's *hallucinating*?" she asked in that soft, monotone voice that commanded attention and pause.

Vashti wavered. "She's been talking to someone, a man, I think. But it's been *years*. At least a decade."

Min pursed her lip. "A . . . decade," she repeated. "She's been imagining things for a decade."

"I don't know," Vashti whined. At that moment, she

sounded an awful lot like an eighteen-year-old. "I don't know. He . . . helps sometimes. But she *knows* he's not real. It's not a personality, and it's *not* contagious. He's just . . . there sometimes."

Min tightened her robe around her waist. "Vashti. I'm going to ask you a single question. But first, I'm going to summarize what you're telling me. Do not interrupt. When I am finished, I want you to answer my question with a simple yes or no."

Min walked in front of Vashti, blocking Nina from her view. Slowly, the woman squatted in front of her, resting her entire weight on the balls of her feet. "One of my most valuable assets, has, over the last several years, been exhibiting symptoms of some sort of chronic psychiatric condition. And you thought it best to tell nobody. *Is that correct?*"

Nina side-stepped so she could get a better look at Vashti. And as incensed as Nina felt, she couldn't help but harbor pity for the girl.

But Vashti maintained eye contact as she hugged herself, likely from the post-healing soreness. She followed Min's instructions perfectly when she answered.

"Yes."

Nina's breath shuddered as her wife nodded. "Okay. Alright."

Then Min started laughing. A wide toothy grin appeared on her face as the throaty chuckle evolved into something akin to manic glee.

"Min—"

Vashti's voice shattered Min's brief surrender of sanity. The woman spun on her heels and grabbed Vashti's face, squeezing her cheeks between her thumb and fingers. Nina stepped forward but Min held her back with an outstretched hand.

A wordless command. *Don't you dare.*

"Vashti, if you open your mouth again, I will kill you," Min growled. Her voice had fallen back to its usual low timber. "I don't care what you have to say anymore. You've had *years* to open your damn mouth." She shoved her back with that last word. The push was so violent Vashti nearly fell off the couch.

"Min," Nina said softly. "Min, please."

"Taking this one in was your idea," Min scowled, pointing at Vashti.

Nina scoffed. "You're joking. Are you blaming *me* for this?"

"No. But now she's a liability. They're *both* liabilities. And *that's* your fault."

Vashti opened her mouth again, briefly forgetting Min's instruction. But Nina interrupted before Vashti could test Min further. "How is Vashti a liability? She was supposed to be *Ruth's* responsibility, not the other way around!"

"Exactly!" Min yelled.

The back of Min's hand collided with Nina's cheek with a deafening *crack*. Nina looked up and gingerly touched her left cheek. Ribbons of blood stained her fingers.

Min was heaving. Vashti was silent. And Nina's vision swam.

"They became dependent. *Reliant*," Min said through a quivering upper lip and tight jaw. "On *each other*. *This* is why we keep our assets separated."

Nina couldn't think. Couldn't see. Couldn't tell it was even her speaking when she stuttered. "But you agreed—"

Min took a half-step forward and Nina felt herself flinch. And she hated that.

"No, *you* wanted," Min seethed. "*You* wanted to make a team."

"No, we—"

"You wanted to make a new *family* for yourself. You and your *fucking* penchant for co-dependency—"

Nina growled, standing up straight. "No — no, your assets kept disappearing! We'd find them in Argentina or Bora Bora months later with new identities that you didn't even know existed. You asked them to do the impossible and when things got hot, they ran. And each time, I cleaned up all your loose ends and tied them up with a bow so nothing came back to you—"

Min had the audacity to look bored. "Oh, shut up."

Nina could never hurt Min back. Not physically at least. And Min knew it. Nina had the capacity to break and re-create anyone into any image of her choosing.

But she would never — could *never* — touch Min.

She loved her.

"You *agreed*," Nina continued anyway. Salt stung at the wound on her cheek. "Don't forget that you agreed to try this. It was my idea to have them work together, to give them a reason to stay. Since your *money* wasn't even enough to keep them."

Min rubbed at her forehead lazily. "I don't have time for this."

"*No*, you can't just ignore me—"

"Kill her," Min said, readjusting her robe. "Do what you do best, then. Clean up. Tie up loose ends. Take care of it."

"Uh, wait a minute." Vashti quickly muttered.

Nina hesitated. No, she couldn't. Why would Min say that?

"We'll talk later," Min promised, her tone soft, still low, still commanding attention and respect. But recognizable, again. "Take care of them. Please, dear." She walked towards the door, as if this conversation was over simply because she willed it to be.

"Min," Nina begged. She couldn't. She *wouldn't*. "Hey, come on—"

"Why not?" Min asked.

She didn't answer.

"I'm your family," Min reminded her softly. An encouragement. A reminder.

It was true. Min never left. She'd *never* left. "Yes . . ."

Min's hand was on the door handle. "And you'll always have me. So take care of this. And then we can talk."

She shouldn't.

Nina hesitated.

And then Min's hand disappeared.

Anthony

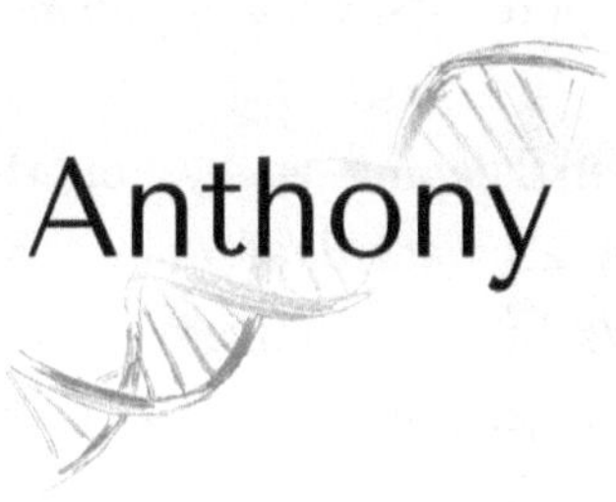

"Is it working?"

"You're stressing me out, V." Simi slapped Vanessa's hand away from her mouse. "Stop touching shit."

Vanessa retracted her hand and held it up behind her head, fingers interlocked as she paced the room. "And where the *hell* is Holly?" she muttered. The back of Vanessa's arm shimmered, the pattern beneath her tattoos breaking through as her resolve wavered.

Simi tapped at the keyboard of her computer furiously, eyebrows furrowed. "She's on her way, V. You need to chill."

"Simi, I swear to God, don't tell me to chill."

Simi rolled her eyes and looked at Anthony expectantly. "Can you handle her?"

Vanessa's eyes darkened. "*Handle* me?"

Yikes.

Anthony stood in front of Simi before Vanessa spontaneously combusted. "She's right. You need to calm down."

"It's been *hours!*" Vanessa yelled, embers and flames

seeping from her pores. "She fell off our radar hours ago. How did we miss this?"

Simi had been keeping an eye on the motel's security cameras but they all went dead a few hours ago. Then, just moments ago, Vashti had activated her panic button. The 'emergencies only get me out of this mess right now' panic button.

"I gave it to Vashti just before she left," Simi explained.: "In a few minutes I'll be able to access to Min's network and every-thing connected to it: cameras, TVs, even her air conditioning. But I need to focus."

"Hey, V, look at me." Anthony stood in front of his sister. "She's gong to be fine, okay? We know where she is. She's *fine*. We'll get her out."

Vanessa nodded, lips parted slightly. Before she could respond, the door to the office flew open and Holly rushed into the room, red curls trailing behind her like angry sails. "I'm here. Are we ready? How did Vashti find a blood sample so quickly?"

Anthony shook his head. "We didn't. Vashti's in trouble. Can you get us into Min's place?"

Holly's cheeks paled. "You're joking."

"Can you?" Anthony pushed.

Simi tapped at her computer monitor, specifically at the bottom left quadrant that displayed Min and Nina arguing at each other. Vashti was silent, her arms wrapped around herself as the two adults in the room gestured wildly at each other.

"I can't hear anything," Vanessa said. "No audio?"

"Working on it," Simi said. "Holly? Can you get us in here?"

Holly peered over Simi's shoulder. "Shouldn't be a prob-lem. I can portal out Vashti. But what about the rest of the plan? What about the hard drive?"

"We have an idea," an unfamiliar voice added. The trio

turned to see Amari, the young fighter who had just earned her place in their monthly tournament, leaning against the open door. Anthony spotted Ender and Wyatt behind her, itching to catch any stray pieces of the conversation.

"What are you guys doing here?" Vanessa asked.

Simi attempted to kick the door shut, but Amari caught the door with her foot before it could close. "Strategizing."

Vanessa, Simi, and Anthony shared a look. Anthony wasn't sure what the others were thinking, but he was willing to accept any available assistance at this point.

Amari stepped into the room. "We can still get Vashti out *and* the data we need to open the drive. Fingerprints and a blood sample, right?"

Simi hesitated. "Wait, how do you know about—" She paused, realizing. "Oh . . ."

Amari nodded and tapped her earlobe with her finger.

Oh. Super-hearing. She'd probably known everything they'd been planning for weeks.

"It's ok. I don't tell people things," she added.

"What things?" Anthony asked.

"I don't tell."

Ender spoke up next. "Do you take bribes?"

"*Focus*," Vanessa turned her attention towards Amari again. "Welcome to the brainstorming session. I hope you have some suggestions."

"I do."

"And?"

"I don't think you'll like it."

Wyatt nodded dramatically. "Oh, you'll like it."

Vanessa motioned towards Wyatt. "I thought you didn't tell people things."

Amari shrugged. "He's a good sounding board."

Vanessa rolled her eyes but motioned everyone in towards

the office. The space wasn't large enough for all of them, so the door was left open. Wyatt and Ender celebrated their inclusion with a high five and scooted closer to be as active of participants as Vanessa would allow.

Anthony glared at both of them. *Behave* he mouthed.

"We have an idea," Wyatt said.

Vanessa blinked. "*We?*"

Amari, for the first time since making herself known, looked nervous. "Well, it was Wyatt's idea," she said, gesturing towards him without making eye contact. "You should tell them."

Wyatt shook his head, throwing a pretzel into his mouth. Where the hell did that come from? "Nah, I just suggested the concept. You tell them."

"I think you could . . ."

Vanessa looked at Anthony with wide eyes, clearly exasperated and mouthed, *Are they serious?*

"You guys are cute, but we're going to need that power point presentation right now," Simi said.

Amari blushed. "We were thinking . . . maybe nobody has to go in there. We *technically* just need her finger, right? To open the drive?"

Simi's lips parted slightly, considering this with narrowed eyes. "That's . . . true."

Amari explained the details of her plan. Anthony thought it was messy, but clever.

Vanessa, vehemently disagreed.

"It's too dangerous. They'll kill Vashti the moment we show up. We can't do this."

"They'll be a *little* preoccupied," Amari said. "We'll have the element of surprise. And we're not going to leave her there. She'll have back-up," Simi reminded her.

"Fine," Vanessa said. "Then I'll go."

Simi snorted. "You're literally the only person Min wants right now. We can't give that to her. You disqualified yourself from going the day you stole the hard drive from her in the first place."

"I'll go," Anthony volunteered. "She won't expect me, and she won't kill me — not before questioning me first."

Vanessa's eyes widened. "Absolutely not."

"I'll go with him," Wyatt said. "I won't let him out of my sight. Pinky promise."

"*No*," Vanessa said. She yanked Anthony's hand back. "I just got your Popsicle ass back, you are *not* leaving!"

"V," Anthony said softly. "This makes sense. This is how I can help. Besides . . . I owe Vashti, remember?"

The way Anthony saw it, Vashti had been there for his sister when he hadn't. He'd kept her sane these last two years. After he was taken. After Logan died. Vanessa survived because Vashti had been there. This meant Vashti was non-negotiable. She had to survive. At all costs. Because if something *did* happen to Anthony, only Vashti could help pick up the pieces.

That was how he could help.

"We got this," Wyatt said with an encouraging smile, slipping on a pair of suppressors. "We've fought hundreds of Gifted. We can take Min."

His sister looked defeated and desperate. But after a tense moment, she bowed her head. "Fine," she whispered. "Fine. Holly, drop them off somewhere discreet."

Holly nodded. "You got it."

"And Wyatt—"

"I'll bring him home," Wyatt said without hesitation. "Promise."

Min Liu

Min's hand was outstretched, gesturing towards Vashti, when it disappeared.

It was so sudden, so quick. As if the appendage had never been there in the first place. The portal appeared around her wrist, an ethereal shimmering light that widened then snapped shut before she could even understand what was happening. Now, the only evidence of the limb's existence was her own blood seeping out of the stump.

The pain was excruciating. Incredibly distracting.

But worst of all, she hadn't seen this coming. This entire evening had been just one blindside after another. Everything in her life was in flux. Her relationship with her wife. The loyalty of her mercenaries. Her secrets and her control slipped between her nonexistent fingers while blood dripped onto the cold floor beneath her feet and marred her stark white robe.

Vashti's mouth hung open in complete shock. Nina was crying and blubbering about Min's hand — or the lack thereof. That Min needed to go to a hospital. That she wasn't going to be able to re-attach it here, if it could be re-attached at all. And where was her hand? Where did it go?

And yet Vashti sat there, shocked, completely horrified. And somehow . . .

She *knew* something.

That bitch knew something. And Min, with all her drive, tenacity, foresight, and planning, had no idea what it was. With all her money and power and a Gifted empath safely stored in her pocket, she still didn't know whatever it was that Vashti knew.

She looked at Vashti, a feral anger rising within her that she had never felt before.

Talk, Min commanded.

Vanessa

There was blood *everywhere*. On the floors, the table, the keyboard and all over the Scanner. Once they'd opened the drive, Min's severed hand rolled away from them until it rested a mere six inches behind Simi's chair.

And all eyes were trained on Simi's monitor.

"Talk to me, Simi," Vanessa muttered breathlessly. Of course, everything was still in Mandarin. So it was up to Simi to translate the highlights as quickly as possible. "What do we have? Holly, get Wyatt and Anthony in there *now*."

Holly looked like she'd run two marathons. "I need . . . I'm gonna need just a minute," she heaved, catching her breath. Her pattern flickered as she composed herself. "I've never done a trip that fast. I need a minute."

"What is this?" Anthony asked, referring to the computer screen.

"I . . ." Simi looked confused. "I'm not . . . sure. It's not making sense."

Vanessa's heart sank. If this was a dead end that would mean she'd endangered the lives of everyone here for nothing.

"Talk to me anyway," Vanessa pleaded.

Simi exhaled through pursed lips. Her fingers, red and sticky with Min's blood, violently attacked her keyboard until she had pulled up something vaguely recognizable.

Photographs.

Thousands of photographs. Most of them were headshots and each photo was associated with a name, age, and demographic details.

"Jesus," Anthony sighed, his eyes scanning the pages as Simi scrolled through them. "They're just kids."

Simi went through pages and pages of face-sheets and photographs until — "Holy shit."

Vanessa spoke up. "Simi, what—"

"Shut up," Simi said. Her fingers moved as if they had a mind of their own. "Guys," Simi said, her inhales becoming increasingly shallow. "I don't think Min's Gifted."

"But you *told us*—"

Simi's eyes were still focused on the monitors. "Min said . . . Vashti told us that LIUYEN had mutated animals. And the next step was human trials."

"Right . . ."

"They did it years ago," Simi said quickly. "They already mutated a human. They did it *decades* ago."

"Okay, so what does that mean?"

"They *made* her. Min's parents." Simi turned and faced the other teens in the room. "Min was the first person they successfully mutated. Fifteen years ago. Look. They logged every session, every trial, every experiment. All of this research. They did it to her first."

Vanessa shook her head. "She would have been . . . what, eight, nine years old?"

"And look at this — these people, all these kids . . ."

Vanessa's heart froze. "Wait."

Simi stopped scrolling and Vanessa pointed at a grainy photograph. It was of a boy and a girl. The two of them were holding hands. The boy was crying. The girl wore an angry scowl etched into her forehead. The two of them were wearing matching hospital gowns, several sizes too large.

"Anthony . . ." Vanessa whispered.

She'd never seen that photograph in her life. They couldn't be older than three and four. But there they were, clear as day. Hiding in an encrypted secret folder on Min's personal computer.

"Why are *we* in here?" Vanessa said, her voice breaking.

"Min's been keeping tabs on all of you," Simi said. "Or, at least, on every Gifted this side of the Atlantic. Some of these notes are twenty years old, but . . . V, there's something else."

"What?" Vanessa barked.

Simi turned to look at them. She looked terrified. "It's about the arenas."

Vashti

"Talk."

When Min looked at Vashti, with eyes as red as the life spilling onto the floor, Vashti didn't panic. She knew she was looking into the eyes of a crazed megalomaniac who had just realized everything she had worked so hard to maintain was slipping out of her reach. And desperate people did desperate things.

She'd never see Vanessa again. She'd never hold her hand or kiss her goodnight. She'd never get to know Anthony well enough to tease him so the two of them could gang up against Vanessa in that petty way normal families and in-laws could. She'd never know what secrets she'd given her own life to uncover.

She could only hope that it had all been worth it.

But Min didn't kill her. She just spoke to her.

Talk.

It was an instruction. A command. And it was as if her singular purpose on this planet was to complete it.

Talk.

But Vashti didn't want to talk. She had no desire to say a single word. But Min had commanded it. And she would do anything Min told her. Because Min's instruction was her purpose in life. She felt her mind being cleaved in two as her desires yanked and pushed against a base drive to obey.

Min told her to talk. To talk was her purpose. To talk was to live.

It didn't matter that Vashti didn't *want* to talk. Min's command pulled the words from her throat and forced her lips apart.

"I . . . I don't—"

Tell me what the fuck is happening!

Vashti's stomach churned. But only words left her lips. "I don't know! I don't know what's happening, I don't know—"

Tell me why this is happening.

"Vanessa and Anthony probably planned this with Holly. That's why your hand isn't here. She traveled with it. They're using it to—"

Oh my God Oh my God. What was happening?

What was she doing?

She wanted to die.

To take one of her own knives and slit her own throat.

Put that down.

Her hand opened and the knife in her hand clattered to the ground loudly, metal striking solid marble. She hadn't even realized she'd reached for it.

Pick that thing back up.

She did.

Come here.

She did.

Min pointed at the base of Vashti's neck. *Hold it. Right there.*

She did.

Min continued. "*You will not harm yourself in any way until I tell you to. And when I find Anthony and Vanessa and anyone else you have ever cared for in your entire, miserable life, I will kill them. And I will make you watch. And then — and only then — will you have my permission to die. Do you FUCKING UNDERSTAND ME?!*"

Nina hesitated. "Min, what are—"

Min spun around and glared at her. *Shut up.*

Nina did.

Tell me you understand, Vashti.

"I understand." Vashti understood perfectly.

Tell me everything.

And to Vashti's absolute horror, she did.

Secrets, names, things she had somehow been able to keep from Ruth for years. It all came tumbling out of Vashti's mouth like sand through a sieve. She had managed to catch glimpses of Nina as her lips moved of their own accord. She looked sad. Betrayed.

She wanted to apologize to Nina. For years she had kept her at a distance. But Nina had just wanted the same thing Vashti wanted.

Family.

And instead of realizing Nina's dream, even if it was ill-designed, Vashti had escaped and found it elsewhere with Vanessa and the other kids at the parlor. And then she'd had the audacity to keep it away from Nina.

Vashti's lips stopped moving. The thrill in her ears finally quieted. The only sound in the room was that of her own labored breathing.

Min hummed. "Thank you." She stood, slowly. She looked pale. Min's left stump looked . . . older. Almost like an angry burn instead of a sudden amputation. Nina had done well in just a handful of minutes.

Then Min said with eyes glazed over, "Nina will dispose of you, now."

Nina's eyes widened and she shook her head, but her mouth stayed shut. She was crying. *Please*, her eyes pleaded. *Not me too.*

"Wait!" Vashti pleaded.

Before Min could utter another syllable, the power went out in the entire house. The fire alarm wailed and the glass behind Min shattered. Water rushed into the room, catching her feet from under her.

Vashti screamed as the water rose and churned around them like a violent maelstrom. She was thrown to the ground and she winced as shards of glass cut through her hands.

Someone grabbed her arm and she panicked, expecting to see Min looming over her. But it was Wyatt, hoisting her to her feet as the impossible storm surged around Nina and Min.

Anthony stood in front of the most terrifying woman Vashti had ever known. And with gritted teeth, bulging veins, and a blinding pattern, he willed pressured water directly at Min, effectively pinning her against the wall. She couldn't move, couldn't speak — likely couldn't breathe, either. He was so focused he didn't see Nina charging towards him.

Instinct — Vashti's own Gifted instinct — took over.

And *God* it felt good.

Vashti threw the knife sheathed by her ankle. It whipped past Nina, catching her by surprise enough for her to turn. But Vashti was already beside and below her, sweeping her leg. Nina fell onto her back loudly, glass crunching beneath her.

Vashti pounced on top of her and held her knife to Nina's neck. She had to be careful. If Vasthi's skin touched Nina's, she was very likely as good as dead.

Nina reached for her but Vashti jumped up, dodging her hand as she tossed her knife up in the air. She caught it at the hilt and held it out in front of her with her left hand. Her right hand armed with her favorite knife, ready to throw.

"Don't you even *think* about touching him," Vashti warned.

Nina put her hands up in surrender. "Put her down."

Vashti glanced at Anthony. What she saw terrified her. There was nothing but murderous intent in his dark eyes. A bastion of focused determination that saw no way out other than death and destruction.

This was the boy who had survived two years in the arenas.

Vashti wanted nothing more than to see the life snuffed out of Min's eyes. Wouldn't that just be simpler? To just end it all right now?

"Anthony!" Wyatt screamed.

With a pained yell, Anthony released Min. The water crashed to the ground with a force that nearly destabilized Vashti where she stood. Min collapsed as she coughed up the water that had managed to find her lungs.

But when Min looked up at Anthony, the boy had lost his resolve to do the honorable thing. Water lifted from the ground as if it were a single unit, like a rising slab of concrete, before he rammed into Min once again.

"Stop it!" Nina lunged, but Vashti burrowed into the depths of her Gift and allowed her braid to wrap around Nina's neck and squeeze. Nina's eyes bulged and she fell to her knees, her fingers desperately tearing at the strands of hair around her neck.

Wyatt looked up at the wailing siren above them and snapped his fingers. A jolt of electricity left his index finger and flew upwards, directly at the fire alarm, silencing it permanently.

Vashti glared at him. "This *whole* place is covered in water, what the hell is wrong with you?"

Wyatt shrugged. "I'm very precise. Also . . ." he gestured

noncommittally towards her. Vashti risked a brief look down and around her, and immediately caught his meaning.

The room was completely dry, except for the water holding up Min. Anthony had managed to siphon every stray drop of water in the room solely to keep Min hostage. Even their clothes were completely dry.

For the second time, Anthony released Min, leaving her gasping for air on the ground. He kept the water close by, floating beside him like a shadow. Min's stump swung limply below her while her right hand held her up and away from the ground.

"Why did you take us?" Anthony said. When Min didn't answer, he hit her with another wave that crashed into her like a blow across the face.

"Anthony, stop!"

"Why did you take us?"

Vashti didn't understand. What did he mean? Take them from where?

Min was still trying to catch her breath. And Anthony had completely run out of patience. He whipped around, focusing his attention on Nina. "Did you know? Did you *let her*?"

"Know what?"

"The arenas!" Anthony's pattern burned so incredibly bright, it was as if she was looking at a star. His eyes were dark and wild as water whirled around him, searching for something else to destroy.

"It's *her*," he said. "It's been her this whole time. She let it happen. The arenas. She's in charge of all of them. Used the money to fund her *research*."

"Min . . ." The words left Nina's lips carefully. "Min, is this true?"

Vashti watched Min carefully, waiting for any slight movement that would betray her intention. If the inflection was off, if her next sentence began with an instruction and not an admission, Vashti would end her.

But Min wasn't looking at Vashti or Anthony or Wyatt. She was looking at Nina, with solemn, empty eyes.

"Nina . . ." Min pleaded.

Vashti's rage flared. *How fucking dare she?*

The water in the room rose again, and Vashti realized she had made her decision: if Anthony attempted to kill Min, Vashti would not do anything to stop it.

Then, Nina canted her head and gasped. In a soft, uncertain voice, she asked, "Where's Ruth?"

Ruth

She said don't move.

We won't move. Where was it? The Companion? Why hadn't she ever given it a name? It was here. It was always here . . . and she treated it like shit. She kept it safe . . .

No. *It* had kept her safe.

It's alright.

No, it wasn't. Now look at where we are!

I do keep you safe. We've been together for a long time, you know.

For years it had kept her safe, given her hints. Sometimes called her names—

Hey!

—but was always helpful.

I helped! When you were stuck in that sad place. The bad place. I helped.

It picked up on things she missed, sometimes. *I'm right here, you know. You can just say thank you.*

She said don't move.

She can't tell us what to do! it said. It frowned, hands folded across its chest. It looked familiar. But different.

I think she's going to kill us.

That's alright. I'll be here.

She'd been gone a long time. How long had it been? Does it know how long it's been? My feet are tired. My head is tired. My back is tired. Everything hurts and I can't move. Where's Nina. Nina can fix it.

No.

Nina did this. Min did this.

They're going to kill us.

I think we're going to need a shot.

I don't want a shot!

But Nina isn't our friend anymore. She's not a friend, she's not our friend.

It said this would happen. You can't trust *anybody*.

It still *hurts*.

She said don't move but I want to move to a new place. We can sell the old. We have money. Why didn't we move some-where nicer?

Oh. It's you.

Where is she?

We want to go home?

Can we go home?

Vashti

They found Ruth exactly where they'd left her. Sitting knock-kneed, ankles tied to the uneven legs of her chair. Her head hung limply from her neck, her braids swinging, vibrating with the current of the air around them.

"Ruth?"

She didn't move, didn't acknowledge that she had even heard. But as Vashti crept closer, she realized that Ruth wasn't moving with the current in the air or swaying in her chair. She was shaking and shivering. Sobbing violently, but silently, with her mouth slightly ajar. Her lips were cracked and dry, saliva pooled above her bottom lip and cascaded down the corners of her mouth like a sticky waterfall.

"Ruth, look at me, please, what—"

"Don't . . . don't move . . . she said. Don't move. We won't move. *Mmm,*" she hummed, then closed her eyes tightly. "They're going to come and take you. I can't move. we can't move. Don't move. She said don't move, please."

"It's okay. You can move."

But she didn't. She couldn't.

"Ruth? Please look at me."

And then, somehow, Ruth looked at Vashti with empty, unrecognizable eyes.

Vashti's heart shattered. She looked so tired.

"Can we go home?" Ruth asked.

Simi

Min was arrested within hours. Nina, within days.

Simi released a few choice documents to the press detailing LIUYEN's illegal experimentation and the true origin and purpose of the arenas, along with the very long list of benefactors and patrons who frequented them. The arenas: a nation-wide human trafficking ring, created and organized by Min Liu. A traffic ring that had been frequented by government officials, CEOs, princes, and chancellors. It was a scandal that promised to shake the world. Min used the money made from the arenas to fund LIUYEN's very expensive genetic research.

Simi spent night after night combing over documents that she translated herself. She perused detailed journals that went into almost excruciating scientific detail to explain how Min was genetically altered. Min was the product of years and years of radiation and experimental treatments and therapies. And when the procedure had finally succeeded, she had been subjected to many more years of grueling training until she was in total and perfect control of her Gift. All before she turned nineteen.

Then her parents died. A tragic accident. She remembered reading about it in the news years ago.

Founders of LIUYEN Industries dead after fatal car wreck.

Min did not incriminate herself in any of these documents or files. But after the events of that week, Simi had no doubt in her mind that the accident had been fueled by a singular verbal command:

Drive.

Simi shivered and massaged the back of her neck as she pressed on.

It didn't get better. She found manifestos that documented the inception of the arenas as a way to ensure that Gifted with the most promising talents would properly hone their powers and sharpen their skill among similarly empowered. But then Min realized just how lucrative the business could really be.

And then there was the small matter regarding where the Gifted had *come* from.

Simi hadn't told anyone. It had only been a few days, but she wanted to wait until she fully understood it all herself. Min's research insisted that the Gifted didn't appear because of a spontaneous mutation, but that they were from another world. And there was a way to access this universe through a portal.

Through a Mirror.

The research didn't explain how any of it worked. But it was difficult to ignore the evidence in her hands. Min's parents had gone through this portal *thousands* of times. Stealing children that wouldn't be missed and were too young to maintain their memories of home.

It explained why virtually *no* Gifted knew who their biological parents were. People had assumed they'd been abandoned out of fear, when in reality, they'd been taken from a home they couldn't remember.

"Anything good?"

Simi shrugged noncommittally as Anthony settled down in a chair beside her. "I don't know if I'd use the word *good*," Simi said. She gave him a pointed look with narrowed eyes. "Go to bed, Anthony. You look like death. It's four in the morning."

"Not tired," he said as he yawned and rubbed his eyes aggressively.

Nightmares then, Simi assumed.

She'd caught him once in the throes of a nightmare. It was the night after the tournament. She was the last one to leave for the night and as she did, she passed his room. The door was cracked open, and her bulky bag accidentally pushed the door against its hinges, opening it further. She had reached over to close it when she saw him tangled in sheets, sweating, twitching, and muttering to himself with eyes clenched shut tightly. He didn't cry out. He hardly made any noise except for the hushed, soft muttering. His nose was red and salt stained his cheeks.

She had closed the door and left. But her heart ached for days afterwards at the realization that Anthony crawled into his bed every night, uncertain of the horrors his own mind would conjure at his most vulnerable. He slept with melancholy. He dreamt of anguish. And he did it in silence.

"Is V around?" Anthony asked, ripping Simi away from her thoughts.

Simi shook her head. "She's with Vashti. They went to check up on Ruth at the hospital again."

Anthony's lip twitched and his eyes darkened. "Why?"

Simi sighed. "Because Ruth is still Vashti's family, too."

Anthony sighed. "You're right. I shouldn't . . . be like that."

"She's not *your* family," Simi said. "You don't have to like her at all. I sure as hell don't."

Anthony chuckled, offering her a lopsided grin. She tried to ignore the way her stomach twisted in her gut. That had been happening a lot around him recently. He slumped in his chair and rested his arm on the table beside her.

Anthony's lip twisted in thought. "It gets . . . complicated. When the person who's supposed to be watching out for you is the bad guy, too. In the arenas . . . after a while, you kind of forget the handlers are the reason you're there. They're the ones who give you tips about fighting other Gifted and reward you with first dibs on healings."

He hadn't talked much about his time in the arenas with Simi. The ease of which he was able to speak about it now surprised her. Then again, only a few days ago, they'd utilized a portal to cut a woman's hand off. So maybe recounting his experience in the arenas simply wasn't the most visceral trauma at the moment.

"Did they ever say what was wrong with her?" Anthony asked. "With Ruth?"

Simi shook her head. "They said making an accurate diagnosis this early is hard."

"But she's been seeing things for years?"

"Yeah, but the doctors have only known her for days. I think they're trying to figure it out. But Vashti says the phrase all the doctors keep using is 'trauma response.'"

Anthony nodded and yawned again.

"Go to sleep, Anthony."

He shook his head. "I . . . can't," he admitted as he pretended to clean a stain off his pajama pants.

Nightmares.

Simi picked at her cuticles. She could fix code and computers, but she couldn't figure out what combination of words would fix *this*.

He'd done so much already. Given up *so much*. Now the work was complete and the arenas would shut down one by one as its benefactors and managers were arrested. The authorities would handle Min and Nina. His sister was safe. Vashti was safe. Gifted all over the country wake up tomorrow in a world that still treated them with suspicion, but maybe they could all sleep a little easier.

But Anthony still couldn't.

Anthony's eyes fluttered and his head bobbed. But just before sleep could take him, his eyes flew open again.

Simi sighed then stood up, and decided to try something stupid.

Anthony rubbed his eyes and glanced over his shoulder as Simi left to retrieve as many spare sheets, duvets, and comforters that she could find and laid them on the ground. Once she was satisfied, she sat down and patted the space next to her.

Anthony approached, eyes narrowed.

"Whenever I had nightmares, my brother and I built a fort," Simi said. She handed him a handheld video game console. "Not sure why it worked, but eventually I was able to go back to sleep and I didn't have any dreams again. Usually."

Anthony mashed all the buttons on the handheld, searching for the power button. "What were your nightmares about?" he asked.

"The Loch Ness Monster."

Anthony wrinkled his nose.

"I was nine," Simi said. She pointed at the button on the top of the console and Anthony turned it on.

"I knew that," Anthony said. "Must be the new version."

"It's six years old."

"See, that was the problem."

Simi laughed. "Sure. Look, I know you've been out of the loop for a few years but I think you'll like this one." She pointed at one of the downloaded games on the screen.

Anthony rolled his eyes. "I was only in the arena for two years, you know. I've played Minecraft."

"Yeah, but you're probably a little rusty."

He lay back until his head hit the pillow. Simi did the same so they could both watch him play. And he was *absolutely* rusty. Which was fine. He kept flipping through his inventory too fast and it would take him three attempts to finally get ahold of the item he needed. Simi would offer him suggestions and initially he'd ignore them, explaining that he had a *vision* for the cave he was creating. But minutes later he'd nudge her shoulder and ask her to repeat some of those suggestions with a lopsided grin and knowing smirk. Simi couldn't help but laugh every time he tried to run away from a creeper — because that's when he panicked and ran into trees. Usually the same tree. Over and over and over again.

He tried to fight sleep, but eventually Simi turned off the lamp and powered down her computer. After dropping the console on his face three times, he gave up and set it next to him and closed his eyes.

"I'm just resting my eyes," he insisted. "Too much screen time. Bad for the brain."

"Uh huh," Simi said with a yawn.

"And the battery's almost dead anyway."

"Obviously."

Simi waited until his breathing evened out before she closed her eyes, too. He'd be alright, she decided. They'd all be alright. The cards Vanessa, Vashti, and Anthony had been dealt had been horrific, but they were here. They were safe.

And there was still tomorrow.

Epilogue: What Could Have Been

Raahi hadn't the slightest idea what to expect.

He had checked precedents, scoured every single line of the law and scrutinized the recordings and writings from proceedings and trials past. As far as he could tell, the things his father had done during his lifetime had simply never been done before.

The counsel — the same counsel of which he was a member — would listen to his story, his case, and then decide on judgment and punishment. Usually there'd be a trial among his peers as well. But this case was . . . sensitive. And if it came out that a civilian had kept a Mirror hidden for years and aided and abetted in the illegal transport of hundreds of children off-world? Well, the counsel itself would be questioned as an effective entity. The law would be criticized by the general public. There would be war, outrage, chaos.

The last war had only ended a century ago. Nivea was still enjoying a tenuous peace.

"Mr. Varo."

Raahi stood quickly, straightening out his black tunic.

The Counseling secretary nodded tersely. "The Counsel is ready for you."

He nodded and followed her into the large atrium.

His mentors, his coworkers, and his friends sat in front of Raahi forming a semi-circle around him. For a moment, he considered retreating. He could run out of the room. Change his mind.

"Raahi," Councilor Shravan encouraged, her soft voice a stark contrast to her angular features. "Why did you bring us here today?"

Raahi looked ahead, past Councilor Shravan, past the mosaic wall created by the sweat and tears of Untalented. He imagined seeing his sister, Ruth, an adult now, standing there on the other side of the Mirror.

"On behalf of my father, and in the name of the suffering that has taken place as a direct result of my silence, I would like to report a crime."

Acknowledgements

First and foremost, I'm eternally grateful to God for blessing me with the perfect combination of perseverance, imagination, and ADHD to turn my daydreams into the written word. Without His guidance, I wouldn't be here today, and neither would this book.

To Lauren, thank you so much for being this book's first champion. You were this book's first yes and I'll never forget that. Kota, thank you so much for dealing with my anxiety-riddled self in the months leading up to publication day and special thanks to my editor, May, for shaping this book into its final form.

Thank you so much, Audrie, for being the first person to read this story many, *many* drafts ago — your feedback helped transform this story. Thank you so much to my med school friends, The Suities (Mai, Laura, and Sylvi), and The Snitches (Amrita and Krysia). Your unwavering support kept me going when my self-doubt started to creep in.

Dorian, thank you for being an incredible agent and for

being my partner in (fictional) crime. I'm so looking forward to the coming years!

Thank you SO MUCH to the 2025 Small Press Debut group (and especially you, Ria). Your support has been equal parts radical and rabid, and I wouldn't have it any other way. Thank you, thank you, thank you!

Catherine, thank you so much for all the work, love, and care you put into our practice. Without you, I wouldn't have had the time or energy to live out this dream.

To Tolu, thank you for being unapologetically and wholly yourself. For keeping it one hundred and for providing such banger one-liners over the years. I have S-tier dialogue material because of you.

Mom, Dad — thank you for being the first people to believe in me. For the things you gave up, the sacrifices you made, and for the million and one ways you put my needs ahead of yours. I see you both. And I am so grateful to have you in my life. Mom, thank you for reading my first book about a deer going on an adventure. You were my very first beta reader and your honest, actionable feedback is the reason the stories I write today are *much* better.

To my husband, Tyler, who somehow never doubted that this book would hit the shelves: thank you for your steadfast belief in me. For reminding me to eat regularly and go to bed before midnight. I love you so much. Doing life with you is my absolute favorite thing in the world.

And of course, thank *you*, my readers for picking up this book. I hope it found you at just the right time.

About Dami Salako

Dami is a first-generation Nigerian American who spent the first half of her childhood in England and the second half in Dallas, TX. She graduated from Southern Methodist University with a B.S. in Biology and a B.A. in English with a Creative Writing Specialization. She completed her medical school and residency training at University of Texas at Southwestern.

Dami is a board-certified psychiatrist and owner of her own private practice. She currently resides in Dallas, TX with her husband, two dogs, and two cats.

When she's not working or writing, Dami is cosplaying, playing Stardew Valley or Baldur's Gate, or attending EDM festivals (her favorite artist is Rezz).

Also by Inked in Gray

If you enjoyed *Children with Gifts*, please consider also reading *Harvesting Game*, or any of the other Inked in Gray novels and anthologies. Support our small business by buying direct at InkedinGray.com

We also appreciate any and all reviews! You may leave a review on Goodreads, Amazon, IndieStoryGeek or on our site at Inkedingray.com